Esta Brown in
of Becoming

A 'Legends of the East' Fantasy. Book 2

R.N. Jackson

COPYRIGHT

Contents

DEDICATION

To my daughters,
Lucy, Annabel and Phoebe

Epigraph

It's the past who tells us who we are. Without it, we lose our identity.
  —Stephen Hawking, 21st-Century Physicist

To see where you were born before, look at what you are now. To see where you are going to be born next, look at what you do now.
  —Patrul Rinpoche, 19th-Century Buddhist master

CATCHING UP

WHEN I THINK ABOUT telling people everything that happened to me in the spring of 1986, it sounds kind of insane. (Of course, when I *actually* told people, they sent me—for my own good, of course—to Gatley Gardens hospital for the mentally unstable.)

First of all, there was this temple called Rigpa Gompa which me and my friend Simon sort of stumbled across inside the walls of a rundown house. Nothing too weird about that; plenty of buildings hide secrets behind their walls. Except Rigpa Gompa stood guard over the hidden land of Odiyana, a huge valley surrounded on all sides by snow-peaked mountains. (And no, not, as Doctor Edwards suggested, the Pennines).

Then there was Lama la, the old abbot who drank salty tea by the bucket load and could, with a click of his fingers, conjure up a swirling globe he called *Samsara* in his sitting room.

There were his students, the *Dharmapalas*: four children with magical powers who protected the Rigpa Gompa from attack. Two sisters, Karma Chodron and Sera, one who could run faster than a bullet and one who could double in size. The little monk, Tubten, who could make multiple copies of himself, each one as grubby as the next. And finally Rabjam... the oldest boy. What could he do? I think he just made the tea, to be honest.

PROLOGUE

THE DESERT OF FOREVER

I HOVERED OVER AN endless desert. A blazing evening sun scorched the land brown; hot winds whipped it into twisting clouds of dust.

'Please, not here.'

The clouds engulfed me. Tugged at me. Dragged me down. Shapes emerged out of the sand: half-buried skeletons, bleached white by the sun.

Please, not here.

Something moved on the peak of one of the dunes. My heartbeat quickened.

A dog. Not much more than skin and bones. Hind legs folded uselessly beneath its body, fur hanging off its back in patches. It was gnawing at a limb that poked out from the sand like the waving arm of a drowning sailor.

I landed softly. My feet sinking in the burning sand.

How could it still be alive? How could anything live here?

The creature must have sensed me, because it dropped the limb and growled, the remaining fur on its back raised to points. It sniffed the air and turned to face me.

It had no eyes. Just empty sockets.

I backed away from it, partly in fear, partly in disgust.

The thing dragged itself towards me, back legs trailing behind, toothless jaws opening and shutting, tongue hanging limply out of the side of its mouth.

It came to a stop just a few feet away from me, a sudden hacking cough making its body tremble.

I watched, horrified. Expecting the thing just to keel over right there.

When the coughing finally stopped, the dog raised its head, opened its mouth... and spoke in a voice as dry and grating as rusted iron.

I know...

More coughing.

I stepped closer so I could hear it better.

I know who...

'What?' I asked. 'What did you say?'

I know who you are.

'You know who I-'

The wind howled. The dog pounced.

Darkness.

I was hovering again. Floating through an empty sky. Below me, the dog was just a speck.

Its rasping barks swallowed up by the vastness of the desert.

Another sound.

The nonsense whispering of the wind at first. Then words... recognisable ones. Words like: 'immediately' and 'fever' and 'Doctor Edwards'.

The solid feeling of wall against my back. I blinked. Faces hovered over me. I blinked again. Cold empty windows. I turned my head. A single bed; hard, shiny floor. A man in a white coat. Glasses. Pencil hovering over a file he held in the crook of an arm. He opened his mouth to speak:

I know, he barked. *I know who you are...*

PART ONE

Who Are You?

1

AN UNEXPECTED EXCURSION

SEPTEMBER 23RD 1986

7.30 AM

A gunshot-rapping on my cell door.

My daily alarm clock.

I dragged myself out of bed, threw water in my face, and slipped my Adidas tracksuit top over my pyjamas.

Outside, an impatient orderly swung a bunch of multi-coloured keys on a chain in wide, dangerous circles. 'You're late, Brown.'

We walked in silence down 'Red' corridor, until we reached a locked door. The orderly pulled a red key from the chain, unlocked the door and relocked it behind us once we were through. I followed him down an echoey flight of stairs.

The next door opened into the restricted 'Orange' corridor where some of the resident staff had their rooms.

Another door. Another flight of stairs.

At the bottom we emerged out near the reception. My eyes complained at the blinding square of morning sun streaming through a window.

A final *clunk* opened the door to the canteen.

I collapsed into a plastic chair and stared down at my breakfast.

Meals at Gatley Gardens were bland, pallid and overcooked. The cutlery was plastic; the plates were too. Even the consistency and flavour of the omelettes they served was plastic.

I used my standard issue bendy spoon to push a sliver of egg away from me, watching it glide over a surface of grease. My eyes were drawn to a pair of pink tablets in a plastic container beside the plate. My mouth went dry just looking at them.

I gulped down a beaker of water—they couldn't ruin that at least—and glanced about me.

Twenty of us from my wing sat around a row of scarred wooden tables. To my right, Jake, a large boy of about fifteen had already started weeping into his food. To my left, a skinny girl cut up her omelette into ever decreasing particles, only to push them across her plate without them ever coming close to her mouth. Opposite me was a large gloomy looking girl who stroked her dark, curly shoulder length hair over and over again.

I leaned back. Somewhere down the other end of the table, the wheels of Charlie Bullock's chair poked out.

Ever since taking a fall a two years ago, Charlie had been stuck in a wheelchair. It hadn't just been her back that broke, though. Ever since my dad had found her lying under the stairs in Gatley House, she barely communicated with anyone around her. Even when Simon, her half-brother, came to visit. She hardly interacted with the world at all, in fact.

Well, not with *this* world, anyway.

Even though her body was broken, her mind seemed to function all right... it just wasn't functioning in the same reality as everyone else.

You see, Charlie might not be able to talk, but she could draw. It's just that what she drew was... kind of at an angle. Skew whiff. The last picture of hers I'd seen was of Gatley House. Not the battered old wreck everyone else could see. She'd drawn it as a three-story palace in the folds of a mountain. She'd drawn it as I sometimes saw it: Rigpa Gompa.

It was as if Charlie's physical body existed in one reality. Her mind inhabited another. She sat here with the rest of us, but her eyes were focused elsewhere.

So, what about me? I thought. *Which world am I living in?*

I stared at the sliver of omelette hanging off my fork. It looked like a tongue. I thought of the dog in my dream... and let it drop to the plate.

A shadow hovered over me. A stale smell slid along with it.

'Hurry up,' Bernard said through his teeth.

Bernard was the lead orderly. Skinny as a rake with hair that appeared to be washed in chip fat. This morning, he looked like he'd had even less sleep than me. He had exhaustion bruises under each eye and he smiled at me with all the humour of a dead fish.

'Don't rush me,' I complained. 'I want to savour my breakfast pills.'

Bernard reattached his set of rainbow coloured keys to his belt, then pushed the pills aside. 'None for you this morning, Brown,' he said. 'Don't want you keeling over on the way.'

I swallowed some egg with a grimace. 'Way where?'

He sighed, hitched his trousers up over his non-existent hips, and pulled out a floppy notepad from his back pocket. 'I have to be back by ten and you have to stay with me the whole time.'

'Way where?' I repeated.

He screwed his face up at me as if I were a slug he'd stepped on. 'Doctor Edwards is letting you go visit Daddy's grave, per your request.'

I frowned back at him. 'It's not a grave.'

'Whatever you want to think. You can go say your... prayers or whatever, then straight back here. No sightseeing.' He waved his notepad at me. 'Best behaviour. You've got your review this afternoon and we wouldn't want to blot your copybook, would we?'

I gave him my nicest serial killer smile.

'Now eat up. I need you nice and strong. We're walking.'

I swallowed the remains of my omelette, resisted a gag reflex and then, under Bernard's watchful eye, cleared my table like the *very* good girl I am... He didn't write anything down about that, though.

They only ever recorded the bad stuff in Gatley Gardens.

2

THE LAST VISIT

IF THE INNARDS OF Gatley Gardens were bleak and pale, the grounds were like palace gardens. A ribbon of drive cut through a wide, flat lawn that would have looked at home on a golf course. Trees were set back on either side. Big ones. Conker trees and Oaks, that sort of thing. A wind shook the late summer leaves as we walked, making a calm shushing sound that, if you closed your eyes, sounded like waves lapping on a sandy beach.

My thoughts drifted to Dad. The last time I had visited his memorial stone was four weeks ago.

Mum had laid flowers in front of it while I hung back, staring at the golden inscription:

> MICHAEL RICHARD BROWN,
>
> MISSING,
>
> PRESUMED DEAD.
>
> BOUND AFTER ALL BY LOVE.

I remembered looking down at the poetry book I'd left there for him. Its cover curling after a month of sun and summer rain, the words smudged and faded.

I thought I might cry. But no tears came.

The longer I stood there, the stiller the stone became, the carved inscription deeper, more permanent: *Presumed Dead.*

I had waited while Mum arranged the flowers, breathing in and out, trying to recall the sound of his voice; the same voice I'd heard reciting that poem of his last Spring: *You cannot defeat the devil with hate...*

When Mum finally stepped away, I stepped closer, leaned forward and whispered: 'Where are you?' letting the breeze take my words.

I remained there, standing over his stone for what felt like an hour, waiting for a reply. But all that answered were the sounds of the graveyard: the whistling of birds, the creaking sway of summer branches, the endless droning of planes above.

Afterwards, I walked back to Gatley Gardens Mental Hospital, empty, silent and, despite being surrounded by people, completely alone.

That night I started dreaming about the desert and the dog.

I had not been back since.

And yet, here I was, on my way to see him again. *As per my request,* Bernard had said.

But it hadn't been me who put in the request.

So who had?

As we approached the fancy black iron gates that stood guard at the end of the drive I had a feeling I was about to find out.

3

THE VISITOR AT THE GRAVE

BERNARD PRESSED A BUTTON on a metal panel and answered a tinny voice that crackled out of it. The hinges creaked and the twin gates opened grandly out onto the outside world with all the flourish of scratched vinyl.

We turned right, along Wilmslow Road, as the gates slid shut behind us. We'd have to walk within a quarter of a mile of Gatley House before turning off for the Church. The road was empty. Not a single car to drown out the slap, slap of Bernard's flat feet as he chain-smoked a pack of Benson & Hedges: the cancer-stick of champions. It was just before nine am; Wilmslow Road should have been choked with cars and vans on their way to somewhere more interesting.

I rifled through a mental calendar. Was this a Sunday? No. My monthly review with Doctor Edwards always happened on a Saturday. Sundays were for church, long walks and a roast dinner, he always said. So, if it was Saturday, a silent road meant one thing... roadworks. And *that* meant they'd more than likely started on the airport bypass again. That, or, I don't know, some kind of alien invasion had stopped traffic.

Or then again, I wondered, this could all be part of Graham Spark's genius plan to liberate me. I wouldn't put anything past him. After what he did in spring... the newts, the fluffy handcuffs... I was confident he could pull anything off if he was properly motivated.

We walked another ten minutes in eerie silence before we reached the turnoff for the Church. From here, I could see the stone wall that marked out the grounds of Gatley House from the rest of town. The tops of the poplar trees that stood beside it still waved and bowed in the breeze. If the bypass was happening, those trees would soon be history. I sighed at the thought. It seemed like everything we'd done had only postponed the destruction of Gatley House; a temporary pause against the bulldozer of progress.

I didn't fully understand how the two realities of Rigpa Gompa, and Gatley House were woven together, but I did know one thing. While the realms were connected, if you tore one down, the other would go with it.

No wonder Simon and Graham were impatient to get back.

Bernard flicked his second fag-end of the walk into the middle of the empty road and headed left along Counsellor Lane so we could reach the Church through the back entrance. That would allow us to avoid going through Gatley town centre. I was more than happy with that plan.

Going this way meant you reached the graveyard by cutting through the car park of the White Hart pub. It was closed to drinkers until eleven, so it was empty except for a battered green Ford Escort, which sat like a headache on sagging wheels, its dirty windows reflecting the spire of the church.

Bernard pushed a hip-high gate open and entered the Church grounds. He lit another cigarette, dropping his match next to a dried-up bunch of flowers propped up against a shin high marble cross. 'Which way?' he asked.

I didn't answer. Instead, I was watching the pencil line of smoke rising from the flowers as the heat of the match shook hands with the dried stems. I pictured the bunch catching fire, flames rising, licking and cracking between the stones, spreading across the entire graveyard. For a moment, my eyes itched with the baking, warping heat and I was back in the scorched desert of my dream. Black and twisted limbs; a desperate, hungry growl as an arm uncurled... and for a moment, I thought:

Let it all burn.

'I said, which way?' Bernard repeated impatiently.

I looked at the orderly... and flinched.

The lines of his skull showed beneath the tight skin of his face, his lips were drawn back, revealing rotting teeth, his eyes rolled in their sockets.

I shook the vision from my head like a dog shakes water from its coat and—I never thought I'd ever think it, but—thankfully, Bernard was back. Greasy hair, snide expression and all.

'You're on another planet entirely, aren't you?' he said, cigarette smoke escaping through his yellowing teeth.

I stared down at my feet and stamped on the smouldering flowers. I pointed right. Towards a tall black slab near the main entrance. 'It's over there,' I said, dully.

'Come on then. Let's find this grave.'

I didn't move.

'Bloody 'ell,' Bernard muttered impatiently. 'It's like walking with a waxwork. What's up with you?'

There was someone already there. Not Mum, not Graham or Simon, not Lily either. They were looking right at me.

4

Collapsing Gran

GRAN SMILED. HER EYES were clear. Awake. So different to how she'd been just a few months ago. Like curtains had been drawn back from her face. I looked around the graveyard for a nurse, or Mum. Gran's dementia might have been miraculously cured, but surely they didn't just let the old ladies out by themselves now?

She looked down at Dad's stone. 'I came to see Dickie.'

'Are you sure you should be—'

Her eyes darted over my shoulder, then snapped back to me.

I frowned. 'Is Mum here?'

She rolled her eyes then looked, very deliberately this time, over my shoulder again. I turned round: just Bernard prizing moss from a gravestone with the toe of his shoe. She took my sleeve and pulled me close. 'He's waiting for you.'

'That's Bernard,' I whispered back. 'He's my friendly prison guard for the morning. They think I'm going to run away.'

'Not him.' Her eyes flicked back towards the gate, beyond the orderly. 'You need to go,' she said, nodding at the gate.

I followed her gaze. A familiar tall figure waved at me and realisation dawned. 'Graham?'

She smiled and put a finger to her lips. *Shh.*

'I can't just go with him, Gran. They'll never let me out again.'

'He thought of everything, dear. He's a bright boy. Just like his grandfather.'

I closed my eyes. So *this* was Graham's plan? Play hide and seek with Bernard? And they put *me* in the madhouse? I shook my head. 'Absolutely not. Gran. This is never going to—'

'Shh,' she interrupted, and pointed down at Dad's stone. 'Don't give up on him, Esta.'

'But—',

'This may be our last chance. Now, what your guard's name?'

'Bernard?' I said, obviously loud enough to attract his attention, because he was up and over in a flash, his eyes darting from me to Gran suspiciously.

'Are you done?' he snarled.

Gran let go of me and started whimpering, her bottom lip trembling. I cringed. 'Gran? No, no, no.'

She ignored me and reached out for Bernard. 'Nurse!' she said, touching his upper arms. 'Oh, thank goodness you're here.'

Bernard's face was a mask of horror as she wrapped an arm around him.

'Old dear...' he said, searching around him for some help. But she leaned more heavily on him until he was forced to take her weight.

'Bernard, isn't it?' Gran asked, patting his skinny arm.

'How do you know my—'

She led him away from me. 'They said you'd come, dear.'

He tried to pull away from her. I watched the scene, dumbstruck, shaking my head some more. Gran turned to face me, wafted a hand back at the gate, mouthed 'Go,' and collapsed into Bernard's unwilling arms.

I stood frozen on the spot as she moaned, her weight almost bringing the orderly down on top of her.

It was only Graham whispering my name that brought me to my senses. I stared dumbly at him. He'd not cut his hair since I'd last seen him. Dirt and sweat streaked his face, his clothes looked stale and baggy. 'What the bloody hell, Graham?'

He grabbed my hand, pulling me towards the low wall. 'No time! Tight schedule!'

We climbed, jumped and hit the tarmac opposite the White Hart pub, my hair now on end and covered in twigs. Graham started running.

I stayed put.

'This is your plan?' I snapped.

He stopped. Heaving in deep breaths. 'Look. It'll work, but only if you help me. Otherwise, we're screwed.'

'We're screwed anyway, Graham!' I pointed behind us at the graveyard. 'You think he won't notice I've disappeared? You think he won't come looking? You think he won't report that I've run away?'

'Esta,' he said in whispered desperation. 'Look. Just shut up and come with me, I'll explain in the car.'

I stared at the old saggy Ford Escort we'd passed earlier. '*That's* the getaway car?'

'What's wrong with it?'

Wrong with it?

I gave the sky a despairing glance, then ran after him.

5

GRAHAM'S GENIUS PLAN

THE DOOR COMPLAINED WHEN I opened it; the engine took three goes before it started rumbling. Graham put his hand on my head and pushed me down. 'Keep low in case he's already on the lookout.'

I slid down so my back was resting against the seat. Hot air blew from the vents in the dashboard directly into my face. We hit a bump in the road and the wheels squeaked in protest. Something clunked in the front where I imagined the engine lived. I'm no mechanic, but by the sound of it, we were one pothole away from the engine falling out onto the road.

'Can you turn off the hot air?' I asked as we veered away on to the main street.

'No. That's cooling the engine. Stops it from over-heating.'

'Of course! That's not normal for cars, you know,' I said, as the church spire slid across the top sliver of my window. 'Can I at least get up now?'

Graham checked the wing mirrors, then nodded.

I sat up and whacked his arm. 'What on earth are you doing?'

He checked the rearview mirror. 'No other way to get you out.'

'You made the request for me to go see Dad?'

He nodded, then shrugged. 'Lily did. Pretended she was your mum. Do your seatbelt. I can't guarantee we won't just stop without warning.'

I did, although I doubted we were doing much more than a fast jogging pace. 'Just out of interest,' I said. 'How long have you been driving for?'

'Legally?'

'Have you even got your licence?'

'A provisional one.'

'I don't think that means—' I gave up. What did it matter? The fact that we were driving illegally through town was the least of my worries. 'This is more stupid than standing in front of a wrecking ball with nothing but a pair of fluffy handcuffs.'

He grinned. 'No other way to do it. When's your meeting with the doctor?'

'Oh!' I said in mock surprise. 'Which one's that? Do you mean the one that, if I miss, they'll lock me in a padded cell? That one?'

'Don't be so dramatic.'

I thought of Gran's over-the-top swoon and shook my head again at the hypocrisy of it all. '11:30.'

'That gives...' he glanced down at the clockface in the centre of the dashboard. The hands read roughly four thirty. He tapped the plastic screen. The hands wiggled, he tapped it again, and they both dropped to a lifeless 'half past 6' position.

'The Church clock said about quarter past ten,' I said. 'That was just before Gran won the Oscar for most overacted swallow dive and my so-called friend kidnapped me in what is surely an illegal car.'

'Alright, alright. It's not James Bond. I'm saving up for India and this was the cheapest thing I could find that actually moves.' He let go of the steering wheel with one hand and ran it through his tangled hair. 'So, about an hour to get you there, get inside and get back then?'

We passed the 'Greasy Spoon' café on the right and headed towards the Wilmslow Road junction at about ten miles under the speed limit.

He was right about one thing. Definitely not James Bond.

'Wait,' I said as we left the shops behind. 'Graham, where are we going?'

He looked at me like I was mad. 'Where do you think?'

'But they closed off Wilmslow Road.'

'What do you mean, closed it off?'

We rounded a bend, and I pointed out the helpful and informative NO ENTRY sign that sat in the middle of the road.

'Oh crap.' Graham stamped on the brake. The speed dropped to a crawl. We edged towards the sign with no sign of actually stopping. I looked down. Graham's foot was pumping the pedal with very little effect.

I looked at him despairingly. 'You want me to put a foot out, Gray?'

He grimaced and pulled the handbrake. There was a horrible grating sound and the car finally came to a halt. The bonnet nosing the sign. We both breathed.

'Christ,' Graham said eventually. 'When did that go up?'

6

Have Faith

TWENTY FEET DOWN THE road, a group of men were erecting a tall wood panel fence across the road. There was an entrance at the far right — presumably for works vehicles to access what used to be Grover Close.

'We've got less time than I thought,' he mumbled, crunching the Escort's gears. There was a sound of complaining cogs and grinding bits of metal, an unpleasant whine, and then we were reversing.

'What about the bats, the newts... I thought they weren't allowed to build?'

'They already re-housed the bats,' Graham said, fighting with the gear stick to complete his three-point turn. 'I bet they're dredging the pond now, so they can flatten the whole site.'

'Why the big fence, though?'

'That...' He finally won his battle with the gear stick. There was a crunch, and the car jerked forward. '...I don't know.' He changed again, and we settled back into a rumbling trot. Something clattered behind us, as if we were pulling a load of Coke cans. Graham turned to me and winced. 'Exhaust pipe,' he said. 'I had to use garden string. It should hold though.'

'This is a brilliant getaway plan,' I said, shuffling back down in my seat as we neared the churchyard again.

'We'll take the back way. Over Fletcher's Field. Simon's already there.'

'Tell me again how this is supposed to work?'

'Work?'

'Yes. The plan to avoid having you locked up for abducting me... because, just so you know, that'll be my story when they catch us.'

'One thing at a time, Est. Let's get to Gatley House first.'

I groaned. 'Right. Of course. There's that as well. Getting through security and somehow breaking into a building that has concrete for windows. I mean, the running away bit was the easy part and look how well we're doing?'

He placed his hand back on top of my head. 'Shh. I see your nurse.'

I crouched into the footwell of the seat, letting the hot air blow-dry my face again, trying not to think of the hot winds that swept the desert in my bloody dream.

'Have faith, Est,' Graham said. 'I swear. It'll all work out.'

I looked up at him. I couldn't help noticing he was sweating profusely.

7

DANGER OF DEATH

IT TOOK FIVE MORE minutes to reach the far end of Fletcher's Field. By the time Graham pulled the Escort on to the pavement of Boundary Lane, the exhaust pipe was trailing along about two feet behind us. We got out. Graham didn't bother to lock up. To be fair, who'd want to steal it, right? I doubt anyone could drive it off the pavement without something falling off it.

Fletcher's Field was now just two quarter-mile strips of uncut grass on either side of the newly surfaced road. Two years ago there had been sheep grazing here, but now the road cut a black line through the green. It came to a stop at the copse of trees still shielding Gatley House. There were no diggers on this side. They were all stationed on the remains of Grover Close, half a mile to the south. You could make out flashes of industrial orange through the hedgerows they still had to cut back.

We went through the messy knee-high grass towards the eastern edge of Gatley House where a twenty foot high fence ran through trees and spiky hedges.

'Stay close to the fence,' Graham said.

I counted six bright red KEEP OUT signs as I followed. Blackberry shoots reached out through the metal slats like the starving arms of prisoners trying to get out.

Graham stopped by a metal plate which had a picture of a figure recoiling from a jagged zigzag, beneath it: DANGER OF DEATH in bold letters. 'This is the place.'

'I'm not climbing that. It's got to be twenty feet.'

'We're not going over it,' he said, pulling one of the sign aside. 'We're going through it.'

'Can't you read?'

'Signs are a lot cheaper than running an actual electrical current through, Est.'

I shrugged. It wasn't my hand that was going to fry if he was wrong.

He tugged at the fence, peeling a section away like the lid of a tin of tuna. The gap was wide enough to squeeze between. He stood to one side, nodding at me to go. 'Careful.'

I ducked through, making damn sure no part of my body touched the fence. I might be certifiably insane, but I wasn't crazy. He followed, then carefully bent the metal back, hiding the opening to anyone but the most careful of observers. We slid through into the prickly cover of some holly bushes.

'Watch the mud,' Graham whispered as we pushed our way through the undergrowth 'Don't know how you'd explain muddy shoes to the doctor.'

'He's not trying to understand my feet, Gray.' I placed a finger at my temple. 'It's up here he's bothered about. That's if he can get past the fact I just ran away from my orderly. Exactly what *is* your plan to explain this, by the way?'

'Shh,'

I instinctively looked up and stopped in my tracks. We had emerged from the holly bushes. In front of us were the remains of the old sleeping-beauty hedgerow. And, frowning down at us from above it like an angry neighbour, the bashed-in roof of Gatley House.

Gatley House. Solid and clear and... I took a shallow breath, *real.*

An unpleasant vinegar-burn climbed up my throat. I swallowed it down.

'Bloody hell.'

8

UNDER THE WEEPING WILLOW

'THIS WAY,' GRAHAM SAID, pushing south through more branches. I followed, trying not to look at the leaning chimney that bobbed along above the line of hedge. Engines buzzed into life somewhere nearby. A faint smell of gasoline hung in the air.

He stopped opposite the gap in the hedge where the old gate used to be. Looked to the left along the track leading off towards Grover Close. Freshly gravelled. All ready for the diggers to come. 'Clear,' he whispered, then ran across and straight through into the overgrown lawn beyond.

I hesitated. Deep breaths. *So here we are,* I thought. Back at the gate again. I'd stood here, day after day, for more than a year. Wondering about Dad, wondering what secrets had drawn him to it. And now what? Did it still contain secrets, or was it just the empty shell everyone else saw?

Graham waved at me to follow. I exhaled. If I passed through that gap, I'd see the house again. See it in all its glory. Like some dirty old man opening up his mac to unsuspecting passers by. But I could hardly back out now, could I? I checked down the track for security, then leapt the three paces over, keeping my gaze directed left. Away from the old building. Thankfully, Graham headed the same way. His long legs taking him across the overgrown lawn towards the Weeping Willow and the sound of chainsaws.

'Quick!' the tree seemed to say as we approached. The leaves shook and Simon Taylor's grinning face appeared between them. He made a gap in the drooping branches for us to squeeze through.

'What's happening, Si?' Graham asked, making his way to the branches opposite, peering through them towards Grover Close.

'They've been chopping stuff down all morning, since before I got here.'

'You know they've cordoned off the whole of Wilmslow road?'

Simon nodded. 'There've been black vans coming in and out of Grover Close since I got here.'

'Someone wants to get a move on then?' Graham turned and looked at me. 'You see?'

'How long have we got?' I asked.

He pointed toward the buzzing saws. 'Est. They're getting close. We don't have much time. Days probably. That's why we had to break you out now.'

I looked at them both. I'd spent two months in a mental hospital trying to untangle flashes of memory about Dad, Rigpa Gompa and a bunch of demons that smelt of rotting fruit... Some days the flashes were so vivid I could almost touch them; other days, it was like I was seeing them through a silk screen. But whether they were clear or vague, they were always there... sitting in my mind, waiting for me to lift the curtain.

'You didn't just bring me here to tell me that though, did you?' I said.

Graham exchanged a look with Simon. My jaw stiffened. Without warning, the image of the desert in my dream flashed before me; the pathetic dog growling; the feeling of drifting through endless nothingness... I wanted to fly away. Just as I did every night in that dream. Fly as far away from here as I could.

Because, I thought, *what if that's all that remains? What if there was nothing inside Gatley House but that forever desert?*

The sound of splintering wood brought me back. I blinked.

'Esta?' Simon said. He must have sensed something was wrong, because he had a worried tone.

I blinked again. The vision had gone, but not the sense of hopelessness. 'How?' The question crawled out of my throat like a frightened mouse coming out of its hole. 'I mean, they concreted over the windows.'

Simon touched my arm. 'If we could... would you come? If we found a way in?'

My breath was heavy, painful even. I pulled away from him, staring at him. *Found a way in?*

'I don't know,' I said, backing away.

'You don't know?' he looked at Graham for help. 'We *have* to do this, don't we?'

I closed my eyes, felt the branches against my back. *Did we have to? I mean... really?*

I could hear Simon step closer, could hear him saying something. The chainsaw buzz drowned out most of it, but one word got through. A single word that made me stop.

'Tulku.'

I opened my eyes.

No matter how hard you want to resist... you always lift the curtain, right?

9

— . —

TULKU

'WHEN A MASTER DIES,' the old abbot had explained in the dim light of a single candle flame. 'They return to a new life to continue their training. We call these beings "Tulku".'

It had made little sense then. I *had* been a little preoccupied with some other revelations at the time: like that a parallel world somehow existed inside the walls of Gatley House; that my dad might still be alive. And, of course, we had just escaped a couple of nasty demons too. I'd said something banal in response, as I recall. 'You're saying we've been alive before?'

Lama la had nodded sagely. 'And now, you've come back.'

But we'd never spoken about it again. Never had a chance. He'd changed the subject, started talking about Dad again and we never found out... We never found out who we had been in the past.

'It's how we can see, when no one else can,' Simon was saying. 'The Vajra. The Bell!' He touched my arm again. I didn't recoil this time. It barely even registered in fact.

Another vision, another voice was overlapping Simon's.

A voice echoing in an endless desert.

Simon was saying something about how we were supposed to go back, but in my head the emaciated dog was crawling towards me, its hind legs dragging in the dust.

I know who you are...

I staggered backwards, away from that dog. I probably should have fallen through the branches, but Simon and Graham must have grabbed me, pulling me back under cover. I gulped cool air. The desert, the dog, were gone. We were under the deep green shade of the Willow. I swallowed.

Graham and Simon looked at me. Concern etched across both their faces.

'It's OK,' I said, pushing Simon's hand gently off me. 'It's OK. Just a bad... I don't know. Thing.'

'You sure you're OK?'

'It's the meds they give me,' I said, trying to control my breathing, reminding myself that the dog was just a dream. The desert was just a dream. 'I get the odd funny turn, that's all.'

Graham and Simon exchanged another look. Graham shrugged.

'Est,' Simon said. 'Rigpa Gompa, Lama la, the Dharmapalas... everything is still here. They need our help.'

I brushed hair from my eyes; hoped I looked all recovered and… you know, sane again. 'How do you know?'

He pulled something from inside his jacket, started unfolding it. I snatched it off him and finished the job: Charlie's pencil line drawing of Rigpa Gompa.

'My sister sees,' Simon said, nodding down at the drawing. 'She sees it all. And she's still drawing stuff. It's still here!'

I handed the paper back. Simon refolded it and put it back in his jacket pocket.

I inspected my shoes. They were muddy. Doctor Edwards would definitely find that strange. He'd ask where I'd been. If he knew what we were discussing right now under this tree, he'd strap a straight-jacket round me faster than tying his shoelace.

I sighed, pushed hair from my eyes. What were we contemplating? 'Even if,' I said carefully, 'we somehow climb the barbed wire fence around the wall.' I raised my eyebrows. 'There are the concrete filled windows to smash through. I notice neither of you are carrying a sledgehammer.'

Simon glanced at Graham again. I cocked my head wearily in his direction too. 'Alright,' I said. 'You have a plan. Of course you do.'

'I can get you both in,' he confirmed.

'Then there are the keys,' I argued. 'We still don't have the Vajra and the Bell, do we? They stayed in Rigpa Gompa. We can't get inside without them.'

Graham looked at Simon. 'Actually…'

'You're kidding?'

Simon raised his eyebrows with what I took to be his way of expressing bristling pride. 'You up for it?'

I shook my head, but I felt a smile spreading across my face.

'I mean, with the meds and the funny turns?'

'I'll manage. But how? I mean, how did you—'

The chainsaw buzz stopped. We turned as one towards the eerie silence that followed it. There was the unmistakable cracking sound of a tree collapsing into the bushes.

'I'll tell you on the way,' Simon said as he plunged through the branches. Graham and I followed.

'Graham?' I hissed as we ran towards the old building. 'What exactly are we about to do?'

Graham winked, then looked down at my muddy trainers as they landed on the broken driveway. 'You got grips on the soles of those?'

10

—.—

Up a Wall...

I'D NOT BEEN FAR off with my image of the flasher. Gatley House was a grisly and exhausted looking thing. It looked like it would topple over all by itself. The council had fully imprisoned it in tall fencing and barbed wire. The boards over the windows had been replaced with breeze blocks. The place was a crumbling shadow overrun by nature. Ivy climbed out of the hole in its battered roof. One chimney had fully collapsed since the summer, leaving a pile of bricks on the ground.

It had the look of a defeated boxer slouched on his stool at the end of the worst beating of his life.

The smells of nature gave way to the vinegary stink of urine. The trees on this side had avoided the chainsaw, so they partly masked the small basement window where Simon, Graham, and I had entered that very first time. A supermarket trolley lay bent and wheel-less on its side. I placed a hand on the metal fence—there was no tearing a gap in this one —and looked through the slats. Someone had daubed blue graffiti all over the breeze blocks covering the window: a symbol that looked like a "3" and a blue arrow pointing skywards. Water dripped from the first-floor window, streaking the brickwork black.

'It's greasy,' Graham said. 'It'll be dangerous today.'

I looked down at my trainers. Hardly climbing gear. I gripped the wire fencing and rattled it. 'We're going to climb that?'

'With a little help.'

'You've already done this, haven't you?'

Simon nodded. 'That's how I know we're still connected. How I know they want us to help them.'

'I thought you needed me—'

'I do. You'll see. Trust me. Up there. Please.' He checked his watch. 'We've got less than half an hour before Esta has to be back. How are we going to do this?'

'Not at all if you keep checking the time,' Graham said, yanking the trolley up against the fence. 'Give us a hand, Si.'

They heaved the trolley upside down and then got on it. The thing wobbled a bit, but Simon leant against the fence to steady them. After a few seconds, he bent his knees and made a cradle of his hands. Graham took off his jacket, then stepped in and clambered up, using the fence, Simon's shoulder and then the top of his head for balance.

'Hurry!' Simon's muffled voice said. 'Your foot's in my face.'

Graham whipped his jacket up and over the barbed wire that was strung all along the top of the fence, then brought one knee up, using the jacket as padding. One hand splayed against the wall for support as the fence wobbled under his weight. He reached up with his other hand until it seemed to sink into the wall. A missing brick. He pulled his other leg up, bringing a sigh of relief from Simon. The fence wobbled. My heart skipped a beat. Graham stayed still for a few seconds and then climbed.

Every fourth brick was missing or half broken away. This is how he climbed. A ladder built into the wall. Ingenious.

Simon jumped down and stood by me, watching Graham make the climb. 'If you think I'm doing that,' I said. 'You can forget it.' If you slipped, the only thing to break your fall would be barbed wire and a shopping trolley.

'Me neither,' Simon replied.

Graham was at the first-floor window now. Back in spring, this had been overgrown, with branches pushing through the boards. Now the branches had been cut back and breeze blocks guarded the way. I looked further up. The wall looked flat above him. No more holes. So what was he going to do? Kick the breeze block in? He rested on the windowsill, checked back at us, smiled, then reached up once more and started climbing again. I frowned. How was he doing this?

Simon answered my unasked question. 'He hammered in a few metal rods between the bricks for foot holds. We didn't think anyone would notice.'

'Where'd he learn this stuff?' I asked, staring in amazement as Graham did a Spiderman impression up the wall.

'His dad's in the army, isn't he?'

After another minute of careful climbing, he reached the roof, using the gutter for support. I gulped. 'That's going to snap.'

'Dad told me,' Simon said, 'whoever fixed in the guttering meant business. None of your plastic tat. Victorian iron works. It's all riveted into the brick. Look. It doesn't even bend.'

'I don't see how I could do that,' I said. 'I mean, my trainers are slippy and—'

'Wait.'

The end of a rope landed with a thump against the trolley.

Simon looked at me and grinned. 'It's safe,' he said. 'It's wrapped round the chimney. Just use the fence for a foothold, then the missing bricks and then—'

I held up a hand. 'I got it, thanks, Si.'

'OK,' he said, looking up, hands on his waist. 'So... ladies first?'

11

—.—

And Down a Hole

WHEN I WAS ABOUT halfway up, Simon whispered: 'You OK?' I looked down and cursed myself. Surely I'd learned by now? Simon looked about the size of a jelly baby. Around him were piles of bricks, fallen branches and other really hard looking things. I paused, trying to control the wobble in my legs. *Come on Esta...* I told myself. *We got over this, didn't we? Feel the fear and everything?*

When I got to the top, Graham's hand appeared, and he helped me up over the gutter. I lay back against the tiles, let out a deep, steadying breath and looked out across the hedgerow to Fletcher's Field... correction, what used to be Fletcher's Field. From up here you could see the dark strip of road: a black stain flowing through the a blanket of green. I looked south towards the Weeping Willow and the thinning belt of trees between it and what used to be Grover Close. They'd sent the bulldozers away for a few months over summer, no doubt tearing up some more grass in another part of the county. Now they were back with a vengeance. Taylor hadn't stopped. He'd only paused while the council re-housed the roosting bats and dredged the pond.

Simon's head emerged over the gutter.

'I can't believe you two planned all this,' I said as Graham yanked him up.

Simon grinned. 'Nothing much else to do during the summer holidays.'

'You're both nut cases, you know that?.'

Simon sidled next to me and grinned.

'What now?' I asked.

Graham sighed and rubbed his hands against his shirt. 'You two go on. Simon. You know what to do. Go slow—'

'Wait. Aren't you coming?'

'No. I promised Simon it would just be you two the first time.'

'What was the point of you coming up here, then?'

'Cos he's the only one who can make the climb without having a wobble,' Simon said.

'And anyway,' Graham said, picking up the rope and glancing down. 'I need to get the engine running on your getaway car.' He leaned out. 'I'd say you've got about twenty minutes. Good luck.' And with that, he let himself down.

By the time I leaned out far enough to look, he was already at the bottom. He landed, looked up, and saluted. Then he ran to the gap in the hedge, checked up the track, and disappeared behind the hedge.

I leaned back against the roof tiles. 'What did he mean, the first time?'

I think Simon pretended not to hear me. Instead, he started shuffling along the side of the roof, crab-like; heels dug into the gutter, palms and backside against the tiles. I followed. Slowly. Reminding myself that Victorians made gutters to last.

Simon stopped at the corner. 'You have to push out a bit, swing your leg round. Graham fastened a hook between the tiles to hang on to in case... you know.'

I watched as he carefully hitched himself over and round the corner, knuckles white around the hook. When it was my turn, I didn't look down. Or breathe. And I held on to that hook so hard I was afraid I might have ripped it out of its fixings.

I breathed heavily when I was flat against the tiles again, then slid on after Simon towards the semi-destroyed roof.

The tear was about twenty feet wide.

I'd been right underneath when the wrecking ball made matchsticks of the walls. The council, it seemed, had the funds to surround Gatley House with barbed wire and breeze-block the windows, but not to seal off a collapsed roof.

I reached the edge and peered down. The floor directly below was smashed to pieces. Harry Sparks had removed the floor below that years ago. So I stared through a gaping hole down to the main staircase forty or fifty feet below.

A jungle had taken over down there; nature reclaiming the land before Taylor could wipe it out completely and replace it with his beloved tarmac.

'Watch your feet,' Simon said. 'That beam's not secure.'

Simon went first. The beam, I noticed, was propped up by a pile of bricks. Nice.When he landed safely on the remaining bit of floor, I breathed another sigh of relief, followed and landed on the broken floor as lightly as I could.

The floorboards creaked under our weight; I peered over the edge, half expecting to see Dad swimming down there in the grey sea again. Not this time. Just bricks and fragments of plaster littering the stairwell. *Had I really fallen down there and survived?*

'Come here. Look.' Simon held my hand and pulled me back towards the wall so we were under the shade of the remaining bit of roof. A small wooden table stood on the floorboards, untouched by the surrounding chaos. The only bit of furniture in the hollowed out room. On top of it were three rows of dusty trash. Spoons, knives, a couple of plates, steel goblets, a pair of wire-rimmed glasses.

'I told you, didn't I?' Simon whispered, his hand hovering over what looked like an old door-bolt. 'Everything laid out for us. Just like the first time.'

I reached out towards an object in the centre of the table: a rusty old hinge. I ran a finger along its familiar edge. It was warm to touch. A trickle of electricity ran beneath my fingertip. I heard the scrape of metal as Simon lifted his door-bolt.

I gulped. If I picked it up, I knew, everything could change. Was sure of it.

'They want us back,' Simon said. 'Why else would these be here? They need us.'

I curled a finger around the hinge. Maybe nothing would happen today. Maybe today the junk would just be junk.

I picked it up and looked at Simon as I did. A web of blue strands of light crackled and sparkled in his eyes.

The surrounding space darkened and suddenly became so cold that my breath turned to steam. 'It's happening, Est,' Simon whispered.

A vague, rose-coloured shape flickered into view about fifteen feet away from me.

I swiped at the air, parting the cloud of breath.

The walls and floor swam in and out of focus. The room seemed to shift.

In the middle of it all, a figure dressed in wine-coloured monk's robes stood in what was—what should have been—mid-air.

PART TWO

I Know Who You Are

12

WHISPERS FROM THE WHEEL

WHERE THERE HAD BEEN crumbling bricks and jagged strips of wood, there were now walls covered with painted images. Where there had been broken floorboards and a dangerous dark hole, there was now a shimmering of greys, greens and browns. Each colour bleeding into another, collecting into a new, solid floor that emerged from the chaos of quivering light.

A couple of cushions lay on the new floor. To the left, a small shrine: six bowls lined up in front of a little brass statue.

I blinked. Lifted my head towards the sky. A wash of slate grey mist hung over us. What was left of the daylight seemed to drain out of the sky like dirty water down a drain. A pale blue and misty grey swirled and slowly gathered into a floating ball of light that hung just above the ground.

A polite cough.

I lowered my gaze.

The figure in the wine-coloured robes beckoned us towards him. 'Come.'

And just like that, all my doubts and confusion about Rigpa Gompa disappeared. Gatley, the mental hospital... even Mum were distant pin pricks, fluffs of dust on a window screen. I walked forwards, ignoring the fact that I was walking on ground that moments before hadn't been there.

My feet trod the solid wooden boards of Rigpa Gompa now. There were signs of destruction everywhere, but unlike Gatley House, this place had been patched up with wooden boards and white paint.

I stood and looked around for a few moments, memories flooding back to me: the first time we met the four Dharmapalas in their multi-coloured robes; the enormous statue of Padmakara, so big, its head poked through the ceiling; the battle with the Mamo; the smell of their rotting flesh; Mara's face looming over me as I hung on the rope. All of it real. All of it suddenly more real than anything else.

Lama la stopped beside the floating sphere of light. It seemed to grow, spinning slowly, pulsing, *breathing*, as if it were alive. 'Time is moving quickly,' he said. 'The Dharmapalas have been away for too long, they cannot do it all.'

The sphere expanded, become brighter, larger, blotting out the rest of the room.

I moved closer, mesmerised by it.

'Lama la?' Simon said, his voice barely audible.

I reached out towards the light, my fingers magnetised by its glow. I was close enough now to see movement within each of the six realms. My eyes skated across the surface of each one: the Gods, the Jealous Gods, Animals, Hungry Ghosts, Hell Beings and this one... the Human Realm. What had Lama la said about it? *The Wheel of Samsara: A place where living beings are caught in worlds of their own making.*

I thought of Dad. *Which one are you caught in?*

Simon spoke, but his words were dim and unclear. Lama la may have responded, but a whispering sound coming from within the Wheel drew in me; a voice speaking right at the edge of my hearing:

'*Esta...*'

Not a dog's growl, but a woman's voice.

'*Esta Brown?*'

A voice I wanted to answer. Wanted to follow.

'*I know who you are.*' Such a lovely, safe voice.

My fingers touched the light. Static electricity crackled across its surface, drawing my body to it.

'*I can show you.*'

And now my feet lifted effortlessly from the ground like my body was filled with helium. I felt insubstantial. Hardly there at all. The feeling was so peaceful, so pleasant, like stepping into the cool waters of a pool on a hot summer's day...

'Not yet!'

Lama la's face loomed out at me from within the globe. The shock of him was like being slapped in the face.

I dropped to the floor, my body solid again, my breath coming in sharp gasps. Lama la raised his eyebrows, then strode right through the middle of the Wheel like it wasn't there at all. 'No point going in,' he said, his words suddenly all too loud and clear, 'when you don't even know what you're looking for!'

'You alright?' Simon whispered in my ear as he helped me to stand.

'Just a bit freaked out,' I glanced guiltily at *Samsara,* like someone on a strict diet looks at a cream cake in the corner of the room.

'It's just...' I said. 'You know, a lot to take in.'

'I'm getting my head round it too.'

'Here,' Lama la said. 'Take a seat. Have some tea. I had Rabjam make a pot before he and the others left. It's still warm. I'll give you a moment to catch up.'

We sat on the cushions by the shrine, drank our butter tea, and gazed at *Samsara* as it hung in the centre of the room. At more of a distance, its pull on me was barely there at all. But the memory of that whispering voice still echoed in my ears:

I know who you are...

The tea helped clear my mind a bit, and after a second cup, I was even able to tear my eyes away from the light. I breathed in the salty aroma of the drink, the spice of incense hanging in the air, the acrid twist from the butter lamps on the shrine.

I ran my fingers over the smooth wooden floor. Last time I'd been here, Mara had smashed this floor into pieces. It felt solid now. Not a dream, not an illusion, not just a line of poetry.

It was all real. As real as Gatley Gardens was, anyway.

I glanced over at Simon. He was watching me. A faint smile on his lips.

'What?'

'We're really back,' he said. 'We're really here, aren't we?'

I smiled back. 'Yes.' I glanced over at Lama la. He was studying his fingernails.

But why?

Lama la looked up suddenly, noticed our empty cups, raised his eyebrows: 'So... are you ready to begin?'

13

THE POISONED ARROW

'HOW LONG HAS IT been?'

'Just a couple of months,' Simon said.

Lama la nodded. 'I see. I see. And... everything is... as it should be in the human realm?'

'No,' Simon said. 'Esta's locked away in a hospital and the bulldozers are back. I don't know how we're going to stop them this time.'

He nodded again. 'Apart from that? Everything is running... smoothly and... predictably?'

'Cause and effect,' I said. 'You mean, is everything...' I searched for a word other than "normal".

'Flowing correctly,' Lama la finished. 'Does the sun rise in the morning? Does the rain fall down, not up? That kind of thing.'

I thought for a second. Everything did seem disjointed in Gatley Gardens, but keys still opened locked doors. Breakfast was always reliably awful. Mum visited at 4 o'clock every day.

'Yes,' Simon said, a little impatiently. 'Cause and effect is fine. But they're coming to pull Gatley House down.'

'The attacks have been getting stronger here as well,' Lama la said. 'We have little time. It is fortunate you came when you did.'

I waited for him to tell us more, but he was squinting at us, as if maybe Simon and me had vanished, and he was searching for us.

'Why us?' I said, after a minute of uncomfortable silence.

Lama la's eyes refocused. He smiled, briefly. 'Because you have returned after many lifetimes.'

'Tulku,' I repeated quietly.

'Lama la,' Simon said, and asked the burning question. 'You never told us who we were. You said we used to be important, but you never told us anything more.'

I held my breath, waiting for the answer. *I know who you are...*

Lama la had set out the Vajra and the Bell for us to find. He had led us to the teachings we had supposedly written and hidden hundreds of years ago. If anyone could answer the question, it was him.

'I never told you,' Lama la said at last. 'Because I'm not completely sure.'

My breath escaped me in a long, slow, disappointed sigh. *How could he not know?*

'Hundreds of lives have come and gone. You have returned, but it is not clear by which route and it is only the greatest masters who can trace the tangled web of lives each of us weaves.'

I touched my forehead. Cold sweat was beading there. *How could he not be completely sure?*

'But what about the objects we found?' Simon asked. 'And you said you'd been waiting for us.'

'It would be foolish to speculate,' Lama la replied. 'Sometimes it's better to know nothing rather than half a truth.'

I shook my head, and a dry laugh escaped my lips. 'So, you want us to help you, but you won't tell us who we are and why it has to be us?'

Lama la gave me a fierce glare. 'When a man is shot with a poisoned arrow, does he ask who shot it?'

'What?'

He pushed himself to his feet and pointed to something behind us. I turned. The Wheel. It had changed colour. It was greyer than before. It looked sort of... older. He stepped over his low table. 'No,' he said, as he shuffled between us towards it. 'The man's first question should be: "How do I get it out?"'

14

—·—

THE BROKEN WHEEL

LAMA LA SILENTLY EXAMINED the rotating sphere of light. Simon and I got up and joined him. Me, a bit nervously. The closer I got, the more powerful the pull it had over me.

I can show you who you are...

My stomach lurched.

'Samsara continues to fail,' Lama la said when we reached him, pointing to a spot on the north-east section of the globe. I gripped Simon's hand for security and focused on the old man's words.

'The division between each realm is disintegrating. You see that?' he said, pointing at the foot of an enormous mountain which dominated the top part of *Samsara.* 'The Chitapali tree sits on the lower slopes of Mount Meru.'

Simon stood on his tiptoes to get a better look.

'It is the great tree that separates the Gods from the Ashura.'

'Ashura?' Simon asked.

'Jealous gods.'

'There's smoke coming from it,' Simon said, peering even more closely at the area just below the tree. 'God, this is so detailed. It looks like a battlefield.'

'It is.'

'Who are they fighting?'

'The Long-lived Ones themselves. The Ashura have everything they could want, and yet they're never satisfied. They want it all.'

I looked up towards Mount Meru. The lower slopes were covered in what looked like fields of flowers, swishing grasses and sparkling streams. I frowned. There was no opposing army. 'There's no one fighting back,' I said, looking back at the tree. Some of its branches were now alight. Black smoke rose from fires on the field below it.

'The Gods are so refined that they never suffer,' Lama la said. 'They don't even know they're being attacked. The tree protects them. It's an endless battle that the Ashura—by their very nature—have never won. No matter how much they throw at the Gods, they have never—'

A branch snapped off the tree and cart-wheeled to the earth.

'They looked pretty determined to me,' Simon said.

I looked at Lama la. The light from the Wheel made him look ghostly, like an old photograph fading from view. He saw me looking at him and immediately turned away.

'For the first time,' he said. 'The Ashura are winning.'

'That's bad isn't it?' Simon muttered. 'If they beat the Gods...'

'... Then what hope do the other realms have?' Lama la completed Simon's thought.

I looked back at the burning tree. It was like staring down on a Lego world, or some super advanced computer game. It was hard to believe real actual people were living, suffering and dying down there.

'The reality of *Samsara* is changing,' Lama la said. 'We are entering the Bardo of Becoming. The laws of cause and effect are loosening.'

The Wheel turned. The grasslands of the Ashura realm ended at a wide river which ran from the edge of Samsara into the centre, like the single spoke of a wheel. Beyond it was what looked like... I peered closer... dust, smoke.

'The realm of the animals,' Lama la said.

'What's wrong with it?' I said. I'd seen a documentary about deforestation in the Amazon jungle where acres and acres of jungle had been scythed away, leaving bare clumps of earth and barren hills. Once rich, life-giving soil turned into dead sand. Hair rose on the nape of my neck. A desert as far as the eye could see.

'Nothing lives there now,' Lama la said quietly. 'The Preta have consumed the *forest*: Hungry Ghosts out of control. The animals have fled.'

'What can we do?' Simon said. I heard him, but his voice was distant again. I had to focus. I had to concentrate on the here. On the Now. But the spinning wheel pulsed. It ebbed and flowed and the woman's voice called out to me again:

Esta Brown... Let me show you... The sands below whipped and spun in a rising cloud. Patterns forming in the swirling dust. An image emerged of my dad's face: a haunted look, hollow cheeks, scratchy beard. Then it was gone. Something else: the rounded spiky leaves of the Fly Trap in Harry Sparks' room, the twitching leg of the insect in its clutches. *Shadows... close around you. Consume you.*

Then the woman spoke once more. This time just one word, clear as a church bell.

Beautiful.

15

THE PRECIOUS CANOPY

I BIT THE INSIDE of my mouth. Sharp pain brought tears to my eyes. I shook my head vigorously, breathed and took a step away from the Wheel. Simon squeezed my hand, gave me a questioning look. I nodded: *I'm OK.*

'There is a temple,' Lama la was saying, 'like this one, in every realm of *Samsara*. Each one protects a key in the form of a symbol.' He looked at me. Checking I was still with him.

I nodded again. 'Like the Kila.'

He gave me a reassuring smile. Wagged his head from side to side. 'A little like the Kila.'

'It's missing,' Simon said. 'You want us to find the key?'

'I cannot leave Rigpa Gompa unprotected.'

'You want us to go in there,' I said, staring at the desert land passing below us. 'And find some kind of key?'

'Nothing can harm you. You will be protected.'

I shook my head. 'I don't think we should—'

Simon cut across me. 'What does it look like?'

I glared at him. Always eager to play the hero.

Lama la pointed to the wall to the left of the doorway. There were a series of wall hangings. 'The second one along on the top row.'

'It looks like an umbrella,' Simon said.

'A parasol, actually. It has the power to protect the one who possesses it from the burning heat of suffering.'

'You want us to go inside there and find an umbrella in a desert that's inhabited by ghosts?'

'A precious parasol... and it's *Hungry* Ghosts,' Lama la corrected.

'Well, of course,' I murmured. 'Who wouldn't be hungry in a place like that?'

'Where will we find it?' Simon asked.

'There will be a statue of Padmakara. Just like here in Rigpa Gompa. The symbol will be placed before it. Remove it. Hold on to it and I will retrieve you.'

'Retrieve us?' Simon asked sceptically.

'The key will create a bridge between the two realms. I will be able to retrieve you without leaving here.'

'So...' I sighed. 'That all seems simple enough. When do you want us to come back to do this?'

Lama la snapped his fingers. The Wheel stopped spinning.

I smiled stiffly. 'Cool. No time like the present.'

Lama la held up the finger he'd just snapped. 'No. There's no time *but* the present!'

We sat around the sphere, looking at the wide expanse of desert, which crawled across the surface. *Stretching to the horizon. I hope we don't meet any dogs.*

Lama la ran his bead necklace through his fingers, lips moving in silent prayer.

I tapped Simon's knee. 'You're an idiot,' I whispered.

'Why?'

'Because this is your fault.'

'My fault?'

'You couldn't help yourself, could you? It's like when you ran back into Gatley House. You have to be the hero.'

'Says the girl who took a wrecking ball in the face.'

'I didn't *choose* to—'

Lama la coughed politely. 'The Hungry Ghost realm is a mentally created reality. You remember when I took you into *Samsara* last time? You should be able to move using the power of thought. Just focus on something and you'll travel there. Remember that.'

We both nodded. The last time Lama la had taken us within the Wheel it had taken me a while to breathe again. Actually, we'd spent the first few minutes floating around, disembodied, so strictly speaking, it had taken a while for me to even have lungs to breathe *with*.

'Don't stay long. If you don't find the key, then fly back to the Gompa. The longer you stay in the Wheel, the deeper an impression you'll make. If your body begins to take on substantial form, you may be weaved in.'

'What does that mean?' Simon asked.

'It means you'll begin to feel the heat, you'll sweat, the Preta will *smell* you. If that happens... you must return to the Gompa immediately or you'll be stuck in the realm of Hungry Ghosts.'

I looked at Simon. He returned my look with a little wince. I shook my head. *Idiot,* I mouthed, then gripped his hand.

Lama la made his final incantations and the sphere of light expanded, the desert land filling the room.

'Go straight to the Gompa. You will find the key on the shrine.'

A sandstorm billowed upwards.

'Just find the key, remove it from the shrine and call me! Don't be distract—'

A tornado of dust tore apart his last words. It filled the room, snuffed out the candles. Grains of swirling sand filled my nostrils, my eyes, my ears, lifting me, spinning me and finally, sucking me inside. I felt Simon's fingers slip from mine. Oh God, I thought. Please, not here...

16

INTO THE REALM OF HUNGRY GHOSTS

'SIMON?' I WHISPERED AS the sandstorm settled. My invisible body drifted through a thinning dust cloud. 'Simon?' I called.

A current of hot air brought a hollow smell of decay, and with it the vivid sense of having been here many times before. As the dust cleared, I saw the familiar landscape of my dreams. The bleached remains of things that might have once been people. *Nothing,* I thought. *Nothing could live here.*

I searched the sky for Simon, but it was an ocean of empty blue. I searched the dunes for the dog. Terrified of seeing it, but desperate to see something. *Anything* that moved. In my dream, there was *always* the dog.

I drifted on. Tears dried on my skin, my skin dried on my flesh, my flesh cooked. The sands were endless sleep. My mind a parched fog. Where was Simon? Was he drifting like me? Had Lama la flung us into this deserted place on purpose?

This wasn't my dream. I was sure of that. This seemed *realer* somehow.

The temple, I thought. Lama la said there would be a temple, just like Rigpa Gompa. *Move by the power of thought,* Lama la had said. *Focus on something and you will travel there.* I closed my eyes and conjured an image of Rigpa Gompa. Focused on it.

I felt myself glide. I opened my eyes, relieved. Something glinted down there in the sands. A pinprick of light which grew into a rose-coloured line. Vibrant against the grey of the desert.

I dropped. If there was a stream, it might lead me to the Gompa.

But my heart sank as I got closer. The pink 'stream' was drooling across the sands from a foul-looking mud pool covered in thick scum. I hung in mid-air, staring down at it, breathing in poisonous smelling fumes. *Focus and you will travel there... Focus...*

A noise made me twist around: a bubbling groaning sound like an old smoker clearing his throat. I lifted into the sky to see what was making it.

A human figure limped across the desert.

My heart leapt. 'Simon?' I called.

The figure collapsed on to its knees.

I flew downwards. 'Simon!'

But even before I reached the figure, I knew it wasn't him.

The thing was barely human at all. A bulbous head sat on top of a long, scrawny neck. Beneath that, its stomach was so enormous that it spread out on either side of four skinny limbs. It reminded me of a jellyfish I'd once seen lying on the beach: all pale, gelatinous and veiny.

I backed away, momentarily transfixed by the sight of its pathetic attempts to right itself. A movement in the corner of my eye made me tear my gaze from the creature.

More were coming.

17

A Hundred Lunch Bells

HUNGRY GHOSTS.

The dipping sun stretched their long, drawn out shadows across the dunes. Each one of them dragged itself forward, head bowed, back arched over, pulled down by the weight of its huge, sagging belly. The mud-pool bubbled beneath me, letting out a *ppff* of trapped air. Green and yellow gunk oozed out in rivulets like some kind of tie-dye lava flow. I gagged at the stench.

To my disgust, the closest figures scrambled towards it, diving into the slime wherever it seeped, plunging their faces through the scum floating on its surface, guzzling it hungrily.

I was about to rise high up again when one creature caught my eye. Most of the others were bald, but this one had long, stringy brown hair that hung limply from its sunburnt scalp, ends dipping in the ooze.

I tilted my head for a better look. Blinked in disbelief. This creature wore what looked like an ancient pair of blue jeans and... around the fourth finger of its left hand: a golden ring.

'It's just a dream,' I whispered to myself. I hovered lower, heart pounding in my ears. The smell was almost too much now, but I had to see its face. *Long hair, blue jeans, wedding ring...*

As it drank, a strand of hair slid away, revealing a straggly beard.

My feet touched the ground. Solid ground. I checked to make sure the stream flowed between me and the line of Hungry Ghosts. I was sure that all of this was just a dream, but Lama la had talked about being 'weaved in' and I didn't want to be anyone's dinner. Not even in a dream.

I lowered into a crouch. I knew I was torturing myself. I knew what I would find. If this was some sort of mind-created reality, then none of this was really true, was it? I should have just stopped. Flown away, left them to their disgusting meal.

But I couldn't. Because, if I could just see its eyes...

The creature next to it stopped slurping. It sniffed. Slowly, very slowly, its nose twitched. Its head came up from the gunk. A single red-rimmed eye twitched in its socket, then paused, fixing on me. The thing drew a slimy arm from the mud, strings of snotty stuff hanging off it. Its mouth opened, revealing a row of brown teeth.

I backed away, briefly checking upwards, hoping to god that I'd be able to take off again.

The creature grunted: a wet farting sound. Even the noise of these things was disgusting.

'Time to go,' I whispered to myself. But my feet stayed firmly in the grit. Grit that felt pretty hot beneath my feet. '*You'll begin to feel the heat,*' Lama la had said. '*The Preta will smell you.*'

I stared up at the empty sky. 'Come on,' I said through gritted teeth. 'Fly.' The sound was barely above a whisper, but I might as well have rung a hundred lunch bells. The line of creatures stopped guzzling and raised their marble-glass eyes as one.

I took a shuffling step backwards. And as I did, just in case I wasn't freaked out enough already, the rusty penny of a sun dropped over the horizon, instantly turning everything blood-red.

'Bugger,' I whispered.

18

ATTACK OF THE HUNGRY GHOSTS

I TOOK A BREATH. Regretted it immediately. Gagged on the stench of rotten eggs. Almost threw up my omelette.

You can fly, I told myself. *You can flipping well fly! Focus on something and travel to it.* How hard was that? But my feet were concrete blocks and I could barely even shuffle backwards. *At least,* I thought hopefully, *they're on the other side of the stream.*

But that was never going to last, was it? They could have side-stepped a few feet to the left or right and it would have been narrow enough to step over, but apparently Hungry Ghosts don't think like that. Hungry Ghosts are all about beelines.

They crawled towards me through the slime, clambering over each other to get at me.

The dipping sun sucked all the heat from the atmosphere, and as the night sky turned everything from red to purple, the surrounding air froze. The skin on my face burned with the cold and my panic-stricken breath hung in clouds around me.

There was a grating, crunching sound.

My eyes snapped back towards the mass of Hungry Ghosts. They'd stopped in the middle of the stream, the thick goo hardening and cracking into ice around them. The tangle of slime-coated limbs stiffened and slowly sank under the freezing surface.

My own limbs locked with the sudden cold. I took in a tiny shallow breath, then stared up towards the blackening sky. I had to get out of here, or I'd be a block of ice in minutes.

A loud cracking noise made me look back at the frozen stream.

A single hand had broken through the crusted surface. A hand, I noticed in the fading light, with a golden ring around its fourth finger. It reached for the bank, scrabbling for grip. A head emerged. Hair pasted against its skull, green, unblinking eyes fixed on me, jaws working silently, swollen tongue rolling in its toothless mouth.

No, no, no. Not here. Not like this. I glanced back up at the empty sky again. *Focus on something.* But the sky was a black hole with nothing to move towards, nothing to fix on, just the hissing, bubbling sound of the Hungry Ghost as it heaved itself onto dry land only fifteen feet away.

I thought of Simon. Those hopeful blue eyes hiding behind a flick of straight blonde hair. A faint nervous smile.

I whispered his name.

But the sound died on my lips. I was alone in this empty place. "Weaved in" or whatever Lama la called it. And so what was the point of running? Where would I go?

The sound of shuffling feet and groaning increased. More Hungry Ghosts. Coming from behind me now. *Even if I escape*, I thought. *How long will it be before I become one of them?*

I closed my eyes. *Just like...*

But I couldn't say it. Couldn't even think the word.

I felt an immense weight, like the whole of the sky was pushing down on me. My shoulders dropped, my head bowed under the pressure.

So heavy, my thoughts seemed to hiss.

I frowned. Tried to bring back the image of Simon. But the whispering thoughts persisted: *Forget running. Running is exhausting.* I shook my head to dislodge them, but they became more numerous. Chattering voices: *Take the path of least resistance...*

I might have listened to them. Might have just given up right there, if it hadn't been for the sound of another voice. This one was distant, from somewhere far away.

I know you, it said.

Simon? Lama la?

No. A strange, but familiar voice calling to me. A beautiful, lilting sound that cut across the gurgling and shuffling of the approaching creatures.

I know who you are.

I clung to it as if it were a rope ladder hauling me to safety. And suddenly, thankfully, the ground disappeared from beneath me, the groans of starvation faded, and I surged upwards into the ink black of space.

Upwards towards a woman's soft voice.

A voice that said: *I can show you who you are...*

19

TRISNA

THE STENCH WAS GONE, the horrible sounds of the creatures were gone too. I was no longer bitterly cold. The woman's voice came to me from, I don't know, maybe above, maybe below. Hard to tell.

'A human girl shouldn't be visiting in the realm of the *Hungry* Ghosts.' She whispered the word "hungry". 'You've too much flesh on you. *Beautiful.*' This last word was more of a hiss too. A breathy word.

Silence.

I searched for whoever had saved me, but there was just inky darkness.

She knows who I am, I thought. *One of the Dharmapalas?* Two of them were female. Karma Chodron? No. This voice was far too serene. The other one. Sera? Could it be her? I couldn't remember her actually ever speaking, but she'd seemed kind of shy and this voice was anything but that.

I drifted a little longer in silence. After a while, I thought that maybe I'd imagined the voice. Maybe I was still somehow sitting in the desert. Or back in Gatley House having insane dreams under the stairs. Just like Charlie Bullock.

I breathed. *Calm down Esta. You're losing it. This is all in the mind.* 'None of this is real,' I said into the silence.

The woman's voice responded immediately. This time, there was a tinge of humour: 'You keep telling yourself that, human. *Excellent.*' That gentle hissing of the final word again sending an unpleasant shiver up my spine.

'Who are you?' I asked, straining my eyes to look into the darkness.

'Who are *you?*' she echoed back. '*Come* with me. You *want* to.'

Despite all my 'stranger danger' alarm bells going off all at once, I began drifting toward the voice. Why did I follow? Why didn't I resist? Because she had saved me from being eaten by... whatever *that* was down there? Sure. Maybe. But also, because apart from her voice, there was nothing else to focus on, just blank, empty nothingness. And anything, no matter how creepy, was preferable to that.

'Trisna,' the woman said. She followed this with: '*Adorable.*'

I gulped. I *really* didn't like the way she wove those little whisperings into her sentences.

'What are you *searching* for?' asked the woman.

I twisted round, looking for some landmark to focus on, anything to cling to, to anchor me down. Something that would allow me to escape this mysterious voice. And that's when I first set eyes on her.

She was twenty feet above me; a figure picked out by a growing light on the horizon.

She was the very opposite of a Hungry Ghost. Thin and sleek as a sports car; a beautiful but severe face; straight black hair flowing behind her. She looked down at me with eyes that glittered like a couple of knife points: 'What is it you *want*, Esta Brown?'

I wrenched my gaze away from her. *She knows my name.* 'I'm good, thanks,' I mumbled.

'You're *searching* for someone.'

Simon. I want Simon to come and bloody rescue me. 'My friend. I have a really powerful friend that's looking for me right now.'

'I don't think so,' she replied. And then came closer, so I couldn't avoid her face. She smiled. It was a toothy smile. You know; all soap-star white. '*Delicious.*'

I spun away from those eyes. They were sharp as razors. Bright as sunlight through a magnifying glass.

'Where are you taking me?' I asked.

'Wherever you *want* to go. Whatever you *want* to find. Just tell me your *desire* and it will be done.'

'To be honest, Trish,' I said, trying to keep absolute panic out of my voice at least. 'Is that your name? I was thinking of just... you know, leaving?'

But as soon as the words left my mouth, we plunged into dense smoke and ash. I coughed as it filled my imaginary lungs. *Imaginary lungs, Esta,* I tried to tell myself. *It's only real if you let it be—*

'Let me go,' I said in a strangled voice. 'I don't want to go with you.'

'You're right. None of this is real,' said the voice, reading my thoughts again. 'It's a mirror. Now tell me what you are *yearning* for.'

A stifling heat gathered around me like an unwelcome cuddle. Somewhere out there, beyond the ash cloud, a man was crying. No. He was pleading; his voice echoing and swirling around in the hot ash. A deafening crack of a whip; then the pleading turned into howls of pain.

'Dad?'

The choking clouds seemed to shake. Every individual particle within them vibrated and *shished* like grains of sand in a sieve.

Then the blackness spoke. This time, the voice was a deep growl: 'I know who you are... Esta Brown.'

Then all sounds ceased again. The smoke shifted and dissolved. My lungs unclenched and I sucked in cool air.

Now the woman's voice was back. All mellow and light and pleasant and she said: '*Follow* me Esta Brown. And I promise to show you what you *want...*'

20

—·—

THE GOLDEN CARRIAGE

THE BLACK CLOUD THINNED, parted, cleared.

We descended towards a land I recognised. Fresh green grass, blue waters, villages separated by fields and even oceans in the distance. I filled my lungs with the sweet, clear air.

Mountains reared up ahead of us and we plunged past shining waterfalls, between enormous rainbow arcs and then along a dark green valley. At its head were the peaks of a snow-topped mountain. Nestled in its arms was a small square courtyard and a white building with a curved golden roof.

The place was so familiar, as if from a distant memory or a forgotten dream. It wasn't Rigpa Gompa. It couldn't be Rigpa Gompa, but somehow I knew this place.

People in different coloured robes filled the courtyard.

'I've been here,' I whispered.

'You remember? Of course you do. But wait until we see the main... *attraction*.'

I floated closer to the building. 'Where is it?'

'Not where... who,' replied the mysterious woman.

I turned to her, too intrigued to be afraid anymore. 'Show me.'

She swept an arm in the direction of the valley. At the bottom was a line of monks dressed in blood-red robes. They were climbing a steep path that had been carved into the cliff face. Some held flags that waved in the mountain breeze.

Trisna spoke. 'He's *coming...*'

At the head of the line was a wheel-less carriage. It was like a horse-drawn one but supported by two long poles, a pair of monks taking the weight at each corner. Golden drapes hung over the sides of the vehicle, making it impossible to see inside.

'Who is it?' I started. But surely I already knew the answer. Who else could it be? My guide had already told me she would lead me to the thing I desired most.

Trisna sighed. The sort of satisfied sigh you might give when slipping into a warm bath. Or like sitting down after a job well done.

I drifted away from the courtyard, and down towards the procession; close enough to see the sweat on the brows of the men hauling the carriage up the path; the soft smiles on those following behind.

Could they see me? I didn't think so. I mean, I was hanging in the air as they climbed, so you'd have thought they'd react if they could.

I sank lower until I was on a level with the carriage windows. If I could just part those golden drapes. Look within. If I could just see him.

There was a deep, echoing rumble.

A loud call echoed against the walls of the cliff face: 'Awake!'

No one in the procession batted an eyelid.

I looked around for the source. It didn't sound like Trisna. It sounded more like...

'Enough!' the voice boomed.

I glanced upwards towards Trisna. Beside her, a misty figure had appeared in the sky.

'Esta!' the figure called, as it gained in clarity.

'Lama la?' I said.

'Come away!'

Trisna blocked him. 'You can't protect her. She will *find* him. He will *return*.'

I turned back to the carriage. It rocked and swayed as the men hauled it up the mountainside. If I could just pull at the curtains. If I could just see him.

'Esta,' called Lama la. 'Now is not the time. Follow my voice. Do not...'

The curtain rippled. A man's hand appeared, resting against the sill of the window. A golden ring with a single red symbol embossed in the centre.

'I have to see,' I whispered.

But before the curtain could part any further, a powerful hand gripped my arm and the mountain walls blurred and twisted.

I reached out to touch the fingers of the man behind the curtain, but the golden fabric folded and swirled and the whole world spun like the inside of a washing machine and everything collapsed into smudgy black again.

21

THE GREAT UNCERTAINTY

'WHAT DID YOU SEE?' Lama la asked sternly.

I cringed, my mind still slowly dragging itself back to the present. What had just happened? Where I had come from? Exactly why was I being told off?

I looked around for Simon. He was sitting next to me, innocent as anything, watching me with questioning eyes. I looked back at Lama la, who glared silently at me too, his eyes burrowing into mine. Absolutely typical of my life. Even in a parallel reality, I was always the one to be dragged into someone's office.

'What happened to you?' Simon asked. 'You disappeared. I tried to find you.'

I shook my head. 'I don't know. There was...' memories were flooding back in a rush now: the desert, the putrid stream, the crawling corpses. Acid rose in my mouth.

'Don't believe any of it!' Lama la said angrily. 'Mara may have given up attacking Rigpa Gompa, but his power is undimmed elsewhere. I should never have asked you to enter the Wheel like that!' His voice brought me fully back into the room, and with it, a sense of loss. Lama la had dragged me away from something... from someone. There had been a carriage; a curtain. Lama la had torn me away before I could lift the curtain.

'Why,' I said, a flicker of heat now sparking in me. 'Why did you take me away? Who... who was that?'

Lama la frowned, then let out a breath and dropped his gaze. His fingers went to a bowl, and he picked a small pile of dried rice from it. 'Where did she take you?' he said eventually. Voice calmer now.

'You were there. You tell me.'

He let the rice drop from his fingertips, like sand running through a glass timer. It was slow and deliberate. It was bloody infuriating.

'Why wouldn't you let me see him?' I asked.

'See who?' Simon asked. 'Esta, where did you go?'

Lama la let the last grains of rice drop. 'You may have seen too much...' he paused, considering his words. '... of something that could change everything.'

There was silence. I waited for him to go on, but he merely reached down, took an apple from a plate and placed it on top of the rice pile. He wasn't going to tell me. I remembered his habit of keeping information slightly out of focus when it suited him. So I changed tack.

'Who was the woman who saved me?'

Simon's head snapped up. 'Saved you? What happened, Est?'

'I got weaved in, or whatever, didn't I. I was attacked by Hungry Ghosts.' I thought about those bulbous green eyes and quickly shut the memory down.

'You didn't find the Gompa?' Simon said.

'No Simon! I did not! I suppose you did though? Found the precious umbrella or whatever it is? Saved the day, did you?'

Simon shrugged. 'It wasn't exactly hard,' he scratched his head. 'I just picked it up and came back here.'

'Yeah, well! I got lost, didn't I?'

'How could you get lost? We went straight there.'

'It's not like I meant to go. It just... pulled me in.'

'You were looking for your father,' Lama la said matter-of-factly.

I didn't answer. I hated it when he did that. It was like I had a glass bowl for a skull and all he had to do was peer at me to know what I was thinking.

'Your craving for him distracted you,' he continued. Paused. 'Didn't it.'

I sighed. What would be the point of denying it? 'Last time I was here. When I was facing Mara... I heard Dad's voice. He wanted me to find him. He was in a dusty place. And I've been having dreams...'

'Dreams?' Lama la asked.

'Dreams about... about a desert. And I thought that—'

'So, you thought you'd have a chat with a Hungry Ghost? Did it fulfil your expectations?'

'I wouldn't exactly call it a chat.'

'They saw you?'

I nodded. Saw me, smelt me, almost tasted me.

Lama la's brow furrowed. He leaned forward. 'You're sure?'

I pictured the bodies clawing themselves across that horrible stream. 'That's what I'm trying to tell you. This woman saved me.'

Lama la closed his eyes. Pinched the bridge of his nose.

'What's wrong?' Simon asked.

Lama la looked up at us. He stroked his stubbly chin. 'The realms are collapsing in on each other. Each one bleeds into the next. The machinery of cause and effect is collapsing. The time is almost upon us.'

'Time for what?'

He gave a tired smile. 'To finally act.' He nodded and then became silent again. After a while, he picked an apple from his table and stared at it.

When it became apparent he had finished whatever point he was making, I asked: 'Who was she then? Some sort of goddess?'

Lama la wagged his head wearily from side to side. 'She gave you her name,' he stated. 'She told you who she was.'

'Trisha or something,' I said.

Simon stifled a laugh. I shot him an annoyed look.

'What?' he protested. 'There's honestly a goddess called Trisha?'

I scowled at him. 'It might have been something more exotic. I was busy flying over a land full of disgusting monsters to really get the nuance—'

'Not monsters!' Lama la interrupted. 'Hungry Ghost are trapped by their own craving. They deserve our compassion, not our disgust.'

'But they're—'

He held the apple up. 'Disgust is merely the flip side of craving. And we are *all* guilty of that.' He rubbed the apple on one sleeve. 'We have all wandered our own desert in the past...'

'Well,' I mumbled, 'it's not like they were showing *me* much compassion.'

'You were lucky Simon came back so quickly.'

I looked sideways at Simon. 'What do you mean?'

'He was able to hold the fort while I went in search of you. I should *never* have sent you in! If you had spent *one* more moment in that place...' He turned the newly polished apple between his fingers. Another spinning globe. 'What you might have seen...'

I stared at him, waiting for him to finish his thought.

When he eventually lifted his attention from the apple, his eyes were dark and the creases on his face seemed about half an inch deeper than before. But yet again, whatever he was going to say remained unsaid.

'She offered me a choice,' I said. 'But you stopped me.'

Lama la closed his eyes and nodded.

'Who was behind the curtain?'

'Who was what?' Simon asked. 'You saw someone else?'

I nodded, but didn't take my eyes off Lama la. 'In a carriage heading up towards the Gompa.'

'But the Gompa was abandoned.'

'Not the one you went to,' I said. 'There was a Gompa, just like this one. Trisha took me to—'

'Trisna,' Lama la corrected. 'She's called Trisna.'

'Whatever. She told me she knew who I was, she told me she could show me what I wanted most in the world, and then she brought me to *that* spot. And there was a man. Behind a curtain.'

'Be careful of those who offer you the world, Esta. No one can fulfil that promise. Not even a goddess.'

'Your dad?' Simon said.

I shot him a triumphant look. Then turned to Lama la. 'If that was him behind the curtain... just tell me. I just want to know if he's alive, that's all.'

Lama la gave a heavy sigh. 'It's not that simple.'

I lifted my arms in the air. 'Then help me understand!'

The old man cleared his throat, placed the apple in one of the bowls on the shrine. Then he pinched up a small mound of dried rice. 'Things are not clear,' he said, letting the rice fall back into the bowl. 'It would be dangerous to tell you half-truths.'

'I'd rather half a truth than no truth at all.'

Lama la paused for a while. He had one rice grain left between forefinger and thumb and he rolled it back and forward, contemplating it. 'I told you that we are moving into the Bardo of Becoming,' he finally said. 'A state of reality where the law of cause and effect is impossible to predict.'

Simon and I nodded.

'And yet, everything we say and do in this moment will change the future. And the future is on a knife edge as it is.' He looked up at us both. 'Great uncertainty is coming and we must be ready.'

'Ready to do what?' Simon asked. 'You tell us we're Tulku; that we've been here before in some other life. That we're somehow important in all of this. But you haven't told us who we were and what we're supposed to be doing.'

Lama la snapped the tiny grain of rice in half with his thumbnail. 'Knowing may change everything.' He held each half up between the forefinger and thumb of each hand, scrutinising the broken grain.

'Change what? Know what?' Simon asked.

'Stability. Normality. Certainty. I believe that if we are to bring these qualities back in to the world, we may first have to embrace a little uncertainty.'

'So...?'

'I will need both of you to trust me.'

'But...' I let out an exasperated breath. 'You don't *tell* us anything!'

'The answers to your questions are close. I don't keep them from you lightly. We are close. But I need another to help if we are to succeed.'

'Another?' Simon asked.

'Someone who can travel between our two realms as you two can. Someone with a connection. Someone in your world who has seen Rigpa Gompa.'

Simon and I exchanged looks. I suspected we were both thinking the same thing. I was imagining Charlie Bullock being dragged up the wall of Gatley House.

But Lama la wasn't thinking of Charlie. He had another name in mind.

22

THERE WILL BE A ROPE

'HARRY SPARKS!' I SAID in astonishment. 'But he's an old man.'

'*I'm* an old man,' Lama la replied. 'He has seen. He will see again.'

'No. I mean. He's... he's *old,* old.' I pointed up at the roof. 'You don't understand what we have to do to get up here. He'd have to climb a fifty-foot wall for starters.'

Lama la shrugged. 'Harry Sparks was the man who reestablished the connection. He is the owner of Gatley House. He'll come. We must have all the pieces of the puzzle gathered together. Everything depends on this. Without you two and Harry, the door between realms remains open. We will have no control over the uncertainty that is on our doorstep.'

'How are we supposed to do that?' I said, shaking my head.

Lama la rose slowly to his feet.

Simon got to his feet, too. He held out a hand for me. 'We made it today, Est. Who says we can't do it tomorrow?'

'*We* made it today. But that's not the same as getting *Harry* up here!'

'Obstacles,' Lama la said, 'are more often than not in the mind. And therefore that is where you will find the means to overcome them.' 'Est, he's not the same man you saw before and, you know, Graham. He'll find a way.'

I looked behind me at the spinning wheel. Even from this far away, I could see the smoke rising from Wheel. *All the realms bleeding together.* I thought of the Hungry Ghost realm and the creatures that might escape from there.

'If you bring him,' Lama la said from somewhere behind me, 'I will have an answer for you.'

I saw a swish of golden curtain in my mind's eye; strong fingers; a ruby red ring. I looked up at Simon's still offered hand. 'OK,' I mumbled and took it. 'Of course we'll do it.'

Lama la had turned his attention from the Wheel to the ceiling. He pointed up to the rafters. 'That's where you got in?'

'There's still a hole in the roof where we come from,' Simon said. 'Everything else is blocked off with concrete. Windows, doors...'

'You should probably leave the same way you came in.'

Simon pointed up at the ceiling again. 'Yeah but...'

Lama la shuffled past The Wheel and beckoned us to follow. 'Leave the Vajra and Bell on the table. We can't risk you losing them in the Human Realm. I'll keep them safe for next time.' He pointed at the low table by the back wall. 'Same place as always.'

We followed Lama la through the curtain that hung across his doorway, then along the landing, past the stairs, and the painted images of demons and goddesses coating the walls. At the end, he made a sharp right and went up a set of rickety wooden steps to a faded purple door.

Lama la waited by it. 'It'll be chilly.'

'And then what?' Simon asked.

'You came up with a rope, you said?'

'Yes.'

'Then there will be a rope.'

23

From the Roof

THE STEPS HAD A dusting of snow and a strong breeze blew flakes underneath the door. Simon pushed. It opened with an unpleasant squeak and we walked out into a bright and clear day.

Simon stared out towards the horizon and whistled through his teeth. 'I forgot about this.'

Rigpa Gompa sat huddled halfway up the slopes of a huge mountain. The mountain was at the head of a deep valley and Rigpa Gompa's courtyard ended at the knife edge of a cliff that plummeted into its depths. A range of tooth-like snow-peaks rose either side, and off to the South, the valley narrowed into a thin river that flowed between the steep slopes.

An icy wind brought a hint of something sweet like honey. I breathed it in and gazed down along the valley. Was Dad out there somewhere? In a place just like this one?

I had been a fingertip away from seeing his face; I had been sure of it at the time. But why had Lama la been so nervous about me seeing him? There was, I knew, another possibility... but I didn't want to go there. I'd been attacked by a Hungry Ghost with long hair. It hadn't really even vaguely resembled him, had it? It was just a figment of my overactive imagination. Except... the ring on its finger had looked just like... no. Lots of people wore a wedding ring. Then there were the green eyes.

I stamped an angry foot down into a coating of fresh snow. Trisna had taken me to the thing I wanted the most. If that Hungry Ghost *had* been Dad, Trisna would have just left me back there wouldn't she? But she didn't. She took me to a mountain path leading up to a temple just like this one, a man sitting inside a golden carriage...

Our feet made creaking noises in the snow as we walked. My mind raced. I recalled the glimpse of the hand emerging from the golden curtain. Was *it Dad's hand?* It had looked darker and thicker. He had been gone for more than two years, I suppose. Had he made a new life for himself in *Samsara*? Time seemed to pass differently in the different realms. For one thing, the sun was on its way down in Odiyana, whereas when we left Gatley it had been morning. If it *was* him, what was he doing in a golden carriage? And what was the place he was being carried to? A temple just like Rigpa Gompa. It had been at the head of a valley, too. And yet... it had been full of people.

'Lama la?' I asked. 'You said there are other temples like this one in each realm?'

'Of course,' he replied. 'There's a temple in every realm.'

'All with golden roofs?'

'Some do, some don't. Why?'

'It's just that Trisna took me to a temple full of people.' I tried to recall the scenery around the one I'd seen in Samsara. 'It had a valley. Just like this one. But it looked different somehow.'

'Then it must be a different temple. I only pulled you out of your vision. I did not participate in it.'

'So, you couldn't see what I saw?'

'Only vague suggestions, patterns, colours. Nothing specific.'

Simon shouted from up ahead. 'There's a rope!'

Lama la looked up and shivered. He pointed to Simon. 'The day is almost at an end, Esta Brown. It is time to go. And I must return to the Great Hall and meditate before we have any more unwelcome visitors. Without the Dharmapalas, protection is a little... thin.'

I joined Simon at the edge of the roof and looked down. A rope hung from a decorative gargoyle thing—a lion's head with an elephant's trunk—and dropped into the mist covered courtyard below.

'You sure this'll work?' I wondered aloud.

Simon shrugged. 'I don't know. What happens at the bottom?' he asked Lama la. 'Do we flip back to Gatley?'

'If this is how you came,' Lama la said mysteriously. He peered over the lip of the roof. 'Then this must be how you return. As to what you will find down there.' He stepped back and shrugged his shoulders. 'Who knows?'

24

SO GREAT TO BE BACK

'YOU WANT TO GO, Simon?' I suggested.

'Ladies first?'

I frowned at him. 'This was all your idea, Taylor, step up man.'

He peered over the edge. 'What do you reckon? I don't want to get stuck between the house and the fence.'

'Push off after the last window,' I said confidently. 'You'll clear it.'

'And security?'

'I think they'll be more scared of you just appearing out of nowhere.'

'I know, but...'

'Or... we just stay here until they knock us down.'

He picked up the rope and tugged it. 'Right then.' He turned reluctantly, facing me, back to the drop, then clasped both hands around the rope. 'I'll see you at the bottom.'

'Come back tomorrow,' Lama la said.

'Sure. Piece of cake.'

Simon lowered himself, using his feet to 'walk' down the wall. When he reached the last window, he glanced up at me. I gave him a thumbs up. He spent thirty seconds staring at the wall and then bent his knees and pushed off... and disappeared into a sudden, swirling mist. A second later, the rope went limp.

I gulped and looked back at Lama la. His face was in shadow. Beyond him, the sun was dipping behind the western mountains. 'Bring Harry Sparks, Esta. And you will have your answers. Now leave here before darkness falls. Mara may have left, but the Mamo still come to visit.'

I grabbed the rope, took one last look down into the valley, which was almost all in shade now. 'See you, then.'

Lama la bowed.

I slowly let myself down. At the window, I wrapped one arm around the rope to free my hand, scraped some snow from the ledge, squeezed it into something resembling a ball and threw it into the courtyard. The snowball vanished into the soft mist.

So where did you go then, little snowball?

I pushed away from the wall and dropped, letting the rope slide through the crook of my arm. There was a breathless moment where my stomach flipped over like a tossed pancake. Everything went cotton-wool white for a second and then the grounds of Rigpa Gompa retreated. In their place, the damaged lawns of Gatley House came back into view.

I landed with both feet on broken bricks. The breeze felt warm. It smelt of urine and gasoline. I banged my shin against the shopping trolley and winced.

So great to be back in my world.

PART THREE

How to Get Back

25

BOOTS ON THE GROUND

'ESTA?' SIMON WHISPERED. HE was sweeping snow from his thigh. I grinned. That answered the question about where the snow went, at least. I was about to laugh at the look on his face when he dropped to his knees. I instinctively did the same.

The sound of tyres on gravel. A flashing orange light flickering through the branches of the sleeping-beauty hedge just south of the gate. Simon pulled me away from the house. 'Stay low.'

We crouched, our backs to the hedge. The sound of the vehicles got louder. A radio crackled. We sidled behind the trunk of one of the old Hawthorne trees.

'What time is it?' I whispered.

He checked his watch. '11.17.'

'I have to be in a meeting with my Mum in about ten minutes.'

Simon shushed me and pointed along the hedgerow. 'Bigger problems.'

A black van turned on to the driveway.

'You don't get how serious this is, do you?' I whispered. 'What do you think will happen when the hospital notices I'm gone? They'll never let me out again—'

He raised a hand at me to shut up. 'Graham's plan,' he said, without explanation.

'What plan?' I hissed. 'This isn't a plan, this is a—' I stopped. Another, louder crackle of radio static. Someone shouted something to our left.

'What's with the radios?' I whispered.

'Nothing to do with my dad. These aren't his guys.'

The van came to a halt. Someone got out.

'They don't look like builders,' I whispered.

'I told you, these aren't anything to do with Dad.'

'Police?'

'No. Police have blue lights. It'll be something to do with the council. Environmental health stuff.'

'Maybe they found the newts after all.'

Simon looked up at the branches of the tree. 'You reckon we could climb this without being seen?'

I followed his gaze. The trunk had been part swallowed up by the hedge; the branches were gnarled and prickly, but if you could get through the first tangle of twigs, there was one branch that you might be able to drop down off on to the other side.

I craned my neck round the trunk at the van. It was about thirty or forty feet away. If we made a noise, they'd probably see us, but we'd be over the hedge before they could reach us. 'It's worth a shot,' I said and made to move.

Simon pulled me back. 'Wait.' There were more voices now, the sound of boots hitting gravel as two men got out of the van.

'Bloody hell,' I breathed. 'What are they wearing?'

Simon lay next to me, cheek against the trunk. 'Definitely not my dad's guys.'

From where I was crouched, the branches of the tree meant I couldn't see their heads, just their heavy boots and white trousers tucked into them. They could have been astronauts from a 1950s movie.

We watched in silence as they took stuff from the back of the van. Instruments of some sort... and not the musical kind.

'They'll see us if we stay here,' I whispered.

'Wait a minute,' he said.

'We don't have a minute. I have to get back.' I reached for the lowest branch and heaved myself up, resisting the urge to squeal as I got a face full of thorns.

Simon swore silently below me. I forced myself through the unbending twigs and somehow reached the overhanging branch.

'Stop!' Simon whispered. I peered through the branches back at the van. *What the hell is going on?* There were two more vans now. These were black, too. Unmarked. More figures climbed out, joining the first two, each dressed in white overalls and all obviously far too busy to notice little old me sitting in a tree.

'Esta,' Simon whispered again. 'Go! Go!'

26

THE CHARGE OF THE SPACEMEN

I LOOKED ROUND. SIMON'S head peeped at me from through the twigs below. He had scratches all over his pretty face and twigs sticking out of his hair like pins in a pincushion. I cast my eyes one more time over the activity in Gatley House and then swung myself over the top of the hedge, landing in a rhododendron bush. Quiet as a herd of wildebeest. Nice one, Esta.

Simon scrambled over too, landing almost slap bang on top of me. Fortunately, a branch caught his fall. I think it caught something else as well because... well, I've only ever heard the high-pitched squeak he made once before and that was on a David Attenborough nature programme about monkeys.

He lay frozen next to me for a moment, both hands between his legs, eyes squeezed shut, face pale, lips pursed like he was whistling a tune. There was a sort of hushed silence for a few seconds.

And then everything went crazy.

The men in the suits got all excited. Shouting and running. I hauled Simon up. He opened his eyes and staggered along with me towards the fence, his lips still creased up like he'd just eaten a lemon. Fortunately, we were pretty much in line with the gap Graham had made in the fence. He'd left it open, and we pushed ourselves through. The voices were quieter now. If they were after us, I doubted any of them fancied the climb over the Hawthorne. Not in the weird suits they were in anyway. I chanced a few extra seconds to push the snipped pieces of metal together, slide the yellow DANGER OF DEATH sign back over the top section.

'Where did you park the car?' Simon said through gritted teeth.

'This way,' I said, heading along the fence toward Graham, who was currently climbing out of his old banger.

Simon followed, making little grunting noises as he went. Seriously, boys act tough, but get jabbed between the legs and they're like walking jelly babies. 'Why's he waving at us?'

I looked up. Graham was pointing at something behind us. Then he dived back inside the car. The engine coughed into life.

I turned. Simon was hobbling along about ten paces behind me. About fifty feet behind him were three men in white spacesuits running after us with all the grace of a posse of overweight ghosts. Made it difficult to take them seriously.

'Simon!'

He'd heard the approaching men and almost fell as he upped the pace of his staggering run. He still wasn't moving fast enough though, and I wasn't sure what I could do but... I swore to myself and ran back to him anyway, grabbed his arm and heaved.

There was an explosion, like the sound of gunfire. Simon and I both ducked. *They're shooting at us?* The men in the spacesuits ducked too. *Someone's shooting at all of us?* I turned to face the end of the field. The Ford Escort, exhaust making loud banging noises, was heading right for us, churning up the tall grass under its wheels. I glimpsed Graham through the windscreen. He was wide-eyed with horror and he was waving an arm at us. At the last second, I remembered his appalling brakes and wrenched Simon out of the way. The car missed us by a few feet and slammed into the fence.

The passenger door swung open.

'Get in!'

Simon and I dived in together. Me on top of him, trying to scramble onto the back seat.

Graham crunched the gear into reverse. The wheels ground into the earth. The bonnet pinged away from the fence and we lurched backwards, sending a spray of dirt and pebbles at the lumbering men.

We almost did a full circle in reverse and nearly collided back into the fence.

Graham didn't bother with the brake this time, just went straight into first gear, and we rocketed forwards with another explosion from the back of the car. The sudden change of direction forcing me headfirst into the back seat. We rattled and bumped across the field and by the time I'd turned myself the right way up; we were already bouncing off the curb on to Boundary Lane, leaving the spacemen standing in a cloud of dust.

27

DREAMS WITHIN DREAMS

'WELL, THIS IS GOING swimmingly,' I said as Graham's Escort spluttered along Boundary Lane, heading back towards Gatley Gardens.

'So?' Graham asked, very much ignoring my sarcasm. 'Did it change? Did you flip?'

'Yes,' I said. 'It's still there.'

Graham slapped the steering wheel in triumph. 'Yes!'

'He wants us to bring Harry,' Simon grunted from a curled up position on the front seat. His face had a tiny bit more colour now, but he still looked in pain.

Graham nodded, as if he'd been expecting that all along. 'What else? Did you mention me and Lily?'

'I... I don't know,' I said. 'Why would I have?'

'Because...' For no apparent reason, he slapped Simon on the thigh.

Simon sat up, wincing. 'I told you, it gets fuzzy. When you're there, you can't remember much about here and when you're here, you can't erm...'

'Speaking of which,' I said. 'What time is it?'

Graham checked his watch. 'Nearly half past.'

'Gray, can this thing go any faster?' I pleaded.

He glanced in the mirror at me. 'Don't worry. It'll be OK if you're a bit late.'

I glowered at him. 'Right. The Masterplan. You ever going to tell me what it is?'

'Didn't you tell her, Si?'

'I assumed you did on the way over.'

'No. Well, I tried, but—'

'Why—'

'Boys?' I interrupted.

'Alright.' Graham sighed, slowing the car down even more. 'Here's the story. You went to the graveyard with your nurse, OK?'

'He's an orderly, not a nurse.'

'What's the difference?'

'Nurses are trained professionals. Bernard just knows how to clean tables, ring bells and... I don't know... smoke fags.'

'Anyway — he left you in order to deal with a member of the public.'

'Not a member of the public, Gray. My bloody gran!'

'Yeah, well Bernard doesn't know that, does he? Anyway. He's off dealing with her, leaving you all alone. Me and Simon turn up, just cruising along through our home town as normal—'

'Illegally,' I added.

Graham gave me a sideways look. 'We don't have to broadcast that... and then we see you and bring you back, all worried and concerned about your welfare.'

I leaned back in my seat for a second, absorbing the story. I looked at the scratches on my arms, the rips in my clothes, the streaks of mud on my jeans. 'And how do you explain the fact that I look like a walking scarecrow?'

Graham looked at me in the rear-view mirror. 'You are a bit of a mess. We'll blame it on your nurse.'

I leaned forward. 'He's an orderly! And how are you going to pin it all on him?'

'He wasn't paying attention to you. You wandered into a bush or something.'

'I know I'm in a mental hospital, Gray, but I'm not just going to stumble into a bush because Bernard isn't holding my hand!' I slumped back again. 'This is an actual, literal disaster.'

'Well, I didn't know you were going to get yourself all muddy, did I?'

'The plan, Graham, was to climb up the side of a condemned house, sidle along a roof, and drop down into what is essentially a building site. You thought I might not get a tiny bit dirty doing that?'

'Esta,' Simon said. He was sitting up straighter now, but his voice was still a little hoarse. 'Give him a break. We had to get you out there. You saw what they're doing. It can only be a couple of days now.'

'This was the only way. And anyway, your gran will back you up.'

Graham indicated left, and we joined the open part of Wilmslow Road and trundled towards the grounds of Gatley Gardens. I placed my face in both my hands. 'I'm dead. They'll never let me out again. I can't believe you did this to me.'

Simon turned round in his seat. 'We have to. We have to go again tomorrow.'

I laughed from behind my fingers. 'No chance!'

'Samsara,' Simon said. 'Remember. The Wheel was broken and Lama la needed us to help fix it. You must remember.'

I closed my eyes. What were we planning here? I thought of Bernard, Doctor Edwards, and all the locked doors at the hospital. I thought about Gran swooning in the graveyard, Graham's old banger; about the new fences going up around Gatley House; about the rope and the corner of the roof where you had to push out over the edge. Thought about the men in their spacesuits. All of those things seemed very real to me right then. Very real and very solid.

The threat to Samsara, on the other hand, seemed distant... dream-like. Like part of a T.V. show I'd seen and half forgotten. 'I can't see how.'

I felt the brakes grinding underneath me and looked out of the windscreen. Graham was slowing the car well before we reached the wrought-iron gates of the hospital. I half expected us to clang right into them, but this time Graham judged it right and we came to a stop with roughly three inches to spare.

He got out of the car to press the attention button.

'Your dad,' Simon whispered. 'You remember? You said you found your dad. Lama la said he'd show you.'

I dropped my hands and looked at him. I dimly remembered the hand of the man I'd seen behind the golden curtain. Memories rushed back in random flashes. I blinked them away. They were the chaotic memories of a dream. Of a dream *within* a dream, whereas this... I listened to the heavy gates open for us on their rusted hinges. I thought of Doctor Edwards and Mum waiting for me.

This is real.

And, I thought glumly, if Dad was stuck in a dream. Then maybe...

... maybe that's where he should stay.

28

MEDICAL EMERGENCY

BERNARD WAS WAITING FOR us.

He was leaning against the front door of the hospital, cigarette between finger and thumb.

This time, the boys got out before the car finally came to rest. Simon—apparently well on the mend now—pushed against the door and Graham raced round to the bonnet to stop the car from flattening a row of flowers. They seemed pretty well practised at the procedure.

Bernard ground the end of his fag against the wall and dropped it. He pushed himself away from the door, folded his arms and grinned as I nervously got out of the Escort. Graham's plan seemed even worse than ever now, looking at Bernard's cruel and gleeful expression. A part of me wondered whether we shouldn't just pile back into the car and go back the way we'd come. The black gates clanging shut at the end of the drive put an end to that little fantasy though, and I had a brief image of Graham trying to plough them down in his Ford. That was never going to end well.

Bernard sauntered forward. He seemed taller and smugger than ever, like some horrible cartoon of a baddy in a Wild West movie. 'Where the bloody hell did you go, Brown?'

I felt myself shrink under his gaze.

'And where the bloody hell were you!'

I looked to my left in surprise. Graham was pacing towards Bernard, finger pointing at him, anger making his face go red. 'You were supposed to be looking after my friend!'

Bernard stopped advancing. His right eye twitched, the corners of his lips wobbled.

Graham stopped less than a foot away from the orderly. Bernard seemed to shrivel up in Graham's shadow.

'We found her in the graveyard all by herself! Worried sick we were!'

'She,' Bernard pointed at me, 'ran away from me!'

Graham's finger got to within an inch of Bernard's twitching eye. 'No! You left my friend all alone! And we,' he curled back his finger into a fist, then stuck his thumb out and pointed to Simon with it, 'found her and brought her back here! So the question is... where were you?'

Bernard took a step back. He raised his finger in the air like a schoolboy asking a question. 'I... there was...' Bernard stuttered. '... A medical emergency...'

Graham now pointed at me. '*She's* a medical emergency.'

I rolled my eyes. *Great. Let's pop that comment in the file, shall we?*

'There was an old lady,' Bernard replied. 'She was having a heart attack. I was only gone for a few—'

'Look at her!' Graham shouted. 'She's covered in scratches! You had a duty of care and you failed her. Tell me why I shouldn't go in there and report this to your boss right now!'

He didn't of course. Bernard was very understanding. Full of apologies, explanations and soothing assurances. Eventually, Graham backed down and Bernard promised to give me time to clean up before my meeting. He even bent down to pick up his fag end when Simon stepped up and told him it was unhygienic on hospital grounds.

He took me inside while Graham and Simon watched from the drive. He signed me back in and we stood and watched; me cringing with embarrassment, as Graham got in the driver's seat of the Ford and Simon pushed the thing a few yards before the rattling exhaust—still somehow attached—spewed out some black smoke and the car began a jerky three-point turn.

Simon walked to the passenger side door as they crawled past us. 'Lily's coming this afternoon,' he said. 'Just to, you know, see how things are.' He winked, then climbed in and the Ford grunted its way back up the drive.

There was no doubt. Graham was mad as a hatter. But, as Bernard silently lead me back to my room to get changed, I couldn't help grinning. You had to hand it to him. He somehow always got things done.

29

THE REVIEW

I LOOKED AT MYSELF in the mirror over the mini basin in my room. 'You *do* look like you belong in a mental asylum, Esta,' I whispered to my pale face. I combed twigs out of my hair and dabbed at the scratches on my hands. I looked up at the clock on my wall. Fifteen minutes late for my meeting with Mum and the doctor. Between now and the two-minute walk to his office, I would somehow have to put aside everything that had just happened; put on my most normalest of faces and prepare to smile and nod obediently while adults made decisions about the contents of my brain.

There were three other people in the room. The head doctor obviously, a nervous-looking Mum and—my heart sank—the Governor of the asylum; none other than the chair of school governors, Miss Nuttal. She'd been the one who'd suggested a sojourn at the local loony bin, and with her having—as Mum called it—fingers in both pies, the transfer had not been a difficult one.

All for my own good, of course.

'Thank you so much for inviting me to this meeting,' Nuttal said, her eyes sparkling as she handed out a plate of Rich Tea biscuits to the doctor. She wore one of her vibrantly patterned dresses. A silk scarf was wrapped around her neck, trailing down and over her ample bosom.

The doctor smiled, reached over, took a biscuit, and dipped it into his mug. Doctor Edwards was a weirdly thin man with such skinny wrists, he could probably fit them both through a single shirt sleeve. He had white hair and slick black eyebrows that bopped up and down as he talked. He spoke with the high, bubbly voice of a man who needed to clear his throat. I had a sudden horrible mental echo of one of those things that attacked me in the desert. Him and Bernard would fit right in, I thought. I shook my head a little and tried to distract myself by staring at the row of old medical books on a shelf above us.

'No, thank you for coming, Miss Nuttal,' the doctor said. 'If Miss Brown is to be reintegrated back into school, it's vital you are involved as well. It's so fortunate that you sit on both governing bodies.'

Nuttal nodded and smiled down at the plate of biscuits which sat in the middle of the table — unoffered to mum or me. That should have been the first sign things were not going to go well.

Eventually, she seemed to remember we were in the room. She tore her gaze from the plate and gave us a wide, insincere smile. 'Progress?' she asked and plucked a biscuit without looking at it. I recalled the blue and red fingernails. Today she'd opted for white. White as a set of celebrity teeth.

'Esta has made some,' the doctor replied.

Miss Nuttal crunched her biscuit noisily without dipping it first. Crumbs flecked her lips. She collected them with a flick of her tongue.

'She's acknowledged her father's absence,' Mum said with irritation. 'She's shared her feelings about it with me and her friends.' She smiled at me and squeezed my hand beneath the table.

'Of course. And she's only just returned from visiting his memorial stone, I hear,' Nuttal said brightly.

'Oh?' Mum said, surprised.

Miss Nuttal dipped her head to one side in apparent confusion. 'Doctor Edwards informed me you made the request only yesterday.'

I internally winced. Graham's plan was about to unravel after all.

Mum looked at me uncertainly, then smiled. 'Of course. I'm so glad you allowed her to —'

'Is it true?' Nuttal interrupted. 'That she continues to maintain friendships with Mr Taylor's boy?'

Mum looked at me questioningly. 'Erm. Yes?'

I made a slight nod. In my experience, in situations like this, the adults generally didn't welcome contributions from the child in question. And anyway, it was also my experience that whenever I did open my mouth, somebody much cleverer than me would shut me down with a patronising look, or some complicated question I couldn't answer.

The doctor sniffed. 'One of the key indicators of depression is the wish for isolation so —'

'I understand that, Doctor Edwards, but we have to consider the mental well-being of the other children. Frankly, I'm shocked you allow the boy to visit. We've already seen the effect she has on him.'

The doctor furrowed his thick, black brows and chewed on the end of a plastic pen. 'I see. Although the Taylor boy does have a step-sister who's a resident here.'

'Charlie Bullock,' I said automatically.

'Then,' Miss Nuttal said, ignoring me completely, 'I hope you can reassure us that you will keep visiting times separate—'

'No!' Mum stood, jabbing a finger at the horrible woman.

Miss Nuttal watched her, then looked down and wrote something in her jotter. The doctor did the same.

'Mum,' I whispered. 'Please?'

She ignored me too. 'You can't isolate her from her friends. They're good for her.'

'But Mrs Brown,' Nuttal replied, unruffled by Mum's little outburst. 'It is not clear that *she* is good for *them*. I hardly need to remind you of the danger she put them in last spring at that terrible old ruin. And after all, she won't be entirely isolated. Family are still free to visit.'

Mum turned to the doctor with a pleading gasp, but he was deliberately concentrating on his notepad. I pulled down on Mum's hand, finally making her sit. She folded her arms.

'And the delusions?' Nuttal said to Doctor Edwards. 'Have there been further instances of the dangerous psychosis we saw last month?'

The doctor lifted his notepad and consulted my file, his eyebrows almost touching now. 'Esta has moments of hyperactivity.'

'She exercises,' Mum interjected. I could feel her knee bouncing nervously against my leg.

Miss Nuttal glanced at her and wrote something else in her jotter. She nodded to the doctor for him to continue.

'Preceded by prolonged periods of inactivity.'

'You mean sleep,' Mum responded bitterly.

'No. More, a profound stillness,' Doctor Edwards said, looking up and blinking. 'We have observed her sitting at the foot of her bed.'

'For how long?' Nuttal asked.

He checked the file again. 'Hours at a time.'

Mum leaned over to me. 'Is that true?'

I squirmed in my seat. Nodded.

Miss Nuttal took another biscuit and placed it carefully next to her pad, then she wrote something else. 'Completely still, you say?'

This time the doctor nodded.

'Could it be catatonic?' she asked, as if Mum and I were no longer in the room and she were discussing some random patient and not the one sitting no more than four feet away.

Mum gripped my hand so hard it made me wince.

'When the orderlies enter to bring her water or clean her room,' the doctor said. 'She sometimes doesn't move at all. Apparently makes no sign she's aware they're even there. I myself witnessed such an episode only the other morning.'

I ground my teeth. Pulled my hand from Mum's. 'It's meditation,' I said. 'It helps me to focus my mind.'

The doctor carried on regardless, 'She doesn't wake, even when they shake her.'

I lowered my head and shook it slowly. Honestly, if they think you're mad, everything you do seems to confirm it. If I didn't meditate, I'd probably pace up and down my locked room until they stuck some other label like "Hyperactive" on me.

'I choose to do it,' I said to the tabletop. *But you don't choose the dreams that come, do you?* An unpleasant voice whispered in my head.

'Trance-like state,' the doctor continued as Miss Nuttal scribbled.

'And how does she seem after the episode?'

'Breathless, sweaty. As if she's been running.'

A loud bang made me jerk my head away from contemplating the table. Mum had thwacked the surface with her fist. 'Why don't you ask the Doctor if she's happy?' she shouted, pointing a finger at the thin man, who stared back with a shocked look on his face.

Miss Nuttal merely placed her pen by the side of her pad and lifted the biscuit to her lips. Before she took a bite, she glanced at the doctor: 'Well?'

The doctor flicked through pages in the file, sliding his finger along one of them. 'Yes,' he said finally. 'She does seem a little happier.'

'You see!' Mum said, looking from one to the other. 'Isn't that enough? Isn't that why we're here? So Esta is happy?'

Nuttal chewed on a mouthful of biscuit. I watched her face. Watched her dark, shining eyes, trying not to imagine her as the enormous face that had leered down at me from the hole in the roof of Gatley House. *She isn't Mara,* I told myself. *He just used her likeness to freak me out.* Miss Nuttal was just a stuck up cow — she wasn't the incarnation of chaos itself. At least, I didn't think she was.

A shower of crumbs landed on her silk scarf. She swallowed. 'You are right, Mrs Brown, Esta's time in hospital definitely seems to be working.'

'That's not what I meant!'

'Let me remind you that we are here firstly to prevent harm, Mrs Brown. Harm to Esta and harm to others. When we can guarantee that, then we can work on promoting her happiness.'

'But...'

'But, we are here to determine the risk she poses to the welfare of herself and her friends. What happened at the building site—'

'She was doing it to save her friend!'

'Who,' Miss Nuttal said with one finger up in the air, 'was in there because of Esta's wild stories. She almost got them both killed. If it hadn't been for the heroics of Mr Culter, that wrecking ball would have buried them both. No, the risk Esta took with her own, and more importantly, other's lives was extraordinary and indicates a manic cycle — which I now see is coupled with a catatonic cycle of depression.'

'What about the others? Simon. Graham and Lily?'

'Mum?' I nudged her. God, it was bad enough me being in here without bringing the others in too.

'Neither of those children have any history of mental illness.'

'Neither did Esta until you said she did!'

'Mrs Brown, please calm yourself. Your daughter was living in—by her own admission —an alternate reality. It was you who brought our attention to that fact.'

'She was getting over the disappearance of her dad!'

'Two years is much longer than we would normally expect. Now really, there is no need for argument. We all want what is best for Esta. Surely you agree? Hmm?' Nuttal waited. Mum could hardly object.

'I suggest we keep her under observation for a further twenty-eight days.'

My heart sank.

'What?' Mum breathed. 'I won't agree to that. I want her back home!'

'And if there are any further behavioural issues, next time we would have to conduct more invasive treatments. I'm sure we all want to avoid that for as long as we can. After all, as you say, Esta's happiness is paramount.'

Mum rose. I could sense fury boiling, ready to explode. I gripped her hand more tightly.

'It's OK, Mum,' I whispered. 'It's just a month. I'll stop meditating. I'll be normal. I promise. It's OK.'

She looked down at me, one eye welling up. I smiled back. She wiped her face, shook her head and eventually sat down, defeated. 'One more month. And then I want her back.'

Miss Nuttal smiled and ticked something on her pad. 'One further condition,' she said, looking at me. 'She is not to see the three others: Graham Sparks, Lily Rain or Simon Taylor, until we have concluded our assessments.'

My eyes widened. My heart dropped even further. *Not see Graham, Lily or Simon?* They were my lifeline. They were my Jewel Island. The only thing that made being cooped up in here bearable was the knowledge that I could speak with them every other day.

'Oh, for God's sake!' Mum shouted.

'That is a formal requirement, Mrs Brown. A request from their parents. You don't have a choice about that, dear.' She made another tick. 'In addition, we'll be upping her dose of medicine. She'll be drowsy for a week or so, she won't be much company for anyone.'

Mum leapt to her feet again. 'Drowsy? What are you planning to do to her?'

The doctor half-stood, placing a protective arm between Mum and Miss Nuttal. 'It's alright, Ms Brown,' he said breathlessly. 'Quite normal procedure. It's only temporary. We just need to adjust the dosage until we find the right balance.'

Mum remained standing. Battle pose. Facing the doctor down. 'Well, I don't consent! And it's *Mrs* Brown!'

'You already have,' Miss Nuttal said, pushing a form across the tabletop. 'In our original assessment.'

Mum grabbed it. There was a pause while we waited for her to read. When she finished, she looked back up at Nuttal and then pushed the form back with a sigh. Doctor Edwards sank back into his chair with obvious relief. Miss Nuttal's smug expression never wavered. I briefly wondered if Bernard was one of her offspring. Smug smiles running in the family and all that.

'Can I see Lily at least?' I asked quietly. They had to give me this. 'It's just that she's due to visit today.' I could stay locked up for a month. I'd eat all the rubbish they tried to feed me. I might even swallow all the pills they gave me. I'd be a good girl... but they had to give me this. 'Just one more time?'

Miss Nuttal looked taken aback. She stiffened up, placed a pencil on the table and turned to the doctor. He scratched his head. I placed a hand on Mum's leg. The muscles in her thigh rippling again as she prepared to launch herself across the table.

30

WHATEVER IT TAKES

LILY CAME IN TO the dining room late that afternoon during the final visiting period just before dinner. Her ginger hair had grown past her shoulders. She wore a tonne of makeup and wore a white blouse, black skirt and flat shoes.

'Things changed at the greengrocers then?' I asked, as she sat down opposite me.

'This thing?' she looked down at her blouse. 'I ditched the fruit and veg for the Tea Spoon. Two pounds an hour better pay and you get tips.'

'Right. You're saving for India.'

She nodded, raised her eyebrows. Her finger went to her cheek. She was wearing a lot of foundation, and the eye above her cheek was a little red. 'How was the meeting with your mum?'

'Not amazing. They've got a stack of notes up to my eyes about how crazy I am.'

'But you aren't mad!' Lily said, making a show of looking at the orderlies. 'Surely they can see that!' As she turned, I saw a mark where the foundation stopped just under her jawline. Just a little red line. What was she covering up? She looked back at me and I pretended not to have noticed.

'Thanks. But once they label you, everything else seems to tie in. It's like if I try to act normal, they think I've changed my personality — so they make notes about that too.'

'They can't keep you locked up against your will. They have to let you out. Your mum can insist on it.'

I shrugged. 'It's only for a month.'

She leaned forward and whispered. 'What about tomorrow? Graham told me everything.'

I shook my head. 'I don't know how I'd do it. I can hardly ask Gran to help again, can I?'

Lily smiled. 'Graham told me she was amazing.'

'How did he get her to do it?'

'It wasn't him. It was Harry. He wants to go back to his old house before they tear it down. And, you know him and your gran... they talk.' Her smile turned into a grin. 'They're actually quite sweet together.'

I nodded. 'Well, I don't think she can pull it off in here.'

'Can't you just sneak out?'

'There's always an orderly watching everything I do. They lock every single door throughout the hospital. It's like living in a bank vault. They even watch me when I'm sleeping.'

Lily turned on her chair to look around the canteen as if to inspect its security. 'What about the windows?'

'My cell's three storeys up—'

'We could bring a ladder,' she said hopefully.

'And they have bars across them.'

'Oh.' She touched her cheek again.

'And there are security lights. Lil?' I asked, changing the subject. 'What happened?'

She frowned. Dropped her hand back to her lap. 'What?'

'Your face. The makeup. You've been touching it since you got here.'

She swallowed, her eyes darting this way and that like unsettled birds, bent and fished for a tissue inside her bag.

'Lil,' I reached for her hand over the table. 'What happened? Please tell me it's nothing to do with Graham.'

She shook her head, then dabbed her right eye with a corner of the tissue. 'I...' She sniffed. 'I want to come with you.'

I slid my hand away from hers and sat back in my chair. 'Go with me where?'

'I want...' she lowered her voice. 'I want to see it.'

'You want to see what?'

'Rigpa Gompa. Odiyana. Everything you've seen. I want to... I need to see it.'

'But, Simon and I—'

'Harry's seen it too and Charlie.' Her voice was shaking now. I'd never seen her like this. Lily always smiled. She was the most positive girl I knew. But the heavy makeup, the red eye, the mark on her neck...

'Lily. What's happened?'

She dabbed at her other eye and shook her head again. 'We've been speaking to Harry. He's quite talkative now, you know. He hasn't admitted it outright, but Graham thinks... I do too... that Rigpa Gompa exists.'

'Exists?'

'Yes. In the real world.'

'Real world?'

'Another gateway to the valley. A real, physical place.'

'Physical... What are you saying?'

'You remember, Graham told us Harry was posted in India just after World War Two? He was a civil engineer. Amongst other things, he made maps of the region between India and Tibet.'

'You think that's where this other gateway is?'

'For some reason, he won't say why. We think Harry brought the Kila back to England and used it to make a connection here. But,' she lowered her voice, 'he talks in his sleep... He still has the maps he drew up in India... Graham reckons there'll be a clue in one of them, I know it.'

'So, what? You and Graham are going to go to India to find it? Is that what you're saying?'

'I'm saying that even if Graham and I can't see it here, we might still be able to find it *there*.'

I frowned. 'How...'

'Graham reckons Gatley House and Rigpa Gompa aren't two separate realities at all. They're just somehow bent out of shape. Graham can explain it better than me. But he's sure there's another way in.'

'Don't go to India,' I muttered. 'Please don't leave me.'

'We wouldn't be leaving you. Just the opposite. We'd be trying to find you.'

'How's travelling halfway around the world "finding" me?'

'Esta?' Lily said quietly. 'Simon told us the only way to save Rigpa Gompa is to break the link between it and Gatley House.'

'We tried that.'

'Not with Harry Sparks' help. He knows what to do.'

I shrugged. 'That's assuming we can get him in there.'

'And what will you do if you succeed?'

I tilted my head to one side, confused by the question. 'What do you mean?'

'Which side will you be standing on when the link is cut? Rigpa Gompa or here?'

'This side,' I said without hesitation. I picked up my cup. 'With Mum and you guys.' The surface of the water rippled along with the purring of my heart. I took a nervous sip.

'If it's a choice between staying there to look for your dad and staying in this hellhole?'

'What?' I said. 'No. Not at all. You've got it all wrong.'

She kept on, though, not buying my protests. 'That's why we have to find Rigpa Gompa on a map. So... if we need to, we can find you again.'

'This is my home, Lil.'

'So,' she carried on. 'When you find your dad, you have a route back.'

I placed the cup on the edge of the table. The water wavered, then settled. I thought about Mum. Would I leave her here if it came to that? *No. No. No. Dad's gone, but Mum's still here.* This was my home. This was my place. Lily was wrong.

Before I could protest again, though, Bernard arrived with his little brass hammer and bell.

Ting. Ting. Ting.

Visiting time was over.

'Simon says the Lama la guy needs to speak with Harry,' Lily said.

I grabbed the cup again, downed the tepid water. 'Graham has a plan to get him up, I suppose?'

Bernard was three tables away from us now. He was fingering his set of keys and quietly insisting visitors make a move. A family got up, and I noticed Charlie sitting in her wheelchair opposite an empty table. No one had come to visit. I wondered if she'd notice even if they did, though. What was she looking at now? What world was she a part of?

Lily got up and took her bag from the back of the chair. 'Whatever it takes.'

I shrugged. 'You got a sledgehammer in that bag? Skeleton key? Miniature helicopter?'

Lily fixed me with stern eyes, shook her head in a "this-is-not-a-joke" kind of way. 'It has to be tonight.'

I looked back towards Bernard, at the rainbow of keys jangling from his belt. *A key for every door...* Every door had a colour code matching each different coloured key. If I could somehow lift a set from one of the orderlies... I knew some of the colours already. Red for my floor, a yellow key for the stairs, the next door was orange...

'Esta?' Lily whispered.

I looked at her concerned face. There was almost panic in her eyes. And there was definitely bruising under her left one. I remembered something she had told me months ago when I'd asked her why she was going to India. *"Some travel the world to find new things. Some do it to escape old things."* I began to suspect what it was she might be running from. Lily had never let me down once. She had always believed in me, even though she had no real reason to. And now she needed me.

'Whatever it takes,' I said finally.

'You'll do it?'

I looked over at Bernard's keys. 'It's a long shot, but...'

She beamed. 'We need to be there while it's still dark. We'll be in the car by the gates.'

A shadow fell over the table. 'Time, ladies.' Bernard smelled of vinegar. He might have washed his hair in the stuff because it hung limp over his ears and against his spotty neck. He looked at Lily and licked his lips. The sight made me shudder.

Lily got up. Out of Bernard's line of sight, she held up four fingers. *4 o'clock.*

I nodded.

She mouthed: *'Whatever it takes,'* and left.

Bernard turned to watch her go with those spindly arms folded over his pigeon chest. I stared down at his keys. How was I supposed to get them? They were attached to his belt the whole time.

The door clicked. Lily was gone. An orderly locked the door. Blue Key. The blue key for the canteen door, so—on the remote chance I could get them off one of the orderlies— just three more colours to figure out.

Bernard clapped once. 'Right!' He clapped again. 'Dinner time at the monkey house!'

The other orderlies began shifting tables. I looked across at Charlie. She was staring straight at me, like she was actually looking at me. I smiled. She nodded once, before someone pushed her to the wall to make way for a table. Left her there as if she were just another piece of furniture to arrange.

Lily was right.

If I ever did get out of this place, I could never come back again.

31

MEDS TO BEDS

'EAT,' BERNARD REPEATED, REACHING over and nudging a plate of reconstituted turkey breast under my nose.

'I'm not hungry,' I said, pushing it away.

'It'll help you digest the meds.'

'I don't want the meds tonight,' I said, looking up at him. 'Because tonight, Bernard, I'm not ill.'

'Seriously, eat up.'

I put my hands on the table, ready to stand. If I was going to sneak out, there was no way I could take the meds tonight.

I felt Bernard's hand on my shoulder. 'These are the terms.'

'Doctor Edwards said I'm upping the dose tomorrow.'

'Sooner you start,' he applied greater pressure on my shoulder. 'The sooner we can fix you.'

'I don't need fixing.'

'Take your pills.'

'No.'

'OK then,' Bernard said, releasing me. He sauntered over to a pad that dangled off a hook by the door. He picked it up and scribbled something down. 'I can't force you to take your meds, Esta Brown,' he said, tearing off a sheet of paper.

'Good.'

'Not yet, anyway.' He smiled and sauntered to the door, shouting to one of his colleagues on the other side. 'Adam? Patient is being uncooperative. We're going to need the shirt.'

Jake was sitting next to me. At the mention of the "shirt," he dropped his cutlery and placed the heels of his hands against both ears. I'd heard them talk about the "shirt" before. A jacket with leather straps designed to tie your arms behind your back. Usually it was reserved for kids who were having violent seizures... you know, "for their own good". But once I'd seen them strap down big, lumbering Jake after some idiot freaked him out by accidentally tipping a pile of plates on the floor.

I chewed my lip and stared at the meds. He couldn't just fit me up like that if I stayed calm? The shirt was just for violent behaviour. But then, if the meeting with Nuttal had shown me anything, it was the power of every little scribbled note from the orderlies. Little inky bits of proof of my madness: a "danger to myself and others".

And what if I slammed my food tray across Bernard's stupid nose? What would he jot down then? It'd be the sort of thing any sane person would do when faced with such a weasel.

Instead, I gave in. If it was a choice between being drowsy and being literally strapped up all night, there wasn't much of a choice. Anyway, it took twenty minutes to digest the pills. If I could get to a toilet in time, I could puke them out before they took effect. 'OK, OK,' I called. 'You win! Look, I'm cooperating.'

I waited until Bernard turned round and then put the tablets on my tongue. He folded his arms.

I took the beaker of water and swallowed a mouthful, feeling the hard shells slide down my throat. I opened my mouth wide and waggled my tongue at him. 'Happy?' And with that, I slammed the beaker on the table. Beside me, Jake jumped out of his chair. A screech of metal on plastic tiles echoed around the canteen as he toppled over. Barbara and Georgina put their hands over their ears. The large dark-haired girl giggled.

Bernard nodded at me, pulled opened the folded note and tore it in half, then, oblivious to the shrieking and Jake's shivering body on the tiles, he swaggered out of the door.

'Sorry Jake,' I said, helping him back to his chair. It took him a good five minutes to stop shaking. Everyone else went back to staring at their food. When Jake finally calmed down, I grabbed my tray and took it for washing, then made for the exit, wondering if I still had time to throw up the tablets before I started digesting them.

Bernard grinned at me through the small window in the door. He waggled his finger. 'Twenty minutes,' he said. 'Then you can go stick your fingers down your throat if you like — it won't work though.'

I kicked the base of the door.

That night I lay on the top of my flimsy quilt, my throat dry as a packet of crackers even though I must have sipped twelve cardboard cups of water. I spent the hours from about 11 until 1 am banging on the door of my cell to go to the toilet and, for want of anything better to do, paid close attention to the keys they used when they let me go: Red for the hallway door, as I knew. Green for the toilet block. That left two more colours. One for the doors to each staircase, but none for the main door.

At about 2 o'clock, my heart was beating a jagged rhythm and my options had narrowed to simply trying to beat one of the orderlies over the head with my pillow, steal the keys and make a run for it.

This was hopeless. Even if I managed to take a key, how was I going to get through the main door? How was I going to run all the way to the main gates? My limbs were shaking from the drugs, my mind was as thick as fudge. I'd probably trip over my own feet, or find myself running in circles.

'Focus, Esta Brown,' I said. 'Stop panicking. Think this through. What would Mum tell you to do?'

When you're stuck in a ten foot by ten-foot cell, you don't have many options. Sometimes you just had to change your perspective.

So I did. I sat on the end of my bed, relaxed and focused, just as Mum had taught me. It was calming, peaceful, and warm. I sat there for twenty minutes counting my breaths.

Eventually, even though my eyes were closed, I could picture the cell around me perfectly, as if I were looking at it with open eyes. I stayed still, not daring to react, to move or anything. Just looking. After a few moments, the solid walls seemed to dissolve like a sugar cube in a cup of tea.

I stayed absolutely still.

The grains separated, then blew away.

Something was happening.

32

THE SIDDHI OF SWIFT FEET

LAMA LA WAS SITTING on his cushion in his study, his eyes half closed as if in a trance. He smiled. 'Hello, Esta.'

Drugs. It must be the drugs, I thought groggily.

The room was hot. Uncomfortably hot. I gasped for air. 'Are you really here?'

He smiled. 'Are you?'

I was sitting on a cushion in Lama la's study. I stopped trying to fill my lungs. This wasn't real oxygen I was breathing in. These weren't real lungs that craved it. I hadn't moved an inch. *All this is happening in my head.*

'The Dharmapalas have returned. The Bardo of Becoming is close. It is time for you to return.'

'Yeah, well, I can't. In the *real* world, I'm a prisoner.'

Lama la nodded. 'Although, you may have the means to leave.'

'I can't punch through locked doors.'

Lama la raised a forefinger. 'Ah. But you might be able to *run* through them.'

'Nope.' I shook my head. 'You know, I've heard better plans.'

'You have the *Siddhi,* but you don't know how to control and refine it.'

'Siddhi?'

'Speak with Karma Chodron. She can help.'

'That's the angry nun in the blue robes, right?'

Lama la smiled. I ran the back of my hand against my brow. I was sweating. *Do you sweat in dreams?* 'OK,' I said. 'Whatever. How do I get—'

The room vanished. Everything went black, like someone dropped a blanket over us.

I sat cross-legged on a lumpy cushion in the Great Hall. I looked around me, trying to remember how I'd got here from Lama la's room. I was kind of foggy about details like that at the moment.

I was not alone. The four Dharmapalas were here. To my left, a tall boy dressed in white robes standing just in front of the large shrine. He held a big pot of tea in his hands. That would be Rabjam. Seated at his feet was Tubten. The little monk grinned, then wiped a stream of snot from his nose with the sleeve of his deep red robes. To my right was the high throne. Lama la was sitting on that. His eyes were closed, and he was muttering some sort of prayer. To *his* right, Sera, the nun in yellow robes, sat staring up at me.

'Close your eyes and relax.'

I jumped. Karma Chodron was sitting right next to me. She was scowling. 'I said relax!' She slapped my thigh with a wooden bead necklace.

'Ouch! Alright, alright. I'm relaxed.'

'Now. Focus.'

'Are you going to hit me again?'

'Concentrate!'

'You know, you might want to give this whole relaxing thing a go yourself.'

'Sit with your back straight.'

I straightened obediently. 'I thought I was supposed to relax.'

I got another rapping against the small of my back. 'Not that straight!'

I dropped my shoulders. 'You're not as good as my mum at this, you know?' I said under my breath.

'Good. Now silence.'

'It's not me that's making all the noise.'

Nothing happened. I waited. After a while, I said. 'What do I do now?'

'Be quiet. Wait!'

I waited again. 'What for?'

She didn't respond.

I blinked an eye open. Karma Chodron had her palms resting in her lap. Her forehead was creased into valleys of concentration. Her chest rose behind the deep blue of her robes.

'Close your eyes,' she said, more calmly now.

I did and waited some more. My lungs expanded and fell, my breath fluttered the hairs in my nostrils, a sensation like a velvet cloth ran up within me from my navel to my chest. My body felt light.

'Lama la said that we need you, so that we can bring the realms back into their ordered state. This is why I am helping you. He believes you have the Siddhi of Swift Feet.'

'What's a siddhi?'

'Have you ever Carved before?'

'Carved? Like a leg of lamb?'

'Moved.' Karma Chodron said. 'Through space. Instantaneously.'

I paused, then nodded slowly. I was pretty sure I *had* actually. Three times in fact: when I'd stolen the Kila in the museum; in the Geography classroom when I'd punched Hannah Piranha in the chin, and when I'd run from Mr Blakely just afterwards. 'If Carving means travelling places really quickly by myself. Then, yes, I think so. A few times.'

'Who are you, Esta Brown?'

My mind leapt to that dog in my dream: *I know who you are*. I felt my skin creep. 'No idea,' I said, looking through a slit in my eyelids. Karma Chodron had risen to her feet. She moved her hands together in prayer. 'Stand,' she said.

I stood.

'How do you feel?'

I nodded. I felt fantastic, actually. Light as a feather.

'Do you remember the way to the main door of the Great Hall?'

I frowned. 'Is that it? I thought we were training.'

Karma Chodron's expression stayed the same: 'Do you remember?'

I turned my head, ready to point behind me at the doors, but the fierce nun put a hand against my shoulder. 'Don't look. Visualise it. Do you remember?'

'I guess so.'

'Picture it in your mind. Every detail.'

I pictured the hall.

'Remember the path between the cushions, remember the pillars, the hanging drums. Twenty-five steps from here to there. Can you do that?'

I nodded.

'Close your eyes again.'

I did.

'Place your palms together near your heart.'

I did that too.

'There is no Esta Brown.'

'What?'

'Speak the words, visualise the route and travel to the door.'

I began to turn until I felt Karma Chodron's hand again. 'Not with your feet.'

'Whatever.' But I repeated the phrase and visualised moving towards the door.

Everything seemed to slow down to a standstill. There was a rush of air, a weird blending of colours and sounds, and then a very sharp pain.

And that is how I learned the Siddhi of Swift Feet.

I also learned that although you can travel as fast as light along well remembered pathways, you don't *actually* get to walk through doors. Apparently, that was another siddhi entirely.

Rabjam poured me some of his butter tea and dabbed at my nose with a piece of cloth. 'You did good, English girl.'

The others bustled around, moving tables, relighting lamps on the shrine. I looked up at Lama la, who had stopped his murmuring and was staring at me, like he was trying to figure me out.

I took the cloth off Rabjam and looked at the blood on it. 'If I'm actually here. In this room with you all, why do you need me to escape the hospital? Let's do what we need to do now.'

'This is all merely a temporary projection,' Lama la said. 'To complete the ceremony we need you fully embodied.'

I held up the blood stained cloth. 'How is this not being embodied?'

'I need you to be here,' Lama la insisted. 'In person. Simon and Harry as well. For something... physical.'

I nodded. 'Yeah, well, being able to run quickly is great and everything, but my real physical body is physically locked up inside a—'

Lama la interrupted me by patting his hand against the armrest of his throne two times. I frowned at him. 'What are you doing?'

He did it again. This time with his knuckles. 'Knock, knock.'

I looked around at the others.

Lama la rapped at his armrest again. 'There's somebody at the door, Esta.'

And with the third knock, the Great Hall and everyone in it disappeared.

33

THE MULTI-COLOURED ESCAPE PLAN

I STARED INTO SHADOWS for a moment, confused and disoriented. Above me was a glowing circle. For a second, I thought it was the Wheel of *Samsara*, but it wasn't moving, and it had numbers on it. It took me a second to realise I was back in my cell. I was staring at the wall clock. It was a quarter to four. I checked the window. Darkness. *A quarter to four in the morning, then.* I looked at the door. There had definitely been a knock. Who would knock in the dead of night? The doctor observing my dreaming again?

I listened for footsteps, my senses fully awake. No sound.

I uncurled my legs and got off the bed. The grogginess from the drugs was gone. I touched my nose and winced. My finger came away with a spot of blood. So... *what the hell did that mean?* Had I really just walked into a door in Rigpa Gompa or had I banged my nose on the end of my bed as I slept?

I padded to the door, looked through the square viewing window. An empty hall. I looked down. A napkin lay on the floor by my feet. It must have been pushed under. I bent down to pick it up. On it was a series of parallel lines creating some sort of pattern: arrows, some dashes of colour...

Then, I don't know why I did it—I'd never tried before—but something told me to pull down on the handle.

The door opened silently.

Sticking out of the lock on the other side of the door was a set of multi-coloured keys. I popped my head out and looked up and down the hall. 'Hello?' I whispered.

No answer.

Heart beating hard, I pulled the keys from the lock, ducked back into my room and let the door shut behind me.

'Whoa, whoa, whoa,' I whispered, as I paced around the room. Keys in one shaky hand, napkin in the other, heart pounding, feeling a little dizzy. 'OK, OK,' I said, trying to control my breathing. 'Calm down, Brown, calm down.'

I checked the clock again. I remembered Lily holding up four fingers. *Find a way.* 'Well, here's a way,' I whispered.

I took a deep breath and stopped pacing. Looked at the napkin again. The parallel lines were clearly corridors, the dashes of colour were the locks I'd need to open.

Who would draw me a... *Charlie?*

Had she drawn me an escape route and somehow lifted the keys off some unsuspecting newbie? Who else could it have been?

Now, all I had to do was... I looked at the cell door. All I had to do was... *go.*

I grabbed my Adidas jacket and looked around the room. As dingy and empty as it was, it had been my home for the last couple of months.

Something Lily had asked this afternoon echoed back to me now: *"Which side will you be standing on when the link is severed? Rigpa Gompa or here?"*

I slipped on a pair of trainers, zipped up my jacket, and went to the door.

Which side will you be standing on?

I thought about Dad. Had he been given the same choice? I thought about Mum, imagined her standing in front of *two* memorial stones. I placed my forehead against the door. And what if I just stayed? Went back to bed, took my drugs in the morning, was a good, normal girl?

I kept thinking that, even as I went to the door. I kept telling myself I had a choice; that I could just stay, go back to bed, wake up and play the game. Be ordinary. I kept telling myself that as I tiptoed down the hall. I kept telling myself all of that, right up to the point I placed the red key in the exit to my hall and turned it.

34

THE FOURTH OPTION

I PULLED THE DOOR open and crept down the staircase. At the landing, there was a door and another flight of stairs. A sign pointing downwards read: "LAUNDRY. NO FIRE EXIT." Which didn't look hopeful. I checked the map. According to Charlie's directions, an orange key would open the door. I'd have to walk to the end of this corridor, then turn left before reaching the last flight of stairs to ground level.

There was a sign on the door window. "STAFF ONLY". I peered through the glass. This was where the orderlies slept when they stayed over. It was dark. I couldn't see the end, but I trusted Charlie's map.

The key slid into the lock. As I turned, there was a noise.

I froze.

A strip of light flickered on underneath the third door along to the left, about halfway down the corridor.

Footsteps, a tinkle of metal.

I waited, hardly daring to breathe. The sound of a kettle coming to the boil.

Damn it.

I removed the key and slipped back into the darkness of the stairwell.

If they saw me standing here with a map in one hand and a set of rainbow keys in the other, I'd be toast. They'd put me in the 'Shirt' for sure. I pictured myself being strapped down, Miss Nuttal offering me encouraging and sympathetic words and then telling the doctors to up my dosage until I couldn't even remember my own name.

No. I wasn't getting caught like this.

So, three choices. I could go back to my cell. That was still a possibility; I could stay here in the shadows; or I could take a chance along the staff corridor and hope to God no one came out of that door. Three choices and I didn't like any of them.

There was, of course, a fourth option.

I gulped. Touched my nose. It still hurt from using it as a battering ram earlier.

I'd definitely have to practise first.

Even in a mental hospital, I'd look a bit weird standing in the corridor with my eyes closed, my hands pressed together and chanting: 'There is no Esta Brown,' over and over again.

There was about six feet of landing from one wall to the other on this side of the door. That would take me from one wall to the top of the laundry stairs. Not much to memorise there. If Swift Feet was actually a real life thing I could do... I mean, like not in a dream world, then I should be able to make six feet. And if I could make six feet, then...

I glanced down the corridor. Whoever was making tea wasn't going to bed. Instead, they were humming some unrecognisable ditty. The sort of hum you might make when you're getting ready, or brushing your teeth maybe. Definitely not the knocking-off-for-forty-winks sort of hum, anyway.

Another strip of light appeared at the base of a door on the right. *Jeez! How many of them are on early shift?*

I backed up to the wall, staring at the floor between me and the laundry sign. Barely anything to remember, just flat empty space for six feet. How hard could it be?

I put the keys in one pocket, the map in the other, placed my palms together, and said the words. Heat rose from my solar plexus, the dark landing in my mind became blurry and distorted. I gave a sort of mental push and Carved into it.

35

—·—

WEATHER REPORT

IT DIDN'T FEEL INSTANTANEOUS, even though it must have been. To me, it felt like a couple of leisurely seconds. And for those seconds, I thought *I can do this! I can actually do this!*

When I reckoned I'd reached the far wall, I opened my eyes... and found myself hovering an inch above the top step of the stairs. I dropped, stumbled and just about managed to grab the bannister to prevent an unwanted visit to the laundry.

The sound of my clattering feet and a couple of choice swear words echoed around the walls.

Carefully, I touched my bruised nose. *Overshot a bit. Got to watch that.*

I tiptoed back to the door. Now there were four strips of light. A faint sound of talking: *"... coming in from the north, with gusts of fifteen miles an hour..."* The weather report. Someone had the radio on.

I took a deep breath. The benefit of the increased light filling the hall was that I could see more of the ground and, more importantly, the far wall where the corridor bent left. I stared at it, trying to store a perfect picture in my mind's eye.

How far to the wall, though?

There were four doors on either side. Maybe ten feet between them and a little bit more to the corner. *Fifty feet?* That would have to do.

I turned the key. Opened the door. Stepped through.

Let's make it, say, forty-eight feet. Don't want to use my nose as a paintbrush on that far wall.

I placed my hands together.

There was a clunk of metal to the left. One of the strips of light suddenly became a wedge. The sound of the radio got louder. *"Temperatures today could reach..."*

The humming man was opening their door.

I closed my eyes, brought the mental picture of the corridor to mind...

"Twenty to twenty-one degrees..."

... and whispered: 'There is no Esta Brown.'

The walls warped, the floor twisted, the sound of the weatherman's voice curdled... I opened my eyes.

'... in coastal areas...'

I faced a bare wall.

I turned. The door was still opening... behind me. The radio weatherman was handing over to the DJ.

I slid round the corner, grinning like a Cheshire cat. Checked the map, pulled out the green key, unlocked the door and was already halfway to the ground floor before it shut behind me.

The front door was, of course, locked. I spent two nervy minutes looking for a key, but the sound of footsteps on the stairs cut that short. Soon the place would be crawling with orderlies and I would be dead meat. I could Carve all I liked, but without getting the front door open, I'd just be bopping around the place like a steel ball trapped in a pinball machine.

I jumped over the reception desk in to the little office beyond. A clock on the wall read almost half past four. Would the others still be waiting? What would I do if they weren't there?

What did it matter? I wasn't staying here. I was getting out, and if that meant smashing a window to do it...

36

MISDIRECTION

THE WINDOW WAS A little smaller and a little higher off the ground than I'd have hoped for. Its latch had been bolted down, so I had to punch the glass through with an electric typewriter. I ripped my jeans on the jagged glass as I squeezed through, and just in case they were still unclear about how I'd escaped, I left a streak of blood on the windowsill as a calling card.

A blinding security light clicked on as I dropped, bathing the lawns and the drive in cold white. From inside, I could hear the opening and closing of doors. I think the sound of typewriter on glass might *just* have given me away. After all my tiptoeing, I'll admit, it's just possible I could have been more subtle about the final stage of my escape.

I hastily considered my options again. Going back was out of the question. The cut in my jeans and the blood I'd left behind had definitely burnt that bridge. They'd surely have people watching the drive too and even if I could Carve all the way to the gates— and at several hundreds of feet there was no guarantee of that—they'd be all over me while I was still trying to climbing over them.

The front door opened. I dropped to a crouch and headed round the corner of the building where there was some shadow. If I could reach the trees by the edge of the lawn, I might be able to Carve in stages along the path that ran beside them. One tree to the next. That would get me to the gate without being seen, at least. Then I'd need just a little time to climb over. I'd need a little misdirection.

I know I used to let my anger get the better of me sometimes, but I was never a vandal. Some boys in my form had been done by the police for throwing raw eggs at windows a year ago. That was definitely *not* my bag. However, in my defence, as I had just found out, the sound of breaking glass is an effective way to attract attention. Two more windows along the southern wing of the hospital met their makers before I Carved into the cover of the trees.

I was getting better at this over short distances. A quick scan of the ground (thank you security lights), and, as long as there were no obstacles, I could zip across nearly twenty feet of lawn edge at a go. Trouble is, when you focus so much on the ground, you forget about overhanging branches and twigs. By the time I banged into the gate (which was almost instantly) I had lost hair and some more blood to the trees.

I glanced back at the grounds of the hospital. There were several figures outside now. One by the main door, one inspecting the smashed front window and a couple round the corner where I'd carried out my other acts of vandalism.

'Esta?' a shadow moved on the other side of the metal bars. I peered through. The shadow came closer. 'What took you so long?'

37

Taking the OAP to a Nice Field

I DROPPED TO THE ground. Lily grabbed my hand and led me away from the gate towards Wilmslow Road, where Graham had parked. When we were out of sight of the hospital, she paused under a dim streetlight. Held me at arm's length. 'Whoa, what happened to you? You look like you got into a fight with a cat.'

I touched the scratches on my forehead. My right arm was covered with them too, not to mention the rip in my jeans. 'I had to break a window and then Carve through some brambles to get here.'

'Carve?'

I pointed back at the path I'd taken, opened my mouth to explain... then thought better of it. Superpowers just aren't the same if people don't see you using them. 'I'll tell you later. Kind of hard to describe.'

Simon got out of the passenger's side of the Escort. 'Esta. You made it!' He came over to embrace me and stopped short. 'What happened to you?'

'She had an argument with a bush,' Lily said, opening the rear door.

There was someone else in the back seat.

I bent to look. Mr Sparks. They'd actually brought him.

Graham called out from the car. 'Guys. Get in. We have to go! The sun's up soon.' He turned the ignition, the engine cleared its throat, the exhaust made a snapping sound. Graham slapped the steering wheel and swore. He leaned over. 'What are you bloody waiting for, Taylor? Push!'

Between us, we pushed the car at least twenty feet along the northern section of Wilmslow Road before Graham risked another go with the key. The exhaust belched thick black smoke. The engine rattled into life and the three of us bundled ourselves inside. Simon in the front, Lily and me squeezed in the back alongside Graham's grandad.

Harry Sparks leaned his head against the window. Shock of white hair, scraggly beard, button-up shirt hanging off his body like from a curtain hanger. His arm was stretched out straight, long fingers resting on the top of Graham's seat. Maybe it was the on-and-off light from the passing street lamps, but he didn't look well. He looked out of breath, like he might shatter if he fell over.

He raised his head and looked at me with smoky-coloured eyes. 'Carol?' he whispered. A strand of hair fell over his face.

'My name's Esta. We met already. Do you remember?'

'Carol?' he repeated. He licked his dry lips and his bottom lip wobbled. Then he closed his eyes and rested his head against the window again.

This was hopeless. Graham was wrong. Harry Sparks was as lost as ever.

I turned to Lily. 'Is he OK?'

'He's been asleep. Even that bloody exhaust didn't wake him.'

'Does he even know what we're doing?'

'Yes. Honestly. He's just tired.'

'How on earth is this going to be possible?' I whispered. 'How is it even, you know, good?'

Graham took the sharp right off Wilmslow Road, sending Harry to lean into me. I held his head so it wouldn't bang back against the window when we straightened up.

We began the whirtling way along the back roads towards Fletcher's Field. 'He's a bit wobbly,' Graham said. 'But we'll use the rope.'

'We're going to drag an old man up the side of a building?'

'He'll be fine. He wants to do it.'

I looked at Harry and then at Lily. 'How is this not ten shades of wrong?'

Simon twisted round. 'How d'you get out. Est?' he asked, changing the subject.

'I'm not a hundred per cent sure. Lily? Did you tell Charlie about the keys?'

'Charlie? What keys?'

'I thought one of you must have told her.'

Lily shook her head.

'What about the keys?' Simon asked.

'The orderlies have a set each to open doors. I was trying to think of a way to pinch them, but couldn't. Then this morning I get a knock on the door and there's a set hanging out of the lock.' I pulled the napkin from my jeans and handed it to Simon. 'And this.'

'This is a floor plan of the hospital,' Simon said, looking up at me.

'She drew me an escape route.'

'Maybe she heard you and Lily talking,' Graham said. 'She sees and hears things we don't, doesn't she?'

Simon turned back to face the front. 'Maybe. But that doesn't explain how she half-inched the keys, does it? I mean, apart from her drawing hand, she can barely move.'

There was a squeal as Graham slowed the car near where he'd stopped last time, wheels mounting the curb. The engine shuddered to a stop. 'We're here,' he said.

Harry looked up, blinked at me, then stared out of the window on to Fletcher's Field.

38

TAKING THE OLD MAN HOME

FOR A FEW MOMENTS, there was silence as we all looked towards the dark silhouette of trees surrounding Gatley House. Beyond it, Grover Close was bathed in glaring security lighting and, out of the stillness of early morning, there was the sound of metal clanging against metal.

People were on site.

'What are they doing up this early?' I asked.

Graham unbelted himself. 'Amongst other things, they're decontaminating.'

'Decontaminating?'

'The place is still radioactive after the storm. That's why they've been blocking off the roads.' He grabbed his bag from somewhere down near his feet. 'I went over there after lunch with Dad's Geiger counter. That's why they're in Hazmat suits. They're spraying everything down, excavating the top soil and clearing the bushes.'

'Oh my God.'

'Don't worry. The levels aren't that bad.'

'Could be a good thing, right?' Simon said.

'Good?' Lily said incredulously. 'That there's a radioactive hot spot in the middle of the town? No, Simon. That's not good.'

'I meant good, in that they won't knock it down, will they? Not if they're doing all this decontaminating.'

'No.' Graham said. 'I don't know. It feels like an over-reaction. Like they're using it as an excuse so they can persuade the environment agency to let them push ahead. There's nothing to stop them flattening the place now, digging it all up, removing the poisoned topsoil.'

'Who cares? It changes nothing,' I said, looking at the others. 'We're here, aren't we? I'm not going back to the loony bin. So, what are we waiting for?'

We walked across the field. Harry had woken up well enough. He was slow and cautious, but he only needed his walking stick as support. As we walked past the buckled part of the fence that Graham had crashed into yesterday, I wondered about the men who'd chased Simon and me. Had they seen how we got in? Had they fixed the break?

Graham took a torch out of his bag and trained its beam along the fence as we approached the tree near the way in. The DANGER OF DEATH sign flashed yellow back at us.

I breathed a sigh of relief when he prized the metal apart for us.

'Go straight on,' Graham whispered, pointing at the Hawthorne tree Simon and I had climbed to escape yesterday. 'I cut a gap in the hedge last night. The gate's too exposed to go through now. Stop on the other side and wait for me.'

By the time Simon, Lily, Harry and me had squeezed through the hedge we were a collection of scrapes, scratches and bits of twig. From here we could see the eastern side of Gatley House. In front of it was the pile of bricks; the shopping trolley was still there too. Even now, after all the times I had made the Flip to Odiyana, it seemed impossible that such a dingy place like this could hide a whole reality with mountains, valleys and streams... and demons.

Don't forget the demons, Esta.

A bird sang up in the branches. It didn't seem worried by radioactivity, or the sounds of machines tearing up the bushes. Or then again, maybe it was yelling at everything to just stop. Maybe it was screaming as it watched its universe being torn up. Or maybe it knew there was even more at stake. Maybe it felt reality itself was slowly being torn apart.

Harry pushed himself up, rubbing the dirt off his trousers. He stood still, watching his old home. 'Show me,' he said gruffly. 'I want to see.'

A thrumming noise sounded from somewhere behind the house. It was followed by a rustle of leaves directly behind us. I whirled round to see Graham push himself through the hedge to join us.

'You hear that noise?' he said, standing up. 'What the bloody hell is he doing?'

I twisted back round.

Harry Sparks was on his way out from under the cover of the tree, staggering towards the house.

'He'll give us all away.' Graham hissed. But I could hardly hear him over the sound of the thrumming that seemed to be coming directly from the roof of the house now.

We all stood and watched the old man gazing up at his old home, one arm lifted up as if shielding his eyes from a blinding sun. And then the thrumming noise became a thunderous beating; a heavy gust of wind sent fallen leaves into spirals around him and he became flooded in a pool of white light.

39

HELICOPTERS

A HELICOPTER CAME IN low from over the top of Gatley House, making the branches of the Hawthorne dance madly overhead. Its high intensity beam painted the grounds of Gatley House white. It hovered for a moment and then descended towards Grover Close.

Graham ran out and grabbed Harry, pulling him back under the branches of the Hawthorne just as a second chopper came in, the wind from its blades whipping up the grass at our feet. 'Helicopters?' Lily shouted as a third followed the first two. 'What the hell are helicopters doing here?'

'Special forces?' Graham said as he helped his grandad to his knees. 'They aren't normal army, anyway. I didn't see any markings.'

The third one landed and after a few deafening moments, the noise from the helicopters changed from a heavy throbbing to a metallic whining.

'What does that mean?' Lily asked.

'It means, any minute now, this place'll be crawling with suits.'

'Soldiers? With guns?'

'I don't know, do I!'

I glanced across at Simon. His eyes had a wide, scared look. I think he was thinking exactly what I was thinking. If the military were here in the human realm and the two realms sometimes mirrored each other... then what was happening in Odiyana?

'We have to go,' I said, shuffling my way out. 'Or we'll never get another chance, will we?'

Simon stopped me. 'Wait. Esta. We don't know what's out there.'

'If it's military,' Graham added, 'this is serious. They won't ask questions. We should talk about going back. Just until we know what's going on.'

'I'm never going back,' I said. 'I'm never going back inside that hospital.'

'Maybe, just wait—'

I pulled Simon aside. 'Look. I don't know exactly how, but I met Lama la last night.'

'What? I thought—'

'It doesn't matter. It happened. He needs you, me and Harry, or all of this is just going to get worse.'

Simon stared back at me. For a second, I thought he might just stay crouched under cover. A moment of panic surged through me as I imagined being stranded up on that roof all by myself.

'Simon, you were the one who made me go up last time. It's like you said. We have to do it together.'

After what seemed like an age, Simon seemed to collect himself.

He nodded and held my hand. 'OK, then.' 'Wait for us,' Lily said.

'You sure?' Graham said.

'Whatever it takes, remember?'

40

LAST LOOK

THE ROPE STILL HUNG down from the chimney where we'd left it. Graham pulled the trolley against the fence.

Simon stood, hands on hips, staring up at the roof. 'You ever actually lifted a human being by yourself?'

Graham looked up at the chimney. 'One of us couldn't lift him alone. But three of us might.' He tugged on the rope to make sure it was sturdy and then began to climb, his satchel bobbing against his back as he sped up the wall.

Simon followed.

'You go,' Lily said to me. 'I'll get Harry strapped up.'

I took one last look around at the old place. Listened to the sounds of machines and the crunching of rubble beyond what was left of the tangle of bushes, then grabbed the rope and climbed up the walls of Gatley House for what, I was certain, would be the very last time.

41

DRAGGING THE OAP UP A WALL

GRAHAM, SIMON, AND I sat in a line holding the rope. Simon closest to the chimney, me in the middle and Graham holding the end of the rope. Our feet were jammed against the guttering, which, I was beginning to think, might just be the one thing to resist the wrecking ball when it came again. Graham had swung the rope around the chimney and then told us to thread it through our belts for safety. Down below, Lily had looped the other end under Harry's arms.

'How are you feeling?' Graham asked me.

I held up my hand. It shook surprisingly violently. Mixture of cold, fear and probably the remains of the meds. I had made it up here through sheer will and maybe it was the adrenaline talking, but up here, with the breeze in my hair, I thought maybe we might actually do this.

'That's my granddad down there, Esta. We're not dropping him.'

'I know, I know.' I glanced across the lawn. The sun was a pink glow off to the East, there was enough light in the morning to see smoke curling up from Grover Close. This was it. I had burned my bridges with Gatley Gardens. The bulldozers were closer than ever. There could be no normal anymore, not after all of this.

I looked down. Lily was talking to Harry on the ground. He was nodding.

'Lily?' Graham whispered down. 'Are you sure he's safe?'

Harry looked up, both hands gripping the rope. 'Take me up!' he growled.

'Lily. Are you sure he's tight?'

Lily tried to check the rope around his chest, but the old man shrugged her off. He glared back up at us, his face full of grim determination. 'Now or never,' he said. 'Lift me up. I'll hold my own weight.'

'He thinks he's still a soldier,' Graham said quietly to me. Then he called down: 'Granddad? Just take it easy. I don't want—'

'Boy,' the old man called back. 'I'm coming,' and he started pulling himself up and over the fence.

Graham lent back, gripping the rope. 'Simon!' he shouted. 'Take the slack. Esta? Pull!'

I peered down at Harry, who had already reached the top of the fence.

'Guys, pull when I say. It's got to be in time. Critical. Simon, you can see him best. Keep your eyes on him. When he's ready, say "One". Esta, you say "Two" and I'll say "heave".'

And that's what we did.

It worked like a dream. Within one pull, Harry was clear of the fence, his feet pedalling away against the brick as we took his weight.

Simon: 'One!'

Me: 'Two!'

Graham: 'Heave!'

And we pulled.

Harry shifted upwards three feet. His bony fingers gripping the handholds, his feet jamming into the gaps in the wall.

'He's climbing!' Simon called

'Muscle memory,' Graham said. 'Again. Simon? Ready?'

Simon laughed. 'Unbelievable. Yeah. Ready. One!'

'Two!' I shouted. We were actually doing it. Everything was going to work out. We were actually getting Harry up the damn roof!

'Heave!'

Soon Harry's face, bright red and sweaty, appeared above the gutter. Simon pulled him up and the old man collapsed against the tiles, lungs heaving with exhaustion. Simon held on to him to stop his knees from buckling. When he was secure against the chimney stack, Simon started untying the rope for Lily.

'What are you doing?' Graham hissed. 'Keep him fastened to the rope. Just in case...'

'What about Lily?'

'Lily can manage.'

As he said this, an arm reached up from below and curled around the gutter. Graham pulled her up. Her clothes were muddy from the climb, her hair was as messy as Graham's and she had a grin stretching from ear to ear. 'All here?' she said.

'Well, bloody hell,' Simon mumbled.

42

HAZMATS DISTRACTION

ALL ASSEMBLED. WE SIDLED around the corner of the building, inconspicuous as cake decorations in the brightening morning. From up here you could see the grounded helicopter's blades still slowly rotating; people dressed in those space suit things; diggers gouging strips from the ground. Beyond that, perhaps a quarter of a mile away, a team of workers were erecting yet more perimeter fencing, this time including the whole of Fletcher's Field to the east. The blue lights of police cars flickered every 100 yards along the main road. Other than that, there was no traffic.

'What's with the space suits?' Simon whispered. 'Hazmats,' Graham said. 'Shields them from the radiation. But this is all wrong. If they think it's radioactive, they should evacuate the town, not just erect a fence.'

Lily pointed toward the Willow. 'Someone's coming.'

More men in Hazmats were picking their way through the bushes. They'd be out onto the lawn in a few steps and then they'd have to be blind not to spot four teenagers and an OAP teetering on top of the roof. We couldn't stay put, and I, for one, wasn't risking going back around the deadly corner. So we shuffled towards the hole in the roof. The gutter shook and creaked worryingly beneath our feet.

Graham reached the hole first and had started climbing down into the house when someone, I don't know if it was Simon or Lily, must have dislodged a tile. It knocked against the gutter with a dull clunk and then spiralled down to smash on the driveway below.

We froze, eyes glued to the bushes.

One of the men had emerged. He was standing next to the Willow, looking at the spot where the tile had landed. His helmet shifted as his gaze rose to the roof, then tilted to one side. Another figure appeared, and slowly, raised his arm until it was pointing right at us.

43

CLINGING

'MOVE!' SIMON WHISPERED. AND the three of us jolted into life, sending a few more tiles crashing down. Simon and Lily on either side of Harry, nudging and sliding him along. The next thirty seconds was a rush of sharp tiles, more torn clothes and whispered swearing.

We reached the hole and, trying to ignore the shouting from the men below, I helped Simon and Lily lower Harry over the lip of the broken roof. Graham was underneath. This would have been tough at the best of times; in this panic, and at night, it was close to suicidal. Harry seemed to have found some more strength, though, and to our amazement, could clamber down the last few feet by himself.

Simon and Lily followed.

I took one last look out across the grounds. I had intended to spend a few minutes gazing out at my hometown. You know, just in case I never came back. But that brief glimpse of the choppers, bulldozers and fencing was all I got to see.

I placed a foot on to the crossbeam and lowered myself into a crouch. But as I stretched my foot down to reach the next beam, something snapped beneath me.

There was a sound of tumbling bricks, and before I could pull myself back up on to the roof, the entire beam came away from the external wall and swung out over the hole in the floor below. My trainers slipped and suddenly I found myself clinging on to the beam, feet dangling uselessly above the broken floor.

44

SOMETHING HINGE-SHAPED

'ESTA!' SIMON CALLED, AS I hung stupidly above him. 'Can you move left?'

'No,' I whispered back. 'I don't know what happened.'

'The wood's rotten,' Graham said. 'It broke under you. Can you pull yourself up?'

I looked down. The others were on the safe bit of floor along with the table full of junk. I, however, was over what was essentially a chasm. If I dropped here, I'd probably hit the edge of the jagged bit of floorboard and bounce off down into the overgrown depths of the house. I glanced across at the next beam. There was no way to reach it.

'Idiot!' I hissed. 'Idiot, idiot!'

'Est,' Graham said, obviously trying to sound calm. 'Can you swing?'

'Swing?'

'If you swing and let go at the right moment, you might make it. I'll catch you.'

An explosive laugh escaped me. What were we? The bloody Russian circus? I laughed again and my arm slipped a bit more.

Simon started climbing back up. 'I'm coming up to get you.'

'No. Simon! It's too dangerous,' Graham shouted. He was looking across at the beam I was holding on to, one end just about propped up against the dodgy looking outer wall. 'That beam's not safe, it might break off.'

'Who'd have thought...' I gasped, '... that climbing into a half demolished building would be dangerous?'

Outside, the men in suits were calling to each other. I could just see them through the gaps in the bricks.

The beam jolted. I slipped a bit more.

'It won't take both your weights!' Graham yelled.

'We can't just leave her hanging there!' Simon yelled back.

I couldn't see, but Graham must have stopped him climbing because the beam stopped moving. 'You'll have to pull yourself up,' he said. 'Bring your leg over and then slide towards us.'

I tried. I cocked one leg up like a dog going for a pee. I would have laughed again if I hadn't been so exhausted. 'I can't,' I said, looking down again.

Deja vu.

I had looked down on this drop once before. But there was no rope this time, no swirling ocean, no encouraging mirage of Dad. Just the hard and sure blackness of a broken back... minimum.

Maybe Charlie and I could keep each other company in our wheelchairs.

'Esta?' Lily said. Her voice was high-pitched and desperate. I shifted my head so I could see her. She was looking at Harry, who was inspecting the table. 'I don't know if everything is true, or it's all just in your head. But if it's all true... then it's the only way.'

'What are you talking about, Lil?' Graham whispered. She ignored him. 'Simon, what's your object?'

'Object?'

'Your... thing. The Bell. What am I looking for?'

'In this world, it's a... it's a door bolt.'

My right hand came away from the beam as they talked. My fingers just couldn't grip any more. My left hand was slowly slipping, too. The house seemed to contract. The walls, the remains of the roof, the broken floor all seemed to squeeze in on me.

I closed my eyes. There was no Carving out of this one, there was no route to follow in my mind, there was just gravity and wood and brick and pain.

'Esta!'

My eyes shot open.

Lily's arm was making a sweeping arc. 'Catch!'

Something dull and square came to me through the dusty air.

Something hinge-shaped.

My left hand released and closed around the piece of junk.

Blue crackling light scattered crazily across its surface and the Orb appeared, gold and sparkling in a ray of morning sunlight.

As I fell, I heard Lily scream my name.

PART FOUR

INTO THE BARDO OF BECOMING

45

How's the Nose?

I LANDED, FACE DOWN, on hardwood. The Orb clattered out of my hands and skidded across the floor.

There was the sound of footsteps and I felt myself being gently pulled over.

'Not on her back,' Harry said. 'She might choke.'

Cold hands touched my face. My eyes flickered open. Simon peered down at me with a look of concern. 'You're OK.'

A blurry, milky light to my left cast half his face in shadow. I moved my eyes from his. The Orb lay a few feet away from me. Floating above it, silvery clouds swirling across its surface, was the Wheel of *Samsara*. I turned on to my side and propped myself up on one elbow. 'Lily? Graham?'

Simon shook his head. 'They didn't make the Flip.'

'Are they OK?'

'They're fine,' Harry said from somewhere in the room. 'Nothing we can do for them now though.'

Simon helped me to sit. Harry was gazing at the wall hangings. He lifted one of them, inspected the wall underneath it, then let it drop back. When he turned back to face us, his face was awake. His skin was smoother, his eyes were clear and bright in the strange light of the Wheel. He walked over to us, moving like a man twenty years younger: his back straight, his cane barely supporting him at all. He crouched.

Not even a creaky knee.

'Now we're here,' he said just above a whisper, 'we can finally send this bloody place back to where it came from. That's why you brought me, isn't it?'

'We don't really know why,' Simon said. 'We just know Lama la—'

'Lama la!' Harry spat. 'Who knows why he wants anything?'

'Harry,' I said, propping myself up against the wall, my bones aching. 'What do you know?'

'What do I know?' He let out a dry laugh. 'I know... I should never have brought this place to England. I know I should have finished it off when I had a chance. And I know they've found it now. They must have found it.'

'Who is they?' Simon asked.

'Those who want to keep it open.'

'Mara,' I said.

'What?' Harry looked at me as if I'd said something stupid. 'No! Not him. He's nothing but fire and wind, he's disease and confusion. Mara has no plan. He's just a bull in a china shop.'

'Not Mara?'

'No. Of course not! Someone's using him.'

'Using Mara?' Simon said.

'Who'd use Mara?' I asked.

There was a sound at the door. A swish of curtain. In one graceful movement, Harry grabbed his cane and turned.

Karma Chodron was standing in the doorway. Rabjam, Sera and Tubten behind her.

Harry tapped his cane on the floor, then brought it up in two hands like a sword.

'Where's Lama la?' he growled.

Karma Chodron stepped inside, seemingly unconcerned by Harry's threatening tone. She stared lazily at the cane. 'You want to watch where you put that stick.' She looked past him at me, raised her head in greeting. 'Welcome back,' she said. 'How's the nose?'

46

LAMA LA'S HALF TRUTHS

WE SAT IN AN uncomfortable silence while Rabjam poured butter tea for us. Harry supped his, his hand never relaxing on his cane, his wary eyes never leaving Karma Chodron.

Outside, a wind had risen and gusts of cold air funnelled through the gaps in the ceiling, making the wall hangings shift and the candle flames do little hip jiggles.

I drank my tea. Downed it in three. The cuts and bruises on my face and arms almost immediately seemed to heal. I held out my cup for Rabjam to refill.

'So, this is Harry Sparks,' Karma Chodron said. 'The man who took a whole world home in a suitcase.'

'I saved this place,' he replied evenly. 'Kept it safe for more than thirty years.'

The window rattled.

Karma Chodron glanced at it. 'Well, we don't feel safe.'

For the first time, Harry dropped his gaze. He took a sip of his tea. 'I'd forgotten how unpleasant this is.'

Simon cleared his throat. 'You have to think of it like—'

'Chicken soup.' Harry took another slurp. 'Yeah, I know.'

We listened to the wind. You could hear voices out there too now. Whistles and whispers in the distance and there was that smell. The faint odour of rotting food.

Tubten put down his cup and wiped his mouth with the sleeve of his robes. 'Why are you here, old guy?'

Simon answered. 'Lama la wanted him.'

'I know. But what for?'

'To make you safe again,' Harry said. I noticed his fingers had relaxed around the cane now.

'How?' Tubten pointed at me and Simon. 'They brought the Kila. We're still here.' He pointed at the window. 'Storm's getting worse.'

Harry nodded. Then shook his head. 'I don't know. We'll have to wait for your master to reveal all.'

'Maybe he can help us fight?' Rabjam suggested, looking at Harry's cane.

'Can't you lot count?' Karma Chodron said. 'Look around. How many of us are there?'

Rabjam shrugged. 'Seven.'

'There's eight of us, when Lama la ever turns up. Eight.'

The voices outside became louder. Whispers and words that came and went as if whatever was making them was swooping in circles near the window.

'What's the significance of eight?' I asked.

'The eight symbols?' Rabjam suggested.

Karma Chodron rolled her eyes. 'Of course. Why do you think he sent us out to get them?'

'I thought we just brought them back here to protect them,' Tubten said.

'That was your errand?' Simon said.

'He called it an errand?' Karma Chodron said, clearly unhappy with that as a description. She turned back to the others. 'Why else would Lama la need eight people? He's been planning something ever since we got the Kila back.'

'KC, what are you saying?' Rabjam asked.

'She's saying,' Harry answered, studying Simon and me, 'that Lama la has a habit of concealing the truth or telling people half-truths in aid of a bigger plan.'

Karma Chodron raised an eyebrow at Harry, then she looked at Simon and me. 'Like them?'

'What do you mean, "like us"?' Simon asked.

There was a scream and a thud at the window. The curtain shuddered, some of the lamps shivered and shrivelled to single points of red, Tubten jumped to his feet and started off towards the door.

'The Mamos are attacking,' Karma Chodron said, taking a sip of her tea. 'Same every night.'

'It's getting worse,' Tubten moaned from the doorway.

Rabjam grabbed his kettle and joined the younger monk. 'He's right. We should go downstairs to prepare.'

47

Grade 'A' in Esta Brown Studies

'HE'S A FOOL,' KARMA Chodron whispered as we filed down the second set of steps towards the Great Hall.

'KC,' Rabjam whispered. 'Don't say things like that.'

'He sent us on a fool's mission, Rab. And now he wants to delay and delay, but he won't tell us why. Just gives us rubbish about wheels within wheels. He knows Samsara is broken, and he does nothing. It's almost as if he *wants* it to fail.'

'Lama la is bound to defend this place. We should have faith in him.'

'I do. But he asks us to risk everything and tells us nothing.'

'That's because,' Harry said, his low, growly voice carrying from the back of our little troupe, 'I imagine he doesn't fully know himself. He likes to pretend he's all knowing, but maybe he's just as confused as the rest of us.'

Karma Chodron paused and turned around. 'I don't believe that. How long has he been the abbot of this temple? A hundred years? He knows everything and treats us like children.'

'We are children—' Tubten started.

'You might look like one, Tub,' she snapped, turning back and striding towards the entrance to the hall. 'But don't forget what we had to go through in order to get those symbols for him. You don't send children to places like that.'

'So what do you suggest we do?' Rabjam whispered. 'Because if you are suggesting that we go against Lama la, we won't do it.'

We entered the hall. It glowed golden with a hundred flames that danced in front of the enormous statue of Padmakara. Lama la's throne was empty.

'I agree with Rab,' Tubten said, settling himself down on one of the cushions in front of the shrine.

'You always agree with Rab,' Karma Chodron replied, sitting down next to the young monk. 'But I'm not saying that we go against him. I'm saying that we find out the truth, that's all.'

'I agree,' Sera said. I'm not sure I'd ever heard her speak. She had a gentle, lilting sort of voice. 'But how to know for sure? There are only stories. We don't know if they're true. We can't see what happened. We weren't there.'

'We weren't. But *they* might have been.' Karma Chodron pointed at Simon and me. I checked over my shoulder in case she was talking about someone else, but the angry nun was staring directly at me.

'Us?' I said pointing at my chest.

'Lama la told us all about your little adventure in the Wheel. About the woman who saved you from the Hungry Ghosts. Is that all true? Or was he making that up as well?'

I nodded.

The four Dharmapalas exchanged serious glances with each other.

'And did he tell you who she was?'

I cleared my throat. 'Erm. Trisha or something?' It occurred to me that Lama la had never actually told me who she really was, and I had a horrible feeling that I'd missed something important.

Rahjam looked uncomfortably from me back to Karma Chodron. 'Trisna?'

'She showed me where my dad is.'

'Whatever she said to you. Whatever she showed you — you need to be careful. Trisna wouldn't show you something if she thought it would be helpful to you.'

'Why? Who is she?'

'Trisna,' Harry said. 'Is one of Mara's daughters.'

I froze. 'Mara has a daughter?'

'Not just one.'

'And now,' Karma Chodron added, 'she knows everything important about you.'

That didn't sound like good news, but, then again, so what? After Lama la showed me my dad, with the help of Harry Sparks, we were slamming the door on this world. We were out of here. Mara and his daughters could get an 'A' in Esta Brown Studies for all I cared.

'Whatever,' I said, trying to sound unflustered. 'Let's go find Lama la so we can find my dad and we can get all this over and done with. Isn't that what we're here for?'

'You've got it all wrong,' Karma Chodron said. 'He's not going to show you anything.'

'He promised. Lama la doesn't break a promise.'

'You'd do well to recall exactly what he promised you,' Karma Chodron said. 'Because if I'm right about what, or rather who you saw, there's no way he'll take you back to that place.'

I frowned. What had he promised me in return for bringing Harry? I replayed the conversation in my head. *"I will have an answer for you."* Crap. What exactly did that mean?

'*He* won't take you back to the place you saw with Trisna...' Karma Chodron repeated. Then she walked deeper into the hall and beckoned for me and Simon to do the same. 'But I can.'

48

CONJURING THE WHEEL

KARMA CHODRON MOVED A couple of tables to make a space in the centre of the Great Hall while the others got on with the protection rituals.

Harry, it seemed, had done all this before. He picked up a drumstick and joined in with the chanting without needing to read anything.

'Sit down,' Karma Chodron said, lighting some more lamps on the low tables around us. 'I'll conjure the Wheel. You sit. Meditate while I do it. No talking. I need to focus.'

She read from a small stack of pages for a couple of minutes while Simon and I got ourselves comfortable. We were sitting in a sort of triangle formation. Karma Chodron with her back to the shrine. Simon and I sat six feet apart, facing her.

We watched in silence as little swirling tornados of dust formed in the space between us. They glinted in the candlelight, rotating and dancing together as Karma Chodron chanted.

I'd never seen the Wheel created before and it was mesmerising. The mini tornados of glittering dust gathered together into a slowly spiralling disc. Karma Chodron's voice rose and fell as she turned each page. The disc pulsed with an inner glow, attracting points of light from around the room, sucking up the light given off by the butter lamps near us, until it had expanded into a recognisable globe.

Karma Chodron paused, played a pair of hand-cymbals, then began to chant again, which seemed to cause the globe to divide into the six individual realms.

When she turned over the final page, the Wheel was fully three dimensional, turning slowly between us. It crackled with blueish lightning, like one of those science electricity balls that make your hair stand on end.

'Blimey,' Simon whispered, leaning back so we could see each other. 'It's never looked like that before.'

Karma Chodron appeared now as a vague figure seen through the luminous ball of light. 'The realms are collapsing into each other,' she said. 'The link between cause and effect is almost broken. We can't wait any longer.'

'What's making all this happen?' Simon asked.

Karma Chodron got up and walked through the Wheel towards us. 'Lama la is keeping something from you, from all of us.' She stopped, so it completely enveloped her. 'You have to see. Lama la is wise, but he's old and over-cautious. Mara is amassing outside our walls again and soon he will break us. If we are to defeat him, we need to understand what Trisna was showing you.'

'Do you think,' I said, thinking about the man in the carriage. 'You think my dad has something to do with this?'

Karma Chodron scowled at me. 'You think the Wheel revolves around you and your father?'

'I don't know. Why would the goddess of desire take me to see a man I don't know?'

'Wait,' Simon said. 'Why does Mara want to destroy the whole system, anyway? What does he get out of it?'

Karma Chodron glanced up to her left at the smouldering Chitapali tree. The tree that divided the Ashura from the long-lived gods. 'Nothing,' she said. 'Mara can't help himself.'

'But,' Simon got up from his seat. 'If he destroys,' he waved his hands at the rotating globe, 'all of that, doesn't he destroy himself too? I mean, Mara is nothing without people to feed off, right?'

'Mara is nothing more than disruption and chaos. That's his nature. Like it's the nature of fire to burn.'

'How do we stop him?'

Karma Chodron glared at me for a moment more before answering. 'That's what we need to find out. Simon, go back to your seat. Let's take Esta to see her mysterious man. Perhaps we will discover who he is and what part he plays in all of this.'

I nodded a thanks, but my skin was as cold and clammy as a wet jumper. I didn't like the way she had looked at me when I'd mentioned my dad. Was all this about him or not? Because if it wasn't, I suddenly wasn't keen to go back and lift the curtain of that carriage. I remembered the fingers of the hand I'd almost touched; that strange symbol on the ring. I'd been sure it was his. I mean, who else would it be? I remembered something else Lama la had said when I'd asked about the mysterious man: *"It's not that simple."* Clear as a garage door. Harry was right about that, too. Lama la did have a way with words.

'You already know, don't you?' Simon said, as he took his seat again. 'You know who we're going to find. You know who Esta saw.'

Karma Chodron retreated to her own cushion behind the Wheel. She picked up her mala and began rubbing the beads between her fingers while she spoke. 'Esta, it's time I showed you what Lama la has been keeping from you.'

49

INTO THE ALAYA

I HAD THAT WEIRD floaty feeling as we descended into the wheel — like being suspended in mid-air but with nobody. Far to my right was a horizon of blood-black clouds:

The Hell realms.

The thought that there might be some kind of a leak between there and the realm of humans made my skin crawl.

'This way,' murmured Karma Chodron, and I felt a magnetic tug drawing me away from the dark horizon towards green meadows, mountains and trees; the smell of earth and spring flowers.

'Where are we going?' Simon asked.

'If I'm right about this, it's not where,' Karma Chodron said. 'But when.'

The surrounding scenery blurred out. The valley changed. It was greener. There were rhododendrons of pink and yellow dotted along the slopes. Towering above us was a magnificent temple with blindingly white walls and a golden roof that shimmered in the rays of the sun.

As we approached, I could see movement in the courtyard. The place was teeming with life. People—same as when Trisna brought me here—thirty or forty of them this time, dressed in purple robes.

I turned to look down the valley for the procession that had been climbing the mountain last time, but the path was empty.

I scanned the courtyard. Goats were tied up outside the boundary walls; monks and nuns ran around like kids in a playground.

I swooped lower.

There, around the side of the temple, not far from the side entrance, was the golden carriage, set down and empty. Whoever I'd seen being hauled up that impossible path had seemingly now arrived.

'Where are we?' Simon said.

'Rigpa Gompa.'

'But it's full of people?'

'And so it was, hundreds of years ago.'

My heart stopped. *Hundreds of years ago? How could that be?* If the man behind the golden curtain was my dad, how had he gone back in time?

I followed the ghostly form of Karma Chodron as she took us over the courtyard.

'Whoa,' Simon breathed excitedly. 'We went back in time?'

'Not really,' Karma Chodron replied. 'We're observing, but we're not part of it.'

'Can anyone see us?' I asked.

'Not yet. All of this has already happened. We can't interfere or interact. The past is the past.'

But if I'm honest, I didn't think she sounded all that sure of herself.

'So we're invisible?' Simon asked.

'This is just a projection — a vision we're sharing.'

'Whose vision?'

She looked at me. 'This is the place Trisna brought you to, isn't it?'

I nodded.

'This world is part of your mind stream. That is why we can travel here.'

'So... we're travelling inside my head?'

'Who said anything about a head?' Karma Chodron reached the roof and came to a stop, hovering a few feet above the golden tiles. 'But, if you like, yes.'

'OK... that's not disconcerting at all. So, this really *isn't* about my dad then?'

Karma Chodron threw her hands up in the air. 'Always about your father! You know, other people have fathers too!'

'Alright. Calm down. So this...' I gazed around me. 'Is all about me? About who I used to be in a past life?'

'Of course! Now follow.' She directed her gaze down to the surface of the roof and descended. Her ghostly feet disappeared into the golden tiles as if she were sinking in quicksand and then, slowly, the rest of her body followed.

Simon raised his eyebrows at me and then sank below as well, leaving me hovering over the seemingly solid structure. 'How do you do that?'

Simon was up to his shoulders in roof. He shrugged them.

'Thanks. Not helping.'

'I dunno,' he said, just his face left above the ceiling. 'Pretend it isn't there and imagine yourself going down in a lift.'

I smiled sarcastically. 'This is supposed to be my mind,' I mumbled, then hovered lower, until my feet touched the golden tiles. I closed my eyes, preparing for impact... and imagined myself gracefully passing through the roof.

When I opened my eyes again, I was in the dark interior of the temple. *Piece of cake.* The other two were already drifting along the corridor away from me. 'We have to be quick!' Karma Chodron said when I caught up. 'Before we begin to Weave.'

'I thought we were just observers?'

She turned to me. 'Yes!' she hissed angrily. 'But don't you feel it?'

'What?'

'The floor!'

I looked down. My feet, now more defined, seemed to touch the surface. I could feel the vague pressure of it, like treading on a blast of air. Simon's form was clearer, too. He looked like a colour-it-in outline and the wall that I could see through him was distorted and wobbly.

'I thought you said we can't interact with anything here?'

'The longer we stay, the more your mind accepts us. Draws us into its reality.'

'What are you saying?' Simon whispered.

'That if we stay too long, this will become real for us. We'll be woven into the deepest valleys of Esta's mind.'

'That's why Lama la wanted me out of here so quickly last time,' I said under my breath.

'The less impact on the world you have here, the more you dissolve into the background.'

'Why didn't you say so before you brought us?' Simon hissed. 'I don't want to be stuck in Esta's brain.'

'It's not Esta's brain,' Karma Chodron explained. 'It's the Alaya consciousness. The part of her mind which stores impressions from all her previous lives.' She looked at our vacant expressions. 'If Esta's current mind is like a flower on the surface of a lake. This is the mud where its roots are.'

'That's an even worse thought,' Simon said. 'How long do you think we've got?'

'I don't know.' She glanced at me. 'Ask her.' Then slipped through a solid wall.

I followed, and this time the sensation was like slipping through water. We *were* becoming more real. I was definitely walking on semi-solid surfaces now.

'This is the landing, near Lama la's study,' Simon whispered, pointing at the familiar-looking stairs heading down.

'No paintings on the walls,' I said.

'The paintings came later,' Karma Chodron said. 'Come on. We have to see.'

We stood outside Lama la's room. A beautiful brocade hung over the entrance, ruby red and white, threaded through with silvery leaf patterns.

'In there,' Karma Chodron said, reaching out to touch it. The brocade moved. She froze.

'What's wrong?' Simon asked.

She turned to me. She looked confused. 'You should go in first.'

I frowned. 'Is everything OK?'

She touched the brocade again. This time, her fingers didn't go through the fabric. 'I'm already Weaving! Be quick!'

Simon stepped forward. 'I'll go.' He slid right through the door hanging. It ruffled a little. There was a pause, then Simon's hand appeared back through the material and waved me in.

'I'll wait here,' Karma Chodron said. 'As soon as you feel anything solid, come out. Understand?'

I nodded and made to follow Simon, but Karma Chodron placed a ghostly hand on me. Substantial as a breeze. 'Whatever happens! Whatever you see. Come straight out.'

'I got it!' I whispered and walked through Karma Chodron's arm and the door hanging as if I were plunging through frozen fog.

50

THE TWO DISCIPLES

THE ROOM WAS JUST like the one back in Rigpa Gompa. Shrine to the left; low table beneath the window straight ahead; paintings hanging from the walls. 'Are you OK?' Simon whispered.

'No,' I whispered. 'I don't think we should be here. It doesn't feel right.'

'Where's Karma Chodron?'

'Outside. She's already Weaving, apparently. Can you feel anything?'

'Not really.' He poked my forehead. His finger went right through. 'How about you?'

'Eeww!' I tried to swipe his hand away, but of course failed. I stepped aside instead and headed for the shrine. The statue was more primitive looking than the one on Lama la's shrine. It was difficult to tell the form or shape, other than that it was of a seated man. No painted face on this one.

'This is the same room,' Simon said from behind me.

'Be quiet,' I hissed.

'So what are you showing me?'

'I don't know, do I?'

'It *is* your mind.'

'Sshh!"

There were muffled voices outside. I slipped back towards the wall and sunk into the shadows.

With a flourish, a large man in maroon robes swept the brocade aside. He stormed in, face bright red, sweat beading on his forehead. Simon ducked back to join me as I waited —heart in mouth—to surely see the man who'd been behind the curtain in the carriage.

Two others followed the first into the room. They were arguing with each other.

The next one through the doorway was a large barrel-chested man dressed in golden silks. He had a beard and long black hair that dropped to his shoulders in curls. The last was a younger man — couldn't have been much older than me. No more than a skinny teenager. His head was shaved, and he was dressed in an orange monk's robe.

'Rules!' the man in the golden silks snapped. 'Always with rules!' He swung an arm toward the younger man. 'That's not what Rinpoche means at all! Brother, you're young and naïve! A stickler.'

The younger, skinnier man shook his head and spoke to the floor at the other's feet. 'You've gone too far this time, Rudra.' Then he addressed the first man who had come in.

'Rinpoche, you saw his retinue carrying him up here? There must have been more than a hundred. And... and the gold...'

The man in the golden robes—Rudra—rolled heavy-lidded eyes. His head was enormous, his neck was thick and muscular, and I reckoned the guy was all muscle under those robes, too. 'My brother monk,' he said. 'Freedom means transcending the rules. Liberation means liberation from all limitations. That's basic. I mean...' he addressed the man they were both calling "Rinpoche". 'Even the novices in the courtyard know that.'

'That must be the Abbot of the temple,' Simon whispered as the eldest of the three men stepped over a low table and lowered himself on to a large square cushion beneath the window; the same place Lama la normally took. He sat down with a grunt and wiped his sweaty face with a cloth he retrieved from inside his robes, then he pointed at the young man. 'Padmakara, be seated.'

Simon and I exchanged looks. Padmakara? *The* Padmakara? If he was, he didn't look much like the fierce-looking statue that dominated the Great Hall.

Rudra placed his forearm across his younger companion's chest. 'Surely, master, as we are equals, we should sit down together? At the same time?'

The abbot—if that's what he was—didn't look amused. 'You want me to count to three?'

Rudra forced a smile, removed his arm from Padmakara and dropped easily to his cushion. The young monk shook his head silently and took his own seat. The two disciples—one in gold, one in orange—sat facing the old abbot, just as Simon and I had often done with Lama la.

'You reckon this is us?' Simon whispered.

'What?'

'We're back in time. So d'you think this is me and you?'

I shook my head, but a shiver ran up my spine. Could that be what this was? Were we watching ourselves in a previous life?

'Rinpoche,' Rudra announced. 'I have returned from my travels and brought many offerings. I did as you instructed and have a thousand followers. So, now I have returned for what is mine.'

Simon leaned over: 'If they are, I bet that one's me.'

I frowned at him. *Typical, pick the big manly one... just like your dad.*

The abbot stared at Rudra without speaking, then turned to the other and waited, his face expressionless.

'Master,' said Padmakara. This one had his palms together as if in prayer. His gaze was low, staring at the table in front of the abbot. 'I did as you asked. But I have no followers. I sat in quiet places, caves and forests. I drank from the streams. I ate whatever food I could find on the ground. Mushrooms, nettles. I am weak. But I have done as you instructed. I do not seek what is mine. I offer it to you, master.'

Simon giggled silently. 'And that's definitely you.'

'Sod off,' I hissed, nudging him with my elbow. My arm definitely connected with his this time, though. It went through him like a wooden spoon through jelly. Kind of gross.

The abbot leaned to the right and clicked his shoulder like a weight-lifter before a heavy lift, then he did the same with his left. He shook his head slowly. A heavy silence descended as he shifted his gaze between the two disciples. I glanced across at Simon. Despite his joking, he was glued to the scene; his face a picture of intense concentration.

'What,' the abbot said in a tired voice, 'did I instruct?'

The two disciples exchanged looks, as if waiting for the other to speak. After a moment, Rudra shrugged and answered. 'To develop pride. To transcend mundane reality — to become like gods among men.'

'Like gods?' Padmakara said. 'And when did Rinpoche say that, brother Rudra?'

'He said for us to develop pride in ourselves.'

'Spiritual pride. Not arrogance!'

'Arrogance? You think overcoming my emotional defilements is arrogance? The great masters of old say that when one can sit amongst the people and say without shame that one has transcended the world — then one is to be counted among the gods.'

'You have no shame. You are right about that!'

Rudra laughed at him. A big belly laugh. 'One thousand follow me, little brother! You dream of reaching for the stars, but your false humility holds you back. If only you could grasp the nettle, rather than boiling it into a soup!'

Simon laughed silently. 'This guy's hilarious.'

Padmakara turned away, skinny shoulders slumped like he was sulking. When he turned back, though, his face was serene. He placed his hands together and bowed his head towards the abbot. 'Master. If I have done wrong. If I have misinterpreted your instructions...'

'There you go again!' Rudra guffawed. 'Bowing! Rinpoche is a man with a mind just like you. Just like me.' He turned to his master. 'Aren't you? We're the same — you just have a comfier cushion. Isn't that right, Holy One? Water is still water whatever size and shape the cup.' He planted a hand on Padmakara's back. 'Brother, every time you bow to another, you shame your own true nature.'

I didn't know what Simon was finding so funny about Rudra. The guy was clearly a bully.

Padmakara swatted Rudra's hand away. I inwardly cheered. 'You will not stop me from bowing to my master.' *Go get him, skinny boy!*

'No. You should! He's your teacher. But you should also bow to yourself. To the god within. Then you'll see. It's all the same.' He turned to the abbot, whose expression was dark. 'These are the instructions we were given.'

Rinpoche shuffled again, his gaze moving from one disciple to the other. Eventually, his eyes settled on Rudra and he spoke calmly and evenly. 'Mara is indeed a great force.'

'And only a great force will defeat him,' Rudra replied.

The abbot closed his eyes. 'You cannot defeat the devil with hate...'

I gave an intake of breath—*for his hatred is too great*—Dad's poem.

'I know the line,' Rudra interrupted. 'Spoken by the weak for the weak. But I'm telling you, Mara can be controlled. Mara can be tamed. I will tame him.'

Rinpoche's eyebrows dipped into a deep frown. 'You have learned nothing, Rudra.' He stood up slowly, removing a string of beads that had been wrapped around his enormous forearm. 'Padmakara is right. You are inflated with pride.'

Rudra stayed put. His expression flickered for a second and then froze in a smile. The atmosphere suddenly changed. I could sense the nervous energy increasing in the room. Something was about to happen. Perhaps the thing we were here to see or hear; something that would explain why the realms were collapsing.

'You come here as a god?' The old abbot said, rising to his feet. 'Then you should return to the realm of the Ashura where you belong.'

I look at Simon. *Ashura realm,* I mouthed. But he was running a hand over his arm. His face was pale. 'I can feel myself,' he whispered back. *Damn.* I touched my chest. My finger felt like sponge. *Damn it!* We were becoming solid just as something important was about to happen.

I looked back. Rudra had risen too. He'd grown in size and was suddenly towering over his old master. Beside him, Padmakara remained seated, his head bowed.

'Get out of my temple!' shouted the abbot, the sudden force of his command echoing around the walls. 'Before you infect any more of my students!'

Silence.

Then Rudra belly-laughed again.

'Leave!'

Rudra lifted a finger and pointed it at his master. 'You're frightened, old man. Your hand trembles. Your mala rattles with terror.'

'Not fear.' The old man placed his palms together with the mala dangling between them and whispered something. Then he stretched the beads between the thumb of one hand and forefinger in another — the way you hold a rubber band before twanging it across a room.

The air crackled with energy. Lights—pale at first and then becoming red and orange tongues of flame—shot from the mala.

Rudra immediately placed his own palms together and bowed his head. Blue light emerged from between his fingers. 'Hatred?' he shouted. 'Not fear, but hatred, old Lama? You see, brother? Your master is nothing but an old fraud!'

The red and blue lights clashed in the centre of the room. Simon grabbed my hand. It *hurt.* 'We have to go!'

But I didn't want to go. I was transfixed by the argument. 'Wait!'

Simon tugged at me, dragging me towards the doorway.

'Just a few more seconds!' I brushed him off me. 'I have to see!'

51

THE UNFORGIVABLE SIN

SIMON EMBRACED ME AND dragged me along the wall. I could feel the roughness of the brick. It felt solid. I couldn't take my eyes from the battle brewing, though.

'Your hatred is tempered by your love for me, old man!' Rudra shouted, pulling something from his robes, something long and thin. 'You summon the kings to protect your own power. You are not teaching liberation, master. You just swap our prison bars for golden ones and expect us to thank you?'

'Esta?' Simon pleaded.

I shook him off. I had to know what happened.

Forms emerged out of the red and blue fire that both men had conjured in the middle of the room. Figures, big and bulky as Sumo wrestlers, clothed in silks and scarves.

The red one held an axe in one hand, the blue one emerging from Rudra's palms was slender: a woman, flames crackling from her scalp. Her head was the shape of a lion. Human skulls hung around her neck. She swept a sword in a great arc that sliced through the air, sending sparkling electric blue across the room.

The red figure roared and swung his axe, blasting hot air against my skin. The blue goddess parried with her sword, then rose on to a single leg in some sort of dancing pose and began to spin. Her sword sweeping around the room, faster and faster. While she did, Rudra, only just visible now behind the whirring blue, stepped forward, what looked like a dagger in his outstretched hand.

The master didn't move. His lips still uttered prayers, his eyes on the battle playing out between the two figures of light.

'No!' Padmakara shouted.

The abbot lowered his gaze. But too late.

Rudra plunged the dagger into his master's heart.

Lightning exploded outwards from the wound, filling the room with searing heat. An ear-splitting scream tore at my ears, a jagged crack splintered the floor opening it up to the room below.

Then silence.

The room dimmed back to stuttering candlelight.

Rudra stood, his shoulders heaving, the abbot lying at his feet in a pool of blood. He turned, his face calm, eyes glittering, bright as diamonds. Stared right at me. For a moment I thought he was going to say something, for a split second I was certain he could see me. But he wiped his hands against his robe, turned and crouched next to the young monk.

'You killed him,' Padmakara whispered. 'Your own master.'

'He was an arrogant fraud who didn't like competition. I am stronger and more powerful. His false compassion was his weakness. Don't let it be yours.'

'Don't you know what you've done?' Padmakara whispered. 'Unforgivable. You will experience the consequences, Rudra.'

'My willpower can overcome—'

'No! Whatever you do. However powerful you become... there is no escaping your deeds. Cause and effect is inevitable.'

'No, little brother,' Rudra said, standing up. 'Not inevitable.' He strode over to the shrine, his back to me. 'Only strength is inevitable. You saw the power. Harness the greed and the anger, brother. Don't run from it. Turn it...' he picked something up from the shrine and examined it. '... into gold.'

'Do not underestimate what you have done.' The young monk slowly looked from the ground up towards Rudra. His robe shifted as his body—still in cross-legged position—rose. He flung aside the folds of his robe and drew an object from within. It glinted gold.

Rudra, still facing the shrine, shook his head slowly and laughed once more. This one, a dry and cold laugh. 'You stole it! Very clever, little brother. They only work properly together, don't they?'

'I have one.'

Rudra turned around. 'And now I have the other.'

My body jerked backwards.

'Esta!'

'No!' I shouted, trying to struggle out of Simon's grip. He was too strong and managed to pull me to the doorway.

Another pair of hands appeared through the curtain, dragging me out. Karma Chodron must have come back for us. 'Back the way we came!' she yelled.

As the curtain shut behind me, there was the ringing of a bell, a clash of metal, a roar of anger.

I wrenched myself away, ripping my jacket. 'I have to see!'

Simon stopped. Caught between Karma Chodron and me.

'We have to go,' Karma Chodron said, climbing through the solid wall like she was going through bread dough. 'Her mind is taking shape around us! We'll be trapped if we —' her voice cut off as the wall closed around her.

There was a sound of splintering wood behind the curtain.

'Simon,' I pleaded. Didn't he get it? We had to know... 'Just a minute longer.'

A blood-curdling scream.

Simon yelped, turned and lunged for the wall where Karma Chodron had disappeared. I stood and watched him struggle through, then turned back to the room.

I couldn't leave without knowing.

Just a few seconds. I had to see what happened. Everything depended on it. Surely we had seen ourselves in some previous life a thousand years ago? Two brothers. One a murderer. One possessed the Orb, the other the Bell.

But which was which.

I had to know.

I'd made barely two steps when another shout came from the room, the sound of smashing glass. I ran, but before I could reach the doorway, there was a sudden, biting stench of sulphur, a rush of hot air and then the door curtain exploded outwards. A dazzling golden light flooded the hallway, throwing me back.

Then darkness and silence.

Dazed, I twisted round and clawed at the wall, now desperate to escape. My fingernails filled with plaster and I bruised my knuckles, hammering my fist against it, willing the thing to open up and swallow me.

But the wall was solid. Unmoving.

I had Weaved.

I was trapped inside my own mind.

52

THE BLACK BANNERS

I DON'T KNOW HOW long I lay there in the silence that followed. Probably only moments, but then I'm not sure time has much meaning when you're deep down in the mud of your subconscious. I'm guessing it's like dreams.

I'm told you can dream a decade in the flickering of an eye.

I tapped the back of my head uselessly against the wall. *Prisoner in my own mind.* Then slammed my palm against the hard stone floor.

I was stuck in the one place no one would ever find me.

I let out a dry laugh. I'd always suspected I would end up just like Charlie. And if I was trapped in my own thoughts, where was my body? Was it in the Great Hall of Rigpa Gompa? Were Simon, Karma Chodron and the others trying to bring me back? Or was it lying in the rubble of Gatley House? Maybe Lily hadn't saved me after all. Maybe I really *did* plummet through the floor. Maybe this is exactly what happened to Charlie. I'd heard people could still have dreams, even in a coma. And so what if that was what was happening now?

Deep chanting outside brought me out of my navel-gazing.

I got up and walked into the abbot's room, expecting to find his body sprawled out as I had seen him moments ago.

The room was empty, though. In fact, everything had changed. A rug was laid out in the centre, covering the spot where the floor had split; new wall hangings too. There were freshly filled bowls on the shrine.

Must be a different time. A different memory.

The chanting from outside paused, replaced with the clanging of what sounded like a dozen bells. I walked to the window, lifted the silk drape, and peered out.

There must have been more than a hundred white-robed monks seated in four straight rows, their backs to the temple, facing the valley. The chanting began again and each one, in total unison, made a graceful swirling movement of their arms, which ended with one hand extended away from their body. The chanting stopped abruptly, and a piercing metallic ringing filled the air as each monk wagged a hand bell.

The same sort of bell Simon had chosen.

The noise was high and sharp and made my eardrums itch. When it stopped, the sound echoed around the courtyard for a few moments, slowly fading to a distant hum. And then silence.

When is this? Before the murder? After?

The sun rose in the east, its light making the snow-topped mountains gleam. The slopes dropping into the valley were misty green, the sky a pale, icy blue. My gaze wandered back down to the courtyard wall. A grey cloud was climbing above the edge of the plateau. I wiped the window and squinted.

A dust cloud. Something was coming up the mountain path.

There was nervous chattering in the courtyard now. Some of the monks stood, others tried to pull them back down to their seats.

Something tall and thin and black rose out of the dust cloud, becoming taller and taller as if it were the fast-growing shoot of some enormous tree.

Beneath it, silhouetted by the rising sun, a single person came into view. They held some sort of pole in both hands. When they reached the flat ground at the top of the path, they stopped. After a pause, they thrust the base of the pole into the earth. A great black sheet unfurled from its top.

A banner, its flag rippling in the wind.

The white monks below me raised their voices once more. Their bells clanged noisily in their hands, making the air shimmer blue around them.

Another figure appeared at the top of the path. And then another, and another. More people holding banners slowly poured up and over the lip of the cliff face on to the flat ground of Rigpa Gompa until a row of flags fluttered on the far side of the courtyard wall.

Row upon row of black-robed men and women. Silently waiting—surely—to attack the Gompa.

My heart pounded. What was this? Something from my own mind? From my past? Something that might tell me who I had been? Who I still was?

Maybe it was some ancient memory, or what mum used to call "women's intuition", but suddenly I didn't want to see any more. Those banners. Those black banners folding and rippling in the wind... It wasn't clear, but there was some image, some sort of symbol daubed in white on each one.

And as much as I didn't want to see... I couldn't take my eyes off them.

I watched in silent terror as a gust of wind whipped the dust around the army. It caught at their robes and tugged at their banners until each one unfurled and became—for an instant at least—stiff and wide.

There was no mistaking what that symbol was.

I took a step backwards.

Now the images danced, curled and uncurled as the wind ripped at the material.

The army of black-robed monks was standing beneath the symbol of a single Orb.

53

BROTHERS IN WAR

'THERE YOU ARE!'

I swung round, breath catching in my throat.

'I thought I'd lost you!' Simon stood just inside the doorway.

I almost cried out with relief and had an almost overwhelming urge to run over and wrap my arms around him. Feel him. Solid and real and alive.

I even made the first step.

But stopped.

I glanced behind me at the masses of black-robed monks and nuns with their banners opening and shutting in a rising gale and my stomach dropped.

'We can still leave,' he said. 'But you have to come now.'

I froze. Could I leave? Should I go back into the world knowing what I knew now? Except *what* did I know? Two groups, one in white, the other in black, one wielding the Bell, one with the Orb painted on their banners. Surely one group loyal to Rudra and one to Padmakara...

'What's that ringing sound?' Simon said, nervously entering the room.

I turned, snapped the curtain shut, then hurried over to intercept him. 'How are you still here?' I asked, pushing him away from the window.

He couldn't see those banners. He mustn't see them.

'We got to the roof,' he said. 'When I saw you weren't with us, I came back. KC is up there waiting for us. I've been all over. I just thought I'd check here once more, but everything keeps changing. This memory, or whatever, isn't stable.'

'No. It's a different time,' I said distractedly, half annoyed by the familiar way Simon had referred to Karma Chodron as "KC" and half looking around the shrine for clues. One of the brothers was abbot here, I was sure of it. The other was probably outside the monastery gates.

But which one?

Simon put his arm around me and shepherded me out. 'We have to go.'

Karma Chodron was sitting in the middle of the roof. Above, the sky was grey and there was a smattering of rain and the acrid smell of smoke.

'Jesus. What happened?' Simon said under his breath.

The courtyard below us was scorched, the boundary wall in pieces, columns of black smoke rose from fires that dotted the plateau.

'KC?' he called.

The nun didn't respond. She didn't even open her eyes. Instead, she flicked beads along the string of her *mala* with one hand and beckoned us with the other.

'What happened?' Simon repeated, gazing at the burning fires.

'This is the beginning.'

'The beginning of what?'

She opened her eyes. 'The war.'

Realisation dawned on me. What did it matter who was who? I looked at Simon. Felt dread wash over me.

The two brothers were at war.

Before I could let that fact sink in, Karma Chodron grabbed both of our hands. 'Sit down and hold on to me. We only get one shot at this. Don't let go of me!'

We dropped to the tiles next to her. I grabbed her robes while she chanted. She closed her eyes, then flung one end of the mala above her head. The necklace of beads seemed to stretch into the sky and some invisible force tugged at the other end. I glanced one more time at the broken walls and the billowing smoke. Then we were yanked up off the roof so suddenly I think I left my stomach behind.

54

THE RETURN

I OPENED MY EYES. We were back in the Great Hall. Thankfully, my stomach was back in place too.

The Wheel of *Samsara* spun slowly and innocently before me.

The others were gathered round. Rabjam, Sera, Tubten, Harry. All standing in a semi-circle staring down at me.

I shuddered. *What had happened? Where had we been?* Dizzy spots filled my vision, they became hundreds of black flags swimming before me. Rabjam's tea from earlier rolled around in my stomach and I had to resist the urge to throw it up.

'Get up.'

I coughed, shook my head, looked up, still dizzy. Simon was already standing, his body practically quivering with tension.

Karma Chodron loomed over me. She had something long and pointy in her hands. 'What did you see?' she said, prodding me with what I took to be some sort of spear.

'Ouch!'

'Hey!' Simon called. 'What are you doing?'

'Sera?' Karma Chodron called, not taking her eyes off me. 'Deal with the boy.'

Sera stepped forward, her yellow robe billowing around her as she doubled in size, expanding to fill the space between the pillars. She reached out with one enormous arm and nudged Simon against a pillar. It was a gentle nudge, but it made him grunt.

'Karma Chodron?' Rabjam said. He looked as shocked as I was. 'What are you doing? What happened?'

'Shut up, Rab.' Karma Chodron jabbed me again. The pain was like having a red hot poker against my skin. 'Tubten, send one of your brothers to get Lama la.'

'You better have an exceptional explanation for this,' Harry growled, his cane raised towards Karma Chodron.

She jabbed me again. 'Ask her!'

Harry nudged aside the folds of Sera's robes so he could see both Simon and me. 'What happened? What did you see?'

Simon glanced at me, then at Harry. Shook his head, confused. 'I don't know! It's foggy. There were fires when we left... the place was burning.'

'That mad cow took me inside my mind,' I croaked, rubbing my shoulder. I could still taste smoke at the back of my mouth. I spat it out.

Harry glared at each of us again, then repeated his question slowly, like we were both hard of hearing: 'What. Did. You. See?'

'We s... saw,' Simon stuttered. He had his arms wrapped around himself like he was freezing cold.

I had a flash. A vision of enormous figures made out of light. Something big had happened.

'I don't know. Everything's foggy,' Simon said. 'There were flashing lights. But we were starting to Weave, so...'

'We were there at the very beginning,' Karma Chodron said. 'Just before the battle for Rigpa Gompa. The place was full of monks and nuns. Just as it's written in the Blue Annals.'

'You saw Rudra and Padmakara?' Rabjam asked.

She shook her head, eyes trained on me. 'No. But *she* might have done.'

Rudra. Another flash. This time of golden robes, the glint of a knife... God. What *had* we seen?

'OK,' I said, slowly getting up, my hands out, pacifying. Karma Chodron jabbed at me again. This time, she stopped an inch short of my throat. I peered, cross-eyed, down at the point.

Harry brought his cane down across the tip of the spear, pushing it away. 'OK,' he said, looking directly at Karma Chodron. 'A lot of emotion here. How about we talk this out? Simon and Esta aren't going anywhere, so... Rabjam? You pour us all a nice cup of that soup you call tea and...'

Karma Chodron flipped her spear up, knocking Harry's cane aside and touching my chin with the blade. 'What did you see?'

I gulped. Harry raised his cane again to strike. I put out my hand in a stopping gesture. 'Don't! Mr Sparks. Please? It's OK. Put it down.'

'Only if she does.'

Karma Chodron inclined her head, then lowered her spear a couple of inches so it rested against my chest. 'Remember, whatever you saw happened inside *your* mind,' she said.

I made a sideways glance towards Simon. Had he seen what I had seen? He had been panicking, hadn't he? Did he know what had happened? What *had* happened? It was already a confusion of flashing lights and shadows in my mind's eye. There had been an argument which escalated pretty quickly, but about what? And what did any of it mean?

'We were in Lama la's room,' Simon stammered. 'There were three monks. I think... I think one of them was him.' He pointed at the crossed legs of the gigantic statue behind us.

'Padmakara?' Rabjam said excitedly. 'You saw him!'

Simon nodded. 'I think so. He didn't... I mean, he didn't look much like the statue, but that's what they called him.'

'And the other two?' Harry asked.

Simon looked at the point of the spear, then up at me. He was practically shaking with fear now. I shook my head at him. It was a micro shake, one I hoped he'd spot, but no one else. I didn't like the point of the spear being this close to my neck either, and until I knew why Karma Chodron had turned up her aggression mode to nine, we needed to keep a lid on who we saw... and especially *what* we saw at the end.

'Gendun Rinpoche!' Rabjam said. 'You saw him as well. You must have done!'

'We didn't get any names,' I said quickly, before Simon got us into any deeper trouble. 'But yeah, maybe one of them was called Rinpoche.'

'What were they doing? What did you see?'

'There was an argument,' Simon said.

'More like a discussion,' I corrected, trying to play it down. 'Something philosophical...'

'About rules,' Simon added.

It was about pride, I thought. *Spiritual pride. And Mara. They mentioned Mara.*

I nodded. We needed a break to regroup; think through what had happened. The implications. I suddenly didn't trust anyone in this place. They all knew something we didn't, and any false step now... I glanced down at the spear again, then across at double-sized Sera. For the first time since I had stumbled across Odiyana and its temple, I wanted out of here.

Just me, Simon and Harry. Five minutes to talk through what to do, figure out how to escape.

'You know what this means?' Karma Chodron was saying. She was talking to the others. They all looked tense.

I nodded weakly. I knew what was coming next. My skin goose-fleshed. *Rudra. The man in the golden robes.* The man who had stood over the body of Gendun Rinpoche, dagger dripping with blood.

'No!' Simon complained from a pillar where Sera now had him almost pinned. '*I* don't know what it means. It... could mean anything! Just three monks talking.'

The candles flickered; the wind howled outside; there was a smattering of rain or hail that sounded like the crackle of an untuned radio.

'You chose the Vajra and Bell,' she said. 'Don't you understand?'

'Yes, but—'

Karma Chodron stared at everyone in the room defiantly. She lowered her spear, then pointed it at me and then at Simon. 'Padmakara has finally returned!'

55

THE OPENING OF THE BARDO

I FELT COLD. *One of us is Padmakara?*

'The... the... dude on the shrine?' Simon asked weakly. 'How?' He glanced at me with an expression of... I don't know, hope? Confusion? I tried to smile reassuringly, but he hadn't seen what I had. He hadn't seen what Rudra had done, he hadn't seen the black-robed army amassing on the ground outside Rigpa Gompa with their flags waving the Orb... *my Orb.*

'I mean,' he continued. 'There are two of us.'

Karma Chodron cut him off. 'You chose his objects. The Vajra and the Bell. You used them. There is no other explanation.'

Simon was staring wildly across the room now, his mouth open slightly. I could almost see the cogs whirring around in his brain.

'So...' Simon now stared at me. I liked Simon. Maybe even a lot... you know, after everything we'd been through. But he wasn't the brightest. *He didn't see,* I thought. *He doesn't know what happened.*

'So, me and Esta are *both* the reincarnation of Padmakara?' His voice trailed off once more.

I took an involuntary step backwards towards the door. In my mind's eye, those black banners folded and unfolded over and over again. I felt dizzy suddenly, as if, as if...

... the floor was moving.

Simon flung his arms into the air and half slid down the pillar Sera had pushed him against. Karma Chodron stumbled, her spear striking the ground. I looked wildly around me. The walls were shaking, dust poured from the ceiling. Sera had to cling on to a pillar to stop from falling.

'What's happening?' Tubten called from somewhere. He must have returned after finding Lama la.

The pillar Sera was holding vanished. She sat down hard. The floor vibrated with her weight.

'Everyone stay still,' came a bellowing voice from the edge of the shrine. At those words, the Great Hall stopped shaking. The pillar suddenly flickered back into existence as if it had never been away.

Something rumbled outside: thunder, long and deep.

Almost all the candles were out now. The only light came from the Wheel of *Samsara.* Standing beside it was the unmistakable outline of Lama la, and next to him, Tubten.

'Lama la!' Rabjam whispered. 'What's happening?'
'Be careful what you say and do,' he replied. 'The Bardo has opened!'

56

THE FLIP

LAMA LA'S EYES SWEPT the room. Hail now beat a rat-a-tat against the walls, and a gust of wind made the main doors rumble.

'Lama la,' Karma Chodron said, looking from the doors back to him. 'Begin the ceremony! That's why you brought them here, isn't it?' She swept her spear toward me and Harry. 'Eight symbols. Eight of us!'

'No. Wait.'

'We must act!' she said. 'Or Mara will tear us apart!'

There was a snap of thunder and light flashed through the gaps in the door, casting weird shadows everywhere.

'Lama la!' Karma Chodron raised her spear. 'We can't just sit here and chant anymore!'

Lama la walked slowly towards the glowing Wheel Karma Chodron had created. 'The law of cause and effect is too complicated for any of us to disentangle and every pebble thrown into its waters creates its own ripples.'

Karma Chodron groaned. 'Metaphors! Lama la, don't be blind.'

'It's not blindness that causes us to stumble... it is inattentiveness,' Lama la paused by the Wheel. Its surface was cloudy and indistinct, like a huge goldfish bowl filled with dry ice. 'Karma Chodron. Why have you conjured *Samsara* here in the Great Hall?' She said nothing for a moment. He turned to her slowly and deliberately. 'Karma Chodron, what have you done?'

That seemed to spark her into a response. 'You haven't been inside *Samsara*, like us. You haven't seen what's happening in every single realm. Ever since we started getting the symbols for you. The Preta are on the move, the Ashura are tearing down the Chitapali tree. Soon they'll be on the slopes of Mount Meru itself.' She flung an arm towards the door. 'And now this!'

'You're right,' he said, gazing at the smoky surface of the Wheel. 'The time is almost upon us. But not yet.' He tilted his head. 'Ah! Harry! I knew you would come. You're looking well.'

Harry Sparks bowed his head an inch. 'The nun is right. It's time to act.'

Lama la nodded, but said nothing.

Now Rabjam stepped forwards. 'Lama la, you sent us to retrieve the symbols so we could secure the realms; to protect *Samsara* from chaos.'

'And yet,' Karma Chodron added. 'Ever since we've returned, the Wheel has become *more* unstable.' She swept her spear around her in an arc that took us all in. 'We can perform the ceremony. We can do it now before it's too late!'

Lama la said nothing. He peered down at the table beside his throne, picked up one of the symbols, inspected it, then placed it back. 'There are wheels within wheels and some truths are not yet fully known.'

Outside, the wind became blustery. There was a *whumpf whumpf* that reminded me of flags flapping in the wind.

'What was that?' Tubten whispered.

The flapping noise stopped, replaced by a deep growl and a loud, long *scraaape* like the sound of a spade being dragged along concrete. It was immediately followed by the electronic *beep, beep* of a car horn.

'That sounds like it's coming from Gatley,' I said.

The horn stopped. Just the whispering of a breeze.

'It's going to happen again,' Tubten said with a quivering voice.

The candles sputtered. For an instant, the Great Hall went dim. There was a stale smell of... soil, damp soil. A metallic crunch as if someone had just stood on a tin can. In the poor light, I caught sight of an old staircase where the shrine should have been. The walls were empty; the floor was grey.

'It feels like we're flipping over,' Simon whispered.

We had both done our fair share of shifting between realities. That's what was happening now. Gatley House and Rigpa Gompa were sifting in and out; separate realities flipping and folding between themselves.

The walls and pillars of the Great Hall blinked suddenly back into view.

'Make it stop!' Tubten wailed. 'I don't like it!'

'Reality is breaking up!' Karma Chodron said through gritted teeth. 'If we aren't careful, we'll lose control of the protection circle. Lama la! We have to act!'

But Lama la calmly raised a finger for quiet. 'We are entering the Bardo of Becoming. A knife-edge of deep uncertainty. We are connected to each realm, and each realm is attracted to us. Everything we do now will change the future in ways no one can predict.'

The walls disappeared. Suddenly, we were in the crumbled remains of another temple. It was like Rigpa Gompa, but overgrown with piles of dead branches, dust and a hot, foul-smelling breeze.

I knew that smell.

The last time I'd breathed it in I had almost gagged on it.

57

THE UNEXPECTED MOVE

I STARED INTO THE darkness, thoughts galloping through my head.

We had flipped into the Hungry Ghost Realm... *Dad*?

The air thickened. Flowed around us like liquid, making everything look bendy and melted-looking.

And it was suddenly hot.

Really hot.

The skin on my face itched. Each breath I took burnt my lungs. Around me black strips were being seared into the walls of the Great Hall and I could feel the floor burning the soles of my shoes.

'Hell!' Tubten squealed.

A deafening roar that made the walls shake drowned his cries out. Soot and ash sprayed in to the air. The walls glowed orange.

'Lama la!' Karma Chodron pleaded.

Lama la stood still, one finger held up in the air. 'Be patient!'

'We're being torn apart!'

'Wait...'

The walls faded to black, the burning heat drained from the air. My skin stopped feeling like it was about to split. I sucked in a cool breath. Simon was coughing. He was kneeling over what was now a smooth, hard floor. A ghostly pearl-coloured light reflected off it. The roaring sound became the gentle thrumming of a drum.

'We're safe for now,' Lama la said eventually. 'We're stabilising.'

But I couldn't help noticing that there were still scorch marks on the walls. The floor was buckled, too.

There was one more lurch. Like one last *click* of the Wheel of Fortune in that game show. The light dimmed. The marble floor and walls became the old painted wood of the Great Hall in Rigpa Gompa.

Tubten threw up. I couldn't blame him. It felt like we'd just spun on a merry-go-round at a hundred miles an hour.

Simon, still on his knees, leaned against a pillar, his head bowed; Harry Sparks leaned heavily on his cane; Sera was trying to look big and immovable, but even she looked ill. The only one of us who didn't look sea-sick was Karma Chodron.

She was furious. Glaring at Lama la, spear gripped tight. It looked like she was waiting for him to say or do something.

But he just returned her look, one eye-brow raised.

For a second, I thought they were somehow communicating in some cool mind-to-mind thing. But if they were, he wasn't very good at it, because what Karma Chodron did next was something I don't even think he was expecting.

She did it just as the ground rumbled again. The room seemed to teeter on the edge of flipping over once more. Dust poured from the rafters and there was a flash of blue where Karma Chodron had been standing. I waited, bracing myself for the next reality to twist into this one, but we stayed put this time.

It took me a few moments to realise what *had* changed, though.

Karma Chodron was standing behind Lama la. Her spear now directed at his neck.

58

THE CHOICE

RABJAM TENSED NEXT TO me. 'Karma Chodron, What are you doing?'

Simon got to his feet and tried to run towards her, but Sera pinned him back against a pillar with ease.

Harry advanced as well, ducking under Sera's sweeping arm and raising his stick again. 'Not like this!' he shouted.

Lama la gave Karma Chodron a smile. 'I believe you're speeding up.' He looked up at Harry, who had got within a few feet of them. 'It's OK, old friend. Now is not a time to be pointing weapons at each other.' Then he turned back to Karma Chodron. 'You must know that this is not the solution.'

'I'm sorry, master,' Karma Chodron replied, her face worn and her eyes sparkling with tears, but her voice hard as iron. 'Waiting is tearing us apart.'

'You're making a mistake.'

'There is no mistake. The Bardo is unstable. We must lock the realms back in to place. The Ceremony of the Eight Symbols will begin with or without you. Rab?' She held up one of the oblong prayer books. This one wrapped in emerald green material. 'The instructions for the ceremony.'

Rabjam took the book, sat down, unwrapped it and began to read. One finger tracing the lines of spidery writing.

'Patience.' Lama la held up his hands. Something bound them. 'And you're using one of the Eight to bind me. You will need the Eternal Knot if you hope to complete the ceremony.'

'When everything else is in place, you will have no choice but to help us,' Karma Chodron said.

He lowered his hands and nodded. 'I see.'

'Unless you give me your word that you will help us now.'

Lama la looked down at Rabjam, who was busy flicking through the pages of the prayer book, then up at the rest of us standing in total shock facing the scene. He shook his head. 'I'm afraid I cannot make that promise. Not yet.'

Karma Chodron sighed. 'Sister, you know what we have to do?'

Sera nodded, then started towards Karma Chodron and Lama la.

'Woah!' I said, stepping in front of her. She could have swatted me away, but she stopped, unsure.

'Look around!' Karma Chodron said. 'We have to act! The Dharmapala's loyalty is not to any person, but to Rigpa Gompa!'

I glanced at Lama la. His eyes were closed, his face serene. My gaze moved down to Rabjam. Hunched over, muttering to himself as he read from the book. *What was going on?*

The floor rumbled again. There was an ear-splitting screeching sound and the temperature suddenly plummeted. My skin tightened, my breath clouded up. Ice spread like fingers along the scorched walls, snaking into a crack that had already formed in the plaster.

'Cold hells!' Tubten whispered, frost forming on his eyebrows as he spoke. 'We're in the cold hells.'

The hair on my arms became stiff. *Cold hells? There are cold hells?*

'We have to make a choice!' Karma Chodron announced. 'Do nothing, or do something. Tubten? Are you with me? You've seen. You know what's coming.'

Tubten's eyes roved from Lama la, to Karma Chodron, then to me and Simon. Finally, he looked across at the widening crack in the wall.

'Tub?'

'We're going to save Rigpa Gompa?'

'We all made a vow to protect it.'

Tubten bowed his head towards Lama la. 'I'm sorry, master.'

Karma Chodron turned to Simon. 'What about you?'

Simon said nothing.

'We can't do the ritual without you and Esta,' Rabjam said, looking up from his book.

I frowned. 'Why?'

'We need eight people.'

Simon pointed at Tubten. 'Why can't he just make some more of himself?'

Rabjam stood, pointing down at the open pages of the book he'd been studying. 'It has to be you. When we conduct the ceremony, the conditions will be right for Padmakara to return. Only he can close the circle.'

'So...' Simon said after a moment. 'You're saying that if we do this ceremony thing?'

'Yes. Padmakara will return.'

'Just like that? Esta and me magically become the dude on the shrine?'

Rabjam shook his head. Picked up the book. Tapped the writing on the page. 'No. Not exactly. The physical body of Padmakara does not exist. But his actions remain hidden in your mind-stream like a seed in the ground.'

'When the conditions are right.' Lama la said, almost under his breath. 'You will both remember who you are.'

Another flicker of memory passed through my mind at his words. Clouds of dust hanging in the air above the courtyard, black flags rippling beneath them... I blinked the image away. 'We don't even know if that's us.'

'You chose the objects, you saw him in the alaya!' Karma Chodron said.

Lama la's eyes snapped open. 'Alaya? You took them into the alaya?'

'I showed them what you wouldn't! I showed them who they were!'

The abbot struggled to free his hands, but they were held tight. 'You fool!'

'You kept it from them!'

Lama la stared wildly at me. 'The more they know, the greater the risk!'

A deep hole seemed to widen in my chest where my heart and belly should have been. Another image. Now I was briefly back in the abbot's room, the golden-robed monk reaching forwards, the dagger disappearing into the maroon folds of his master. There had been an explosion of light; the floor split open. *What had I seen?*

'Padmakara will return!' Karma Chodron was saying. 'He can fix all of this!'

She doesn't know what we saw. She doesn't know. We saw someone else. We saw... what did we see?

'Esta! Simon! What did you see?' Lama la croaked. 'Who was behind the curtain?'

I shook my head, squeezing my eyes shut against the images. 'I don't know.'

'Is she right?' he asked. 'Did you see Padmakara?'

I wiped my face with the back of my hand. *Just a moment... I just need a moment to talk... to think through. To untangle everything.*

'I remember the name,' Simon said. 'He was definitely there.'

'Will you help us or not?' Karma Chodron snapped.

I returned Lama la's questioning gaze. He still wanted us to wait. Even while the walls of the Gompa crumbled. But for what?

To know, I thought suddenly. *He wants to know for certain who Simon and I are before he acts.*

The floor rumbled again, the crack in the wall dripped with melting ice. I glanced up at a new cloud of dust. *The black banners rising up from the path in the cliff...*

Screams cut through the air beyond the crumbling walls. I blinked. Lama la wanted us to wait but, with all the noise from outside and the cracks growing in the walls, it was getting difficult to argue that waiting was much of a plan.

'Esta,' Harry said. 'This is real. It's happening and if we don't act now, it's not just a building that's going to fall today.'

I shook my head. Lama la knew. I was sure of it. He was the only one who suspected what Simon and I had seen. If I could just talk to *him.* He'd understand. He'd tell me what to do.

'Look!' Karma Chodron said. 'Make up your damn mind! Or you can go with him!'

'Only for the time it takes to complete the ritual,' Rabjam said quietly. 'After that, we'll release him. No harm done.'

'Choose!'

'Right. OK! I get it!' I shouted. 'You want me to choose: save the world, or let it burn. I understand. Just... just... Lama la?'

The old man raised his head slowly.

'What do I do?' I mouthed.

He spoke without opening his eyes. 'The Bardo is uncertain. That is its nature.'

'And?' I asked desperately.

He shrugged. 'We must wait and see how this unfolds.'

I ground my teeth. *Typical.* A howling scream started up again outside the walls. *Absolutely bloody typical.*

I glanced from Simon, to Lama la, back to Simon, then finally to Karma Chodron. *Make a choice?*

The wind buffeted the door, the walls shook, the wooden rafters in the ceiling squealed in protest. What choice did I have?

I closed my eyes, whispered an apology...

... and gave a single nod.

59

NOT ALL HE SEEMS

I HAD TO LOOK away. I couldn't watch Karma Chodron lead Lama la out of the Great Hall like some kind of petty criminal. But although I could blind myself to the sight, I couldn't blank out the sound of his disappearing footsteps. Apparently, Harry couldn't watch either. He retreated towards the shadows at the far end of the Great Hall.

'This is insane,' Simon whispered. 'Insane.'

The others didn't seem as troubled. The moment Lama la was gone, they sprang into action around us, preparing for the ceremony. I watched in stony silence as Rabjam whispered instructions to Tubten and Sera, who started pushing the low, long prayer tables to one side, making a space in front of the shrine. When Rabjam had finished, Tubten manifested several versions of himself, each one fetching a metal bowl filled with what looked like coloured sand.

How can they be doing all of this while Karma Chodron takes their master to the dungeons? I thought angrily. How could they possibly not trust Lama la? I walked through them all, past the shrine in the direction they had taken him.

Simon held me back. 'Where are you going?'

'I changed my mind. We can't let them do this.'

'What are we supposed to do?'

'Tell them what we saw!'

'What *did* we see?'

'There were three monks in that room, Simon, remember?'

'I know, but...'

'You didn't see, did you? You really didn't see what the other one did?'

'It was all too bright. I don't know...' he looked away. Couldn't hold my gaze. Couldn't look me in the eye.

'Simon? Look at me? What *did* you see?'

He shrugged me off and turned away. 'Nothing!'

Cold realisation hit me. *He had seen!* He had seen everything. He had seen the murder and had pretended not to. I understood that, but now he was pretending to *me*!

'Simon! What if...'

He rounded on me, his eyes full of venom. 'What if what!'

I took a step back, shocked at the sudden change in him. 'There were three men in that room: Gendun Rinpoche, Padmakara and Rudra. What if?'

'What if? What if? Esta! This is crazy. I don't know what you saw. But neither you or me are taking the rap for some stupid argument that happened a thousand years ago!'

I took another step back. Simon's face wasn't scared now, not so innocent. Had I misjudged him? I thought he'd been panicking before. Had it all been an act? Simon seemed to know exactly what he was doing and there was this look on his face now... not *on* his face... *behind* his face. Something I wasn't sure I recognised. Something I wasn't sure I liked.

'This is a mistake,' I said and turned to follow Karma Chodron. 'I have to bring him back. Tell him everything.'

I felt a hand on my shoulder.

'Don't. Esta, it's too late!'

I put my hands together. Nothing's too late when you can travel at the speed of light. I closed my eyes, visualised the corridor leading out of the Hall.

'There is no Esta Brown.'

60

Avichi Hell

I HIT THE SPIRAL staircase going up to the first floor. The rest of the corridor was gloomy, but empty. Karma Chodron couldn't have taken Lama la much farther than this. Carving up a staircase was impossible, so I had to make the climb at what felt like snail's pace.

Nothing up there either.

I took the stairs leading up to the second floor, flung Lama la's door curtain aside. *Empty.*

I swore, running down the corridor, trying every door. Each one *empty, empty, empty!*

It was as if they had simply disappeared.

'Where did she take him?'

Rabjam was still clearing tables away from the space before the shrine. 'Somewhere safe.'

'Dammit,' I hissed. 'Rab, tell me!'

'We agreed. You chose—'

'What if I unchoose? We need Lama la back. This is all wrong!'

'You wouldn't be able to free him without her help. She fastened the Eternal Knot that binds him, so she's the only one that can unfasten it. And just in case you hadn't noticed, once she decides on a course of action, Karma Chodron is unbending. It is one of her great strengths.'

'Or weaknesses. Rab. What if we made a mistake?'

'Perhaps. But the decision has been made now. If she unbinds Lama la, she will never have the opportunity to bind him again. We must proceed. It's only until we have the symbols all in place. Then—'

'But, what if...' I checked around me for Simon. He had walked over to where Harry was sitting at the back of the Hall.

Rabjam followed my gaze. 'Simon?'

I bit my tongue. What could I say? That Simon was... what? That I thought one of us might be Rudra? What would happen if I said that? What would they do? And how could it even be true? I groaned in frustration. 'Rab. We saw three people in the shrine room. What if neither of us are Padmakara? What if one of us is... is the other one?'

'It's OK,' Rabjam said reassuringly. 'Neither of you can be Rudra.'

'What? Why?' Rabjam smiled. 'The Blue Annals explain everything.'

'The Blue Annals?'

'The Histories of Odiyana. If we had time, I could show them to you. They're fascinating.'

'What do they say?'

'That Rudra committed an unforgivable sin. He killed his own master in cold blood.'

I nodded, trying to pretend that this was news to me. 'OK, so?'

'So, when Rudra was defeated by Padmakara he was reborn in the Avichi Hells.'

'Hey!' It was one of the Tubtens. He was sitting cross-legged, drawing the arc of what looked like it was going to be a huge circle on the stone floor. 'Watch where you're walking! It'll smudge!'

Rabjam led me to one side. 'This is the mandala,' he said. 'Normally, it takes a whole day to create, but... Tubten?'

The young monk looked up, nodded once, and another brother flickered into life by his side.

'Start in the middle and go outwards.'

The new boy dropped to his knees and got to work on more circles and designs.

'What's Avichi Hell?' I asked as we watched the mandala take shape around us.

'The worst kind. A place where you can't tell the end of your body from the flames around you.'

'Why can't he come back? I thought it was a wheel. You know. From life to life?'

'Because you don't die in the Avichi Hell. You remain in torment for an incalculable eon.'

My face must have looked blank.

'Millions of years,' he explained. 'So. You see, Padmakara can still return... but not Rudra...' he bent and picked up another piece of chalk. 'Not for a long time.'

I glanced over at Simon again. 'So, we do this ceremony and then what?'

'Everything goes back to normal.'

'I thought, Simon and I are supposed to... you know, change.'

'Momentarily. Then the Six Realms will become separate once more. Odiyana will be safe. And the law of Cause and Effect will return.'

'And... we... I mean, Simon and me... we won't come back as anyone. You know, change or anything?'

'Not according to this manual.' He held up the green prayer book he'd been studying. 'Once the ceremony is complete, Padmakara's consciousness will dissolve back into space. The seed will still be there, but the soil and the water won't be. If that makes any sense.' He tapped my arm. 'Perhaps another time, Esta Brown. Another life.'

I breathed a sigh of relief.

'So,' Rabjam said. 'The sooner we do this...' He held up the chalk as if in explanation. 'The better.'

I couldn't have agreed more.

I was suddenly keen to get this damn ceremony over and done with.

61

THE CEREMONY OF THE EIGHT SYMBOLS

I STEPPED BACKWARDS, ALMOST tripping over yet another Tubten. There were maybe fifteen of them now. Some of them were making chalk marks on the floor, the others sat cross-legged, each waiting by their own bowl of coloured sand. Next to each bowl were two thin, metal implements: a rod and a funnel-shaped pen, wide at one end, then narrowing down to a point at the other.

'This isn't fast enough,' Rabjam muttered. He broke off a piece of chalk and lobbed it into the air. 'Tub? More help. I need to talk Esta through the ritual.'

Tubten number sixteen flickered into life before Rabjam had finished talking and caught the chalk before it hit the ground. He grinned, winked at me, then joined his brother.

'Useful skill when you need to get something done,' I whispered, watching all the young monks beavering away. 'Every home should have a Tubten.'

Rabjam pulled me aside. 'Give them room.'

The two Tubtens in the middle of the circle completed their chalk designs. The others shuffled forwards, bowls between their feet, funnel-shaped tool in one hand, thin metal rod in the other. When they stopped, they each poured a different coloured sand in to the wide end of the funnel. Three of them bent double, noses almost touching the chalk lines, and began rubbing the side of their funnels with the rod. A thin stream of sand flowed out of the end, filling the chalk outlines. It looked like they were piping a ludicrously complicated cake.

The boys worked quickly. The two with chalk furiously scribbling patterns on the floor, the others gradually joining to colour in the outlines with their grains of sand.

'They're drawing the six realms, aren't they?'

Rabjam nodded. 'When he's done, we have to place each key in its corresponding realm.' He pointed to each segment in turn. 'The Treasure Vase in the God realm, the Conch in the Ashura, the Golden Fish in the animal realm, Precious Canopy in the Hungry Ghosts...'

'The umbrella!' I said. 'Simon found that.'

Rabjam nodded and continued, 'The Lotus Flower for the hell realms, and the Victory banner in the human realm.'

'I thought you said there were eight symbols.'

'The first six unite the realms. The seventh,' he pointed to an eight-spoked wheel, 'is for Odiyana.'

'And the eighth?'

He held up a hand to stop me. 'I'll get to that. First, we—you actually—must place the Kila in the middle of the mandala. That will open the other realms.'

I shrugged. That didn't sound too hard.

'When you've done that, we place the six symbols in each realm. One after the other. Each by a different hand. You will place the Victory banner in the human realm. Then Simon, the Canopy.'

'What about Lama la?'

'When he sees what we have done already... I hope Lama la will help us complete the ritual. He will place the Eternal Knot around the Kila, binding it in place. Then the Bardo of Becoming will end.' He let out a long breath.

'What happens then?'

'The Bardo is the moment of uncertainty between one reality and another. When the Bardo ends, there is stability. A new reality.'

'So, what about us? Me, Simon, Harry?'

'When the ceremony ends, we reinforce the divisions between realms. You go back to your world. We stay in ours.'

'And that's it? Clean break? No more mists and flipping backwards and forwards?'

'I hope so.'

I swallowed a lump in my throat. *Dad would be trapped.* I nodded.

'The realms will return to order. Chaos will be defeated. At least for now.'

'Rabjam? We're ready.' It was Karma Chodron. She'd returned from locking up Lama la and was now bossing the others about.

'Is he OK?' I asked her.

'Of course. But the quicker we can do this, the quicker we can free him. Rabjam? Come.'

Rabjam touched my shoulder. 'I must go back and help. You stay here until we call you. Once the drumming stops, the horns will play and thats when you come. Karma Chodron will hand over the Kila, show you where to place it. Don't worry, this will be over in less than an hour.'

'Right,' I said as Rabjam and Karma Chodron walked back to the mandala.

I turned. Simon was talking quietly with Harry, his arms clasped behind his back. I had no idea how reincarnation worked, and even though Rabjam had been reassuring, an unpleasant shiver went up my spine as I watched him.

Let this be over soon, I thought. *Please let this be over.*

62

Watching Each Other

HARRY AND SIMON WERE peering through the gap where the double main doors met. A stream of dust sifted through it. Simon turned round as I approached. 'For someone who can travel faster than Superman, you took your time. I'm guessing you didn't find the old man then?'

I shook my head. Ten minutes ago, all I wanted was a chance to talk alone with Simon. Now, I just wanted all this to end. Things were changing too fast. *He* was changing too fast.

'Harry's been telling me what's happening. Seems like the old man knows plenty.'

Harry spoke, still facing the door. 'I know more than you think.'

'What do you mean?'

Harry straightened slowly. 'You were there at the beginning, weren't you?'

I exchanged a concerned look with Simon.

'And it was no discussion you overheard.' He straightened and turned to face us. 'When I lived here, I spent twenty years studying the histories. It's mainly stories and myth, but if you read between the lines, the glorious history of Rigpa Gompa has a dark beginning.' He took a step towards us and lowered his voice. 'You saw Rudra, didn't you? You saw him murder Gendun Rinpoche.'

Forms emerging from red and blue fire. The golden form of Rudra leaning in towards the abbot...

'Three people in your vision. One of them murdered. You know what that means?'

I glanced at Simon. There was sweat beading on his forehead.

'Rudra's in hell,' I said firmly. 'He can't come back.'

Harry nodded slowly. He touched my chest with his finger and then Simon's. He lowered his voice even more, so it was barely audible. 'That's as well may be. All I'm saying is... watch each other.'

63

—·—

THE KNOCK, KNOCK

IN THE DEPTHS OF the Hall, Sera blew her horn, Rabjam sang, Karma Chodron clashed a cymbal and three Tubtens rattled their hand drums.

'You know what will happen when the ceremony is complete?' Harry asked.

Simon wiped his brow. 'The six lands will be locked again.'

'It will cut the connection between realms.'

He nodded. 'I know.'

Harry looked at me. 'That's what you want?'

'Of course. Why would I want anything else?'

'Because where there's uncertainty, there's still hope.'

'Hope?'

'The Bardo is frightening, but it's full of potential as well. It's the only reason I can think of why Lama la would want us to wait. He must have believed that the chance of changing... something was worth the risk.'

'Like what?'

Harry shrugged. 'You can't make an omelette without breaking eggs.'

'No idea what you mean. But I'm not a big fan of omelettes.'

'What if Lama la knew something... or somebody... was coming? Something inevitable? Something so terrible that anything would be better than it? Even temporary chaos.'

The drumming quickened. Behind the door, the sound of engines started again. I bent down to peek: bright sunlight; a touch of yellow through the trees; the sound of chainsaws; men shouting at each other over the din.

We were back in the human realm.

Home of omelettes.

Harry tapped my shoulder, and I made way to let him look. He nodded. 'Diggers. Not long now. You know, I think there's a Rigpa Gompa in every realm. And in every realm, it's being attacked by something. Bulldozers here, demons in Odiyana, Preta in the Hungry Ghost realm...'

'Mr Sparks?' I asked. 'What did you mean by "still having hope"?'

He moved away from the door, pushed himself up and wiped dust from his trousers. 'Right now, everything is open. Everything is possible. When we lock the Wheel everything will be fixed again...' His voice broke. He looked down at his shoes, like a robot that's been switched off.

I finished his thought. 'If everything is fixed, then we lose them, don't we?'

He gave his shoes a weary smile.

'We cut off Rigpa Gompa and we lose your Carol and my dad.'

The drumming stopped abruptly. There was silence. Not even the sound of chainsaws.

Harry pointed the end of his cane at the strip of golden light filtering through the gap in the door. 'You should take a look, Simon. We're due a god realm.' He tapped the ground where the light touched. 'Heaven,' he sighed. 'Now that would be something, wouldn't it?' Then he leaned on his cane, even though I don't think he needed the support anymore, turned away and walked toward the others, towards the shrine that was flooded with light from a hundred butter lamps.

I stood up too. The drumming had stopped. Sera reached for the long brass horn.

It was time.

'Mr Sparks?' I said.

The old man paused.

'You still think we're doing the right thing? With Lama la and everything?'

'Oh yes.'

'How can you be so sure?'

His head tilted to the side, like he was thinking. 'I'm not *sure*. If I was... I think we'd be doing something wrong.'

He opened his mouth to say something else, but the sound of a horn drowned him out. A long, low trembling noise filling the Great Hall, another higher tone joined it. The two fought with each other for more than a minute before fading away. Then there was silence.

Knock, knock.

The noise came from behind. I frowned. That wasn't a drum. I turned back to the door. Mist was seeping through the bottom, over Simon's shoes.

'What is it?' I asked, moving closer to it.

Simon nudged past me, going the other way. 'Don't Esta,' he warned. 'Don't.'

Another knock. A powerful thud of a knock, like someone or *something* was hitting it with a mallet.

I glanced back around the hall. Despite the rising mist by my ankles, the rest of the hall gleamed with a sort of morning freshness.

My heart raced. The light was unnatural. It was too bright. We were on a knife edge; I realised. A delicate tipping point between realities.

Knock, knock.

I thought about those men in Hazmat suits. Were they outside trying to beat down the door?

'Esta?' Simon whispered, his voice scared. 'Come on. Let's finish the ceremony before something happens.'

Knock, Knock.

This time, the door rattled with the force of the blows.

A musky smell. Sort of sweet and peppery. Something familiar.

'Simon?' I asked, eyes not leaving that door. 'Someone's out there.'

There was a creak. A line of silver appeared, an elongated 'V' of light spilled into the hall. Simon stumbled away from it as if it were molten lava. Fell on his backside. 'Esta! Don't let him in!'

I leaned against the door to stop it from opening any further. It kept coming though.

Whatever was on the other side wanted to get in.

I turned. Planted my back against the wood and pushed back, forcing the door to close an inch. Simon was still down where he'd fallen, one arm out in front of him as if warding something away.

'Are you going to just lie there?' I shouted.

He didn't move. Just kept shaking his head at me.

Then a voice called from the other side of the door.

I stopped. Simon's eyes widened. He tried to scramble to his feet.

The voice was human. A man's voice.

I turned a few degrees. Leaned one shoulder against the door and put everything into it. But this time my head was right next to the gap in the door.

There was a dark figure pushing against me.

Not a demon. Not in protective clothing either. A man: jeans, faded checked shirt, dark hair flopping over his forehead, obscuring the face; a beard that looked like it hadn't been cut for more than a year.

And there was that sweet, soft aroma that reminded me of warmth and safety.

The man must have sensed me. He cocked his head so he could peer through the crack back at me.

Eyes, the green of a summer sea.

'Let me in! Quickly!' he hissed.

My feet lost grip. I slid to my knees.

'Everything's falling apart out here!'

The door opened a little wider. The face appeared.

'Esta?' the figure rasped. 'Esta, is that you?'

64

I Love You

I BACKED AWAY AS Dad squeezed through the half-opened door.

I felt something warm and wet roll down my cheek. My throat was clogged up so badly it felt like I'd swallowed a boiled egg.

He hadn't changed so much after all. His face had a few more creases, his hair was a little longer, his clothes were dusty, but otherwise... it was like he'd stepped right out of my memories.

'You found the Kila?' he said, his words soft as his smile.

I nodded and felt another tear drop from my cheek. *All this time. Every day I spent watching Gatley House; every evening reading those poems he left behind for me... and now, just when I had finally let him go...*

'I knew you'd find it,' he said. 'I always knew.'

'Are you real?' I whispered, reaching out to him. Because what if he was just a desperate dream, a figment of my imagination?

He smiled and met my fingers with his. The feeling of solidity sent shivers up my spine, making me want to laugh out loud.

'I'm real, Esta,' he whispered. 'It's me.'

'That's why you put it there, isn't it?'

He let go of me and raised a finger to my forehead to move a strand of hair. 'I put it there for you, because I knew you'd figure it out.'

I did laugh then. 'You know. You could have been a tiny bit clearer.'

He dipped his head, so hair dropped over his eyes. 'You were brave, Esta. You did it. I know what you did.'

More giddy laughter spilled out of me. My eyes gushed with little-girl tears.

'What is it?' he asked.

'They thought I was crazy,' I blubbed, 'I mean *I* thought I was too.'

His smile became a grin. He handed me a clean handkerchief. 'You're not crazy.'

'I'm sorry.' I wiped my cheeks.

'What for?'

'I think... I think I gave up.' I laughed again and shook my head. 'I gave up on you.'

I thought of what Nuttal's face might look like when she saw him. She'd have to let me out of that bloody hospital now, surely? I wasn't deluded. I had been right. I turned to show Simon... to present my dad to him.

But the words stuck in my throat. Simon was still on the floor, staring up at us in wide-mouthed fear. I twisted back round to check if Dad was OK. He smiled. *Not an illusion,* I thought with relief.

Really here.

And the sight of him was like armour for my soul. My mind was clear, like the surface of an untouched pool.

Dad was back!

'You're breaking the link, aren't you?' he said.

I nodded. 'There's not much time.'

'I'd like to see it before it's too late.'

'See what?'

'The Kila.'

Of course. Dad had been searching for the Kila for two years. I'd somehow called him back by finding the real one. Lama la had told me he would return. And now it was the least I could do before we left for good.

Although a tiny tremor of confusion ruffled the clarity of my thoughts just then. *What had he said? "I put it there for you."* What did *that* mean? That he'd put the Kila inside the old cardboard box for me?

There was something odd about that, wasn't there?

I smiled. What did it matter? All mysteries would be answered. We'd sit... maybe in the Greasy Spoon and he'd tell me everything.

Dad held out his hand. I took it and in the wavering light of a hundred butter lamps; I walked him towards the shrine.

But that tiny, unwelcome voice of doubt niggled at me as we went deeper into the Great Hall. *"I put it there for you..."* Why? Why had he done that? I'd always assumed he'd removed the Kila by accident...

I shut down the thought. *Soon. Soon.* Dad would tell me everything.

We walked slowly between the central pillars; the sand mandala dead ahead, the four Dharmapalas sitting around it, their heads bowed in meditation.

After all the drumming and horn blowing, the place was now filled with an eerie silence. We passed Rabjam and Karma Chodron and came within feet of Sera. No one turned to look at us. No one spoke. No one showed any sign of our presence. We might have been ghosts drifting through space.

Sometimes your eyes see, but you miss everything important. Now, looking back, it's clear to me. Everyone else was stone-still. It was as if Dad and I were moving through a waxwork display: Rabjam and Karma Chodron muttering silent prayers; Sera, staring down the length of her horn; Tubten drawing a line in the sand at the edges of the Wheel.

We reached the shrine. The Kila lay on its side. Waiting for me.

Dad's smile widened, his face golden in the candlelight. 'Thank you, Esta,' he muttered and reached out to caress its handle.

'Dad, don't touch it,' I whispered.

There was a *thwuck* as he lifted the dagger from the shrine. He held its blade, staring at the ornate handle. His face no longer glowed gold, the light around him had turned cold and grey.

He looked directly at me, his eyes gleaming like emeralds. 'I *love* you, Esta.'

The word 'love', drawn out and breathy, clanged like an alarm bell in my head. Dad loved me. I knew he loved me. The last line of the poem he'd left me even used the word. But he'd never said it to me before.

"I put it there for you." If he'd put the Kila in the box for me, what had he been searching for in Odiyana? I'd always thought he'd been out there searching for it. But if he'd known all along?

'Where did you hide it?' I asked.

His smile dropped into a slight frown. 'Darling?' he said in a familiar whisper.

And that's when the spell finally broke.

I think that's when she realised the game was up as well.

But it was too late by then.

I grabbed the handle of the Kila and tried to pull it from him. He wrapped his fingers more tightly around the blade, though.

I took a step backwards towards the throne, still not wanting to believe, unable to accept... 'The Kila, Dad?' I said desperately. 'Where did you hide it?'

He licked his lips. The smile returned. But his hair seemed to grow until it was long and hung limply from what I saw now was a sun-burnt scalp. His hand tightened into a fist, blood seeping through the cracks between his fingers; fingers that had become bony and shrivelled, uncut nails curling over themselves.

'You know, Esta,' he said. 'I have absolutely no goddamned idea.' And then he added in a low and extended hiss: '*Gorgeous.*'

65

LOVELY

THAT VOICE WAS LIKE the hissing of escaping gas inside my brain. Its sound slithered down into my body, filling me with poison.

'*Your father is lost,*' he whispered. '*And now... so are you...*'

His eyes flashed a pale green. He snapped the blade from my grip with so much force that it sent me stumbling backwards. He grinned at me, then *sniffed* the blade. Satisfied, he raised it to his eyebrow in a salute. 'Bye, bye *lovely* Esta Brown.'

I watched in horrified, frozen silence as my dad's face contorted like a crazy reflection in one of those circus mirrors. Dark, matted hair sprouted from his head, falling to his shoulders.

My stomach turned. My mind, trying to make sense of what I was seeing, flailed helplessly around like the desperate flapping of someone drowning.

I made a few staggering steps after him... it. 'No!' I called hoarsely,

The creature barely paused, it just made a flicking motion with the Kila. A blast of hot air battered into me, pushing me into the still unmoving Rabjam, sending his bowl of tea up and over. The creature, meanwhile, carried on walking leisurely towards the main door, the Kila now twirling in its blackened fingers.

'What have you done?' Rabjam muttered. I turned. The monk was staring down at the upturned bowl of tea in his lap. He looked up at me like he was trying to figure out long division in his head.

'Wake up!' I screamed at him, frustration and desperation surging. I grabbed the tea bowl, twisted round and hurled it at the retreating figure. The thing fell way short, clattering loudly against the floor. I spun back to the others. 'Do something!'

Rabjam frowned at me. 'That was a good bowl.'

'Wake up!' I shouted again, pointing behind me. 'He's taking the Kila!'

Rabjam's eyes flicked to the throne, then over my shoulder. 'Oh no,' he muttered.

The figure was already halfway back to the main door.

I stamped into the middle of the mandala, kicked sand at Karma Chodron. She stopped chanting and stared around her as if she'd just woken from a deep sleep. Sera dropped the horn. It clattered against the floor. Tubten jumped to his feet and dived behind her yellow robes.

'Wake up!' I roared.

Rabjam closed his eyes and muttered something, then reached into a metal bowl filled with rice, stirring the grains with his fingertips. He flung a handful of rice towards the retreating figure, blew hard and rasped the word: *'LUNG'*. The rice gathered speed. He turned his fingers like he was turning an invisible door handle: *'MEH'*. Each grain of rice glowed red. They became mini torpedoes of flame, each one tearing holes in the back of the retreating figure.

It staggered for a second. Then straightened.

Its body folded in on itself. It became taller, straighter, thinner, sleeker. Its hair untangled and became longer and shinier, until, walking smoothly down the central aisle of the Great Hall, was the black cloaked form of an impossibly thin woman.

I felt sick to my stomach: *Trisna.*

Karma Chodron jumped to her feet. 'No one enters Rigpa Gompa without a fight.' Then bowed her head and placed her palms together.

Sera tried to stop her. 'No, sister!'

But Karma Chodron whispered the words under her breath and there was a rush of air and a smudge of blue where she'd been standing; in almost the same instant, Trisna spun round and flung an arm out.

There was a crunching thud and Karma Chodron's body appeared crumpled against one of the pillars.

'Karma Chodron!' Sera screamed.

A shadow now emerged from the far wall to stand between Trisna and the main door, a long stick gripped in one hand. Harry's cane glowed in the darkness. 'You finished bullying the kids?' Harry growled. 'How about you pick on someone a little older?'

Trisna turned to face him. Her head cocked to one side. 'Go back to sleep, old man.'

Harry swung at her, his stick making an arc of colour in the dim shadow. Rabjam sent more flaming grains of rice towards her.

In one motion, Trisna ducked beneath Harry's cane and flicked her wrist at the oncoming torpedoes. The flaming rice disappeared into a cloud of steam. She twisted back and pointed the Kila at Harry. Crackling red flames poured from its point, sending him ten feet into the air. He landed in a heap against the back wall, his stick clattering to the ground by his side.

The goddess paused, casting her eyes around her at the two slumped figures of Karma Chodron and Harry. She ran her hands down the sides of her dress, as if to flatten any annoying creases, then looked right at me and smiled.

'Lovely.'

She turned away, slowly walked to the door, opened it with a flick of her wrist and stepped outside into a pale blue light.

The door slammed behind her, leaving the Great Hall in a dreadful, empty silence.

66

JUST RUN

THE KILA IS GONE.

The thought came with a tidal wave of horror and shame. Trisna simply walked in and took it.

No, that wasn't true.

Shame burned a line up my back.

I gave it to her. I gave the Kila to Trisna.

I scanned the ground ahead of me, slapped my palms together, closed my eyes, said the words and the Great Hall became a blur.

I slid through space as if the rest of the world were in slow motion. To my left, the three Dharmapalas were already at Karma Chodron's side. Sera was sitting beside her sister, tending to her. Rabjam was already pouring tea from his pot into a cup. Tubten was crying, fist in his mouth.

I saw all that in a drawn out instant before I reached the far end of the hall and stopped.

Mist seeping under the door, gathering in layers at my feet. Beyond the door: the sound of men calling to each other, the buzz of saws, the clanking of metal. Mixed in with that was another noise: a low growl followed by a slow *sccrraape* that I didn't think had anything to do with machinery.

And bells. There were bells ringing out there, too.

All the six realms bending and folding in and out of each other.

A noise to my left. I whirled round in blind panic.

It was Simon.

He was picking Harry up, propping him against the wall. When the old man was secure, Simon stood, wiped the sweat and grime from his face, and stared at me.

We looked at each other in silence. His mouth was open, his brow creased into a frown.

'What did you do?' he said, eventually.

I gave it away.

'I... tried to...' But I had nothing to say. My face burned hot under Simon's gaze.

'I told you not to open it!'

'I thought...'

'You thought what?'

'I thought it was Dad!'

He stared at me. Confusion turning into a look of horror. He pointed at the door. 'You thought *that* was your dad?'

What could I do? I stood in silence, my jaws clamped tight while Simon continued to gape at me.

'You gave that monster the Kila?'

I nodded.

'The one thing that was going to put an end to all of this? You gave it to her because you thought it was your... your dad?'

I nodded again. But I was falling apart inside. It was like beneath my skin everything important about me was rotting away; turning into dust; an empty shell of a person. Right then, if Simon had poked me, I might have just collapsed in on myself.

'Esta,' he said.

Something touched my arm. It felt warm. I looked down. Simon was holding me. I looked back up, confused.

He looked at me. Blue eyes of concern. 'Esta, we have to get it back.'

'Wait!'

It was Harry. He'd found his cane and was pushing himself up with it. 'If you step outside of that door, you'll be torn apart.'

'What about that thing?' Simon said. 'It seemed to cope.'

'Trisna isn't like us. Normal beings like us don't belong out there in the Bardo. There are creatures out there: *Rakshasa*. They feed on fear, and pain and confusion. You can't defeat them. Not alone.'

Raised voices to my left. Karma Chodron was up, leaning against Sera, speaking to Rabjam and pointing angrily towards us.

Harry turned, following my gaze. 'Stay in the Gompa, Esta. We'll find a way. We'll talk them round.'

But the Dharmapalas didn't look like they were ready to listen. They turned their grim faces towards me. Sera was expanding again, doubling in size; three more Tubtens blinked into life. Karma Chodron locked her eyes on me and placed her palms together...

I spun back to the door, grabbed the handle. 'I'm going to get it back.'

Harry raised his arm. 'Esta, no!'

A streak of blue, a rush of air and Karma Chodron appeared, Carving right into Simon with a sudden ferocity, slamming him into the wall to my left.

Before she could untangle herself from him, I tugged on the handle. The door eased open, blasting me with hot air.

'Esta!' Harry shouted over the noise.

I glanced across at him.

'That scraping noise. If you hear it, promise me...'

'What?'

A soft light touched his face with an amber glow. 'You run, Esta. You run.'

67

Into the Bardo of Becoming

I CLOSED THE DOOR and turned to see what reality or realities I had entered.

Clear blue sky, soft, scudding clouds, buttercups dancing in a gentle breeze, rolling green fields, mountains shimmering a pale grey in the distance.

I inhaled. The air was warm and sweet. There was almost no sound at all, just the *shushing* of grass in the breeze. A place to sit, to stop, to rest...

I glimpsed something in the near distance, though. Something black cut through the meadow. The silhouette of a tall, slim woman; one hand outstretched, caressing the tops of the tall grasses.

Trisna...

My hands bunched into fists at the sight of her. All notions of calm and rest scorched away by one thought.

Trisna.

I stepped from the safety of the doorway.

But as my feet touched the soft earth, the surrounding light shimmered. The whole beautiful scene rippled; fields, flowers, sky, even the distant mountains became sharp and vivid and then, as if I were merely standing inside a page in a kid's picture book, it all just flipped over.

Darkness fell.

A starless night; gloomy courtyard.

Scritching, scratching at my feet.

The goddess came to a stop. Turned. Eyes glistening, reflecting light that wasn't there. She glanced down at the ground, then back at me.

I wanted to stare her down. Didn't want to drop eye contact. Because that's how bullies win, isn't it? They beat you in the mind before they beat the crap out of your body.

'Esta...' she whispered. Her voice carried along with a foul-smelling breeze: 'I know who you are... *delicious.'*

The scratching noises at my feet grew louder. The ground moved at the corner of my eye. I swallowed. *Don't look down,* I told myself.

I looked down.

Bugger.

Insects.

Millions of them.

Crawling over my feet. Big fat, long ones with pincers writhing over each other like the Hungry Ghosts did in that putrid stream.

In the distance, the sound of laughter.

I looked back up. Trisna had lost interest in me and was striding off through the carpet of creepy crawlies.

Not so fast.

I focused on her back. I had no plan other than to burn right through her spindly little frame. I remembered how easily she'd swatted Karma Chodron away, but what else could I do? Carving was the only weapon I had to battle a goddess, and anyway, I had rage and desperation on my side.

More than that: she'd tricked me; pretended to be Dad.

This was personal.

I put my hands together, closed my eyes, pictured the shifting black ground between us and said the words.

The courtyard blurred. The ground rose up and twisted around me. I kept straight at her though: a dart searching for the bullseye, braced for impact.

She turned. The last thing I saw was her toothy smile...

... which faded away like the Cheshire Cat's grin, replaced by a mishmash of flitting shapes: figures in dazzling white Hazmat suits... I felt myself losing control, tilting over...

Flip...

Black, long-limbed creatures glared at me with burning red eyes.

I lost my balance, lost my feet.

Flip...

Trees became pillars of white stone.

Flip...

The sky became scorched black, poisonous cloud...

Flip...

I slammed, shoulder-first, into something hard and immovable.

Everything went blank.

68

BLANK SLATE

WHITE.

Have you heard that stupid joke about the kid who hands his art teacher a blank piece of paper? Tells her, it's a picture of a cow in a field of grass?

'So, where's the grass?' the teacher asks.

The kid says: 'The cow ate it all.'

'Well, where's the cow?'

'It left, cos there's no more grass.'

That's what it was like. *Everything* was white. Not some snowy field or whatever. It was like being back in the desert of the Hungry Ghost realm. Except... cold.

Was I standing? Sitting? I couldn't be sure. There was no up, no down, no left, no right.

I was lost in empty space.

There *were* sounds: mainly men calling out to each other, leaves rustling, birds squawking.

I could hear other voices too as well though. A girl's voice in the distance repeating the same phrase over and over again: '*She did it. She did it...*' until the wind took the words away, like the sound of a radio station as you hit the edge of its signal. I shifted painfully to one side to hear the voice again.

But the channel changed.

A sound like fingernails scraping down a blackboard replaced it.

I tried to jam my hands against my ears, but at that point I don't think I even *had* hands, or ears, for that matter.

Finally, even the sounds stopped.

For a little while, there was nothing to see, nothing to hear, nothing to feel. It was like I wasn't there either.

There is no Esta Brown...

Just thoughts racing through a non-existent skull: random images, feelings, memories tracking backwards and forwards, page flip after page flip: My dad's bristly beard as he bends down to kiss me goodbye; the smell of his aftershave; Hannah Piranha's nose exploding beneath my hand; Mum staring at a TV screen full of white noise; a policeman licking the nib of his pencil; Mr Taylor holding a spade; Charlie's drawings...

Bam, bam, bam. Image after image round and round like a microwave turntable on fast-forward. Now, Dad's memorial stone; now, Georgina, the girl in Gatley Gardens who cut up her food; now Bernard swinging his multi-coloured keys...

Then, without warning, voices returned. High-pitched and cruel, slithering out of the surrounding nothingness: *What are you searching for, Esta Brown?*

Before me, the eyes of the hungry ghost rolled in their sockets, its swollen tongue dangled from its mouth.

What are you yearning for, Esta Brown?

There was the carriage. The hand with the red ring. There were the black banners. The hair drooping over blue eyes...

Ahh. Daddy, the voices mocked.

'Stop!' I cried.

Home...

There was giggling. *We know what you want.*

I sat back and leant my head against the invisible wall. 'I just want everything to be back to—'

Normal. We know...

White eyes... hundreds of them, blinking shut. Each one drifting around me, their mocking words becoming a gust of wind that whipped around me in a whirl of a million tiny fists.

Just as suddenly, the wind dropped. Flakes, cold and feathery, spiralled down in a silent torrent.

Then, out of the quiet came a loud and long scraping sound.

I stopped breathing.

69

— . —

RAKSHASA

SOMETHING HEAVY SHUFFLED OUT beyond the thick curtain of snow. My ears tingled with the sound, my eyes strained trying to cut through for any sign of what made that noise.

A loud screech, like the grinding of iron girders, followed by another horrible, *scrraape.* Behind that, another noise, distant, quieter. A muffled human voice calling out.

The scraping became louder. *What was that?*

The wall behind me was hard and cold. No escape that way. I looked left and right. Could I Carve along it? There was nothing to visualise, I'd be Carving blind. But I had to do something. Whatever made that noise was coming closer.

I stood, palms flat against the wall. I could keep my back protected, at least. Then slide to my right, hope for a door, or something.

A shadow emerged ahead. A grey outline, no more than a vague shape. It was tall, though. Twice as tall as me.

The shape lurched closer; millions of flakes bouncing off a head roughly the size and shape of a stuffed suitcase; what looked like two fangs poked out from the top of a wide mouth and red eyes glowed like brake lights through fog, sweeping right and left as it sniffed the air.

I thought of what Harry had told me.

They feed on fear, and pain and confusion.

A long muscular arm raked the ground: s*crrraaape,* hurling grit in a fan of pebbles that landed at my feet.

I glanced along the blank wall. I could be out of here in an instant. But God knew where. And God knew what else was out there in the snow.

My eyes snapped back to the front. The thing was no more than ten feet away... studying me; flaming eyes distorting the air around them, snow pouring off its massive shoulders. Inky black arms reached almost to the ground, each one ending in a set of curled claws. It brought its right arm back and then dragged something along the ground like it was throwing a bowling ball.

Sccrraaape.

At the end of its reach, it lifted the object up to my eyeline: half a human skull, held in its upturned palm like a begging bowl.

Great. Mystery solved.

The thing gave a throaty, gurgling roar.

Go, go, go, I told myself. But, just as when faced with the Hungry Ghosts, my thoughts froze with panic. *What are the words?* I tried to visualise the curve of the courtyard wall, because, surely, that's where we were.

But what were the words?

Heat touched my face as the Rakshasa leaned forwards. Its burning eyes just a couple of feet from me. I squeezed my own eyes tight.

They were so simple! How could I forget the words?

But my mind was paralysed with fear.

Move, Esta. Move!

The thing breathed out: rotting seaweed, gone off steak, the boy's toilets on a hot afternoon. It smelled like the insides of something's stomach. And if I didn't move now, that's exactly where I would end up.

The fangs grated against the wall above me as the thing opened its jaws. Little smatterings of brick rained down on me.

And something warm and wet.

Dripping.

Just then, there was a sharp metallic noise somewhere out in the courtyard.

The Rakshasa paused. Grunted. A dollop of sludgy saliva dropped against my arm as the beast moved its head to one side. Listening.

There it was again. A clanging sound.

A bell.

I opened my eyes a crack. The Rakshasa had turned away from me, a low guttural growl rumbling in its throat.

The bell rang again. Now it was accompanied by a human voice. Singing. Someone was singing. Badly, admittedly, but there was a melody.

The bell rang out once more. But this time the very ground vibrated with the sound of it. It made my teeth chatter. The cascading snow stopped as if someone had just turned a tap off up in the clouds.

I cautiously opened my eyes a little wider. Stared at my feet. The ground was reassuringly dark. No snow. Looking up, sunlight glimmered through mist.

The Rakshasa was gone.

In its place was a smaller figure that looked no scarier than the Michelin Man.

Its outstretched arm held a sort of black lollipop thing. A persistent clicking came from it.

Just to the right. Another figure.

An old man. On his knees. Walking stick gripped in both hands, propping him up. Chin down at his chest.

'Sarge?' the Michelin Man called, not taking his eyes off me. His voice was muffled and echoey. The clicking increased in intensity, turning into a crackle of white noise.

He held out his other hand as if warding me off. 'Don't worry.'

I didn't know if he was reassuring me, his mate, or himself. 'You're not in any danger.'

I visualised the red-eyed Rakshasa, which; I was absolutely certain, must still be standing behind the thinnest of veils that separated our worlds.

'Joe?' the man called again. 'I got two here. Just appeared out of nowhere. Old man, and a kid.'

I collapsed to the ground, the spiny twigs of a hedge at my back.

Tears rolled down my cheeks.

How was I supposed to believe anything in this crazy world?

Trisna was inside my mind and she was playing games with it, wrapping the rest of me round her little finger.

It wasn't fair. It was like playing chess against a grand master when you don't even know which direction your pawns go.

I looked up as another figure emerged out of the mist, dressed in the same protective gear. Same wavy lollipop linked to something in a backpack.

A Geiger counter.

If Graham's was anything to go by, the greater the clicks, the greater the danger. And, as the person I assumed was "Sarge" or "Joe" approached, both their machines sounded like a bag full of excited crickets.

'Don't move,' the newcomer said. A woman.

'It's off the scale,' the first man whispered, not taking his eyes off me for an instant.

'It's alright,' the woman called Joe said. 'Get a couple of stretchers.' She lowered her lollipop and bent into a crouch. 'It's alright little lady,' she said from behind her protective mask and full body suit. 'We got you now. We'll get you home. Safe. Back to normal in a jiffy.'

PART FIVE

The Normal

70

—·—

HOME

I STARED UP AT an overcast sky waiting for another *flip*; for the snow to fall; or for those hungry red eyes to appear over me again.

Because it was all there. A breath away. As if all you had to do was waft an arm and a new reality would emerge. Like wiping mist from a window.

I let my head fall to the side as someone rolled me over. Next to me, three plastic "bubble-men" were nudging Harry on to a stretcher. I had a momentary flash of him sweeping his glowing cane at Trisna.

Harry moaned as they lifted him. A weak old man again in this world.

We floated side by side on our stretchers through the gap where the old gate used to be. I turned to glance back at the house. It had become weak and old too. Back in its box. Ready for burial.

Harry groaned again somewhere to the side of me.

We were carried onto the track leading to Grover Close. I lifted my head again only a few steps later, but this time, no matter which way I twisted, Gatley House was gone. And that sense of teetering on the edge of a cliff went with it.

I sighed in relief and closed my eyes. Reality felt solid again, more reliable now that we were out of sight of the place.

What had happened, though? What was I doing on a stretcher with Harry Sparks? We'd been somewhere. We'd done something... Reality was solid enough, but my mind was foggy and I was so exhausted if I could just...

A blizzard of images and memories flitted and flickered out of the darkness of my mind. I'd climbed a wall; I'd slipped and fallen... I'd been floating above a building... angry voices... a fight? Simon had been there too.

Simon. Where was Simon?

Sccraaape.

I lurched upwards with a sudden gasp. A gloved hand pushed my head back. 'Rest,' a voice said. 'Somehow, you got away with it. Just a few more tests, then we'll get you back home.'

'Home?' I whispered. And, as the warm darkness smothered me again, wondered what exactly that word meant anymore.

I rested. Smelled the acid stench of tarmac and sulphur and diesel. Listened to the rasping of exhaust pipes, of metal claws ripping up the earth, of the snapping crash of yet another tree as it fell to the ground.

I tried to remember the place I had been: the mountains, the lush green valley, the rainbows... but no sooner had each image came to mind than it rapidly disappeared, like a thin covering of snow dissolves in warm rain.

I lay back and listened to the sound of hard things grinding away and radio crackles and the blades of a landing chopper.

Moments later, I was being moved again. Lifted upwards. The clunk of a door. An engine. A rumbling vibration against my back.

My body hurt. There was a taste of lead in my mouth and when I opened my eyes, they stung like hell. Blinked a few times. A small room with flashing lights. The ground moving beneath me.

Ambulance. They put me in an ambulance. I thought with relief.

I let my head sink back into the stiff pillow. *Unpleasant as this is,* I thought. *At least it's home.*

What was home? To me then, it was a world where it didn't matter who I was: no demons; no past lives; no flipping. Just a bit of misery, a bit of pain.

But at least it was *real* pain.

I closed my eyes again and let the rumbling wheels carry me on.

I knew who I was here.

I was Esta Brown: part-time delinquent, part-time nut job, part-time daughter. But I had friends. I had a mum who loved me and, as far as I could tell, anyway, I had come back from whatever strange place I'd been.

I let out a long, satisfied breath.

The rumbling stopped. A door opened, letting light spill inside.

'There you are!'

I squinted in the direction of the voice. A stick-like figure stood silhouetted in the doorway. It was holding up what looked like a plastic medicine bottle.

My eyes were drawn down to a set of keys hanging off the figure's belt. The light from outside struck them and reflected rainbow colours onto the ceiling.

Rainbows, I thought dreamily, and images of a wide green valley, waterfalls, and mountains flooded my mind.

Home. I frowned. Confused. *Home?*

And then a terrible thought scythed through my meandering thoughts like a knife made of ice.

Simon. Simon.

I attempted to push myself out of bed. *What was I doing here? I had to get back!*

But the figure at the doorway placed a hand on my leg and shook his head. 'Welcome Home, Esta Brown.'

I looked up again at the silhouette.

'And this time,' it said. 'I'll take a bit more care of you.'

Bernard shook the medicine bottle with his free hand.

Ten or more pink pills rattled inside it.

71

THE THIRD TABLET

WE WAITED UNTIL THE effects of the Valium made my speech slur, and my limbs turn to jelly. I certainly wasn't going to be running anywhere for the rest of the day.

'Nice and placid,' Bernard said to no one in particular. 'Just how I like 'em.'

If I'd had the strength, I might have rammed those rainbow keys somewhere painful. But although the mind was willing, my body was becoming more and more useless with every minute.

I had to do *something*, though. Although the Valium was turning my muscles into sludge, my memories were suddenly sharp as pins: the face of my dad as it morphed into the Hungry Ghost; the sight of Trisna striking Harry with blue bolts of lightning; Simon grappling with Karma Chodron as I closed the door on Rigpa Gompa.

Whatever Bernard's plan for me was... I had to escape. I had to get back for Simon.

By any means.

'Give me another one,' I said, my voice loud and clear as I could make it under the circumstances.

'Two's plenty,' he replied.

I coughed. My mouth was going dry already, my lips sticking to my teeth. I held out my hand, palm up, trying to control the shakes.

'Last time you gave me two, I escaped, remember?'

Bernard scowled, picked up the bottle, and studied the label.

My throat burned like hell. I could feel the muscles in my shoulders and arms shutting down.

But I had to be sure.

'No mistakes Bernard,' I grunted. This was a long shot, but... in for a penny and everything.

He looked at me suspiciously.

I held his gaze, refusing to blink.

Eventually, he shrugged and opened the lid of the bottle. 'OK.' He tapped another pill into my outstretched palm. 'Just so long as you can make the walk without me having to carry you.'

I threw my head back and swallowed the third tablet.

'I get what you're doing, you know,' Bernard said as he led me down the driveway towards Gatley Gardens. 'You can't escape out there,' he pointed back to the black gates. 'So, you think you can escape in here.' He touched my forehead. 'I get it. If my life was as messed up as yours, I'd probably turn to drugs an' all.'

He didn't know how right he was.

I smiled grimly, looked behind me and watched as the ambulance drove away into the late afternoon. Then we walked towards Gatley Gardens Mental Hospital while I waited for the full fog of Valium to take over.

The drive started to meander under the soles of my feet. *One foot in front of the other,* I told myself. *Don't fall now, Esta Brown.*

The external walls of the hospital seemed to ripple in the light from the dipping sun. Everything was blurry and far too bright.

My mouth had become as dry as a bag of flour.

I was frog-marched inside.

I was at a door.

I blinked, and suddenly I was at the end of the hall.

Blink.

We were heading down a concrete staircase, my arm wrapped around Bernard's shoulders to stop me from sliding down and breaking my neck on the hard steps.

Blink.

A dark corridor with metal doors lining both sides. So cold I could see my breath.

A hammering noise behind one of the doors.

Monkey hoots.

Each door had a sliding panel at eye level. One was open. A white face stared out at it.

Blink.

On my knees in a white room.

I could have been back in the courtyard at Rigpa Gompa: white walls, white floor, white ceiling.

There was a hissing in my ears.

Mouth dry as desert sand.

I blinked again.

My arms were not my own. I was hugging myself. Bernard was talking softly to me. '... make you feel nice and cosy...'

I tried to speak, but my tongue was a hotdog bun and I just croaked sounds that echoed back at me. I tried to move, but my arms were locked in place and I couldn't stand.

'... Just so you don't hurt yourself...'

I fell to my side, banging my face against the floor. Could barely feel the contact.

'That's right. Sleep it off, Brown. Just a couple of days down here 'Until you're all done struggling.'

I blinked again. Watched a pair of shoes walk away.

A door opened.

A door closed. Something hard slid against it.

The lights went out.

Everything went pitch black.

72

—.—

Remembering How it Works

I LAY STILL AND quiet for what felt like ten minutes or maybe an hour? Listening to the constant banging in one of the other rooms and the dripping water somewhere beyond my door.

I attempted to swallow, but that train had long since gone. It was as if while I was asleep someone had shoved a hairdryer in my mouth and turned it to medium hot for half an hour.

Parched was not the word.

What was the word? Desert...? Dog...? Was "Dog" the word? Why dog?

A noise. Breathing. *Panting.*

I twisted round. Something was staggering towards me in the dark. I could hear it scraping, sniffing, groaning.

The outline of a dog: barely able to walk, front legs straining, hind legs dragging behind.

I shuffled away, arching my back, my hands useless... tied behind me.

The dog clawed its way forwards. So close I could smell the stench of rot and decay peeling off it. Its eyes were sunk deep into their sockets, its jaws dripping with saliva. Toothless gums.

Its bark was deep and low as a bass drum: '*I know who you are*'.

I squeezed my eyes shut and kicked out.

My feet hit fresh air.

I waited. Took a breath. Nothing happened. I opened one eye.

The dog was gone. The room was silent again.

Seeing things, I told myself as I used the wall to shuffle into a seating position.

Hearing things. I crossed my legs, half-closed my eyes.

How does this work again?

I remembered Mum telling me to count my breaths. We'd been sitting in the living room listening to some of Dad's records.

Breathe, Esta.

I exhaled: 'One.'

Now I heard Karma Chodron ordering me to focus. '*Concentrate!*'

'Two.'

Something unlocked in my solar plexus. I smiled. *Oh yeah. I remember.*

The cell walls faded away and a new voice spoke: deep and soft, like the echo of a whisper.

'Hello, Esta,' it said. 'Welcome back.'

73

THE BARDO OF DREAMING

I WAS STANDING ON a dusty plain. Lama la was by my side.

Sitting twenty feet away on a wooden stool, unaware of us, was a man with a child on his lap.

Lama la walked towards him.

'Where are we?' I asked.

He paused and turned his head a touch. 'The Bardo of Dreaming.'

'There's more than one Bardo?'

He didn't reply. Just continued his walk towards the man and, since there was nothing else to do, I followed.

The man on the stool was chewing hungrily on something he held in one hand. A dog sniffed at him warily, obviously attracted by whatever the man was gnawing on.

We watched in silence as the dog crept nearer and nearer. Inch by inch, it came, until eventually, the man noticed it. He bent down, picked a pebble from the ground and flung it at the poor mutt. The dog backed off, whining, but moments later, it was back, its tail between its legs. The man hurled another stone at it.

This little dance played out a couple more times, each time the dog getting a little braver, a little closer.

Finally, Lama la spoke: 'What do you see?'

'I dunno. A man with a baby, trying to eat his dinner. Lama la... What's going on? Are you OK? I need to get back to—'

'Shh. That's Norbu. Look more carefully at what he's eating. Come a little closer. Don't worry. He cannot see us.'

I didn't move. 'You said that about the Hungry Ghosts.'

'This is different,' he said. 'This is just for show. Come.'

I went closer, shaking my head. Ready to run if necessary.

Turns out Norbu was eating raw fish for dinner. I had to wrap the crook of my arm around my face. It smelled like... like raw fish smells. The man tore chunks from it with his teeth.

I took a step back. 'What is this? Why can't you ever show me nice things?'

'Now,' Lama la said, ignoring me. He clicked his fingers. 'Watch this!'

Suddenly, the sky, the street, the house all blanked out. All that remained was the man, the baby, and the remains of his lunch in his hands.

'What?' I whispered. Then stopped.

The fish had begun to move.

74

---·---

Norbu, His Lunch, the Baby and the Dog

AT FIRST IT WAS just a twitch, but then the fish's whole body went into spasm. It made jerky movements, like some kind of zombie fish. Then, as if we were rewinding an old film reel, it regained its flesh and wriggled and twitched Now we were watching a series of flashing images, like flicking through a photo book of the poor fish's miserable life: starting from its grizzly end as Norbu's lunch, then back in time to the basket where it lay with four others; the wriggling frenzy as a net closed around it, then it was swimming free in icy waters, then...

... then I was staring up at a ceiling. A bed in a room with a tiny square window, except... lying on the bed was no fish. Its fins had become the gnarled hands of an old man. Another, younger man bent over him, weeping and dabbing the older man's forehead with a cloth. The weeping man was... was a slightly younger looking Norbu.

'What the hell is going on?' I whispered.

I heard Lama la click his fingers again.

Before I could ask anything else, there was a rush of icy wind and I was dragged away, back into the sunlight and the dusty road, with the older Norbu struggling to keep his lunch from the dog.

'Lama la,' I gasped. 'Who was the man on the bed?'

Norbu kicked at the dog. It yelped and scampered back a few paces, fur raised on its back. Then the man ripped off a strip of bony tail and flung it into the dirt.

The dog pounced on it.

'Now the dog,' Lama la said.

No sooner had the words come out of his mouth than the scene dimmed and images flickered, racing back frame by frame. This time we travelled through the dog's pitiful life, back to its first mewling whines as a newborn puppy, and then into blackness...

And now we were back in the same room as before with the tiny window. This time, the dying man from before was standing at the doorway, very much alive, but looking on in horror while a large, grey-haired woman staggered to the floor, gasping for breath, clutching her chest. She lay, breath rattling in her throat, staring up at the same little window the old man had looked out on. A square of clear blue sky.

Lama la clicked his fingers.

The wind howled, and sent us reeling back into the brightness of Norbu, his lunch, the baby and the dog.

I stared at Lama la, my mind whirring, barely able to keep up with all the backwarding and forwarding he was making me do. 'I don't understand. Why are you showing me this? I have to go back to Rigpa Gompa. I have to save Simon!'

'Do you still not see?' He raised his eyebrows and pointed back at the scene. 'The complexity of cause and effect.'

'What's this got to do with me? We haven't got time—'

'Observe the baby!'

I turned my gaze back to the street and—

This time, the scene went dark almost immediately and there was Norbu. Younger again, standing in a dark spot behind the house. His face was contorted in rage, rock in one hand, ready to swing it at an even younger man who was cowering, arms over his head. As Norbu brought the stone down, the vision blurred...

... and I was once again back on the street and broad daylight and Norbu, wiping the last remains of fish from his mouth. The dog was licking at the discarded bits of skin and bone. The baby cried and Norbu sang to it. A slow and soft lullaby to the child on his knee.

I staggered backwards this time, choking.

'Don't you see?' Lama la said, 'Norbu eats his father's flesh, he kicks his mother away, he sings to the enemy that he killed. And there,' he pointed to the dog. 'The wife gnaws at her husband's bones. Do you see how the wheel turns?'

The sand from the side of the road skipped and danced as a dry wind blew. 'I still don't understand,' I said.

'The course of lives is complicated and yet cause and effect is infallible.' He grabbed a pinch of grit from the rising dust cloud between his forefinger and thumb. 'But who knows which cause is connected to which effect? And whether the effect is also a cause?' Then, like a chef seasoning a pan of food, he released the grit back into the cloud.

Billions of grains of sand spun around each other every which way, forming shapes in the air: a bird flapping its wings, a turtle, a dog.

'What you saw,' Lama la said as he stood watching the shapes slowly fade, becoming solid and flat, '... was just the migration from one life to the next.'

The sand settled around us, blotting out the sky, encasing us within a sort of box shape. Lama la looked behind him and then lowered himself to sit.

'There have been many more lives in your case,' Lama la continued. 'Only Padmakara himself would have the sight to untangle the mess. Too much time has passed.'

We were in a windowless grey room. A dingy cell, in fact. Lama la sat on a straw mat at one end. He looked dishevelled and old.

I sat down opposite him. 'You're trying to show me who I was in the past? Is that it?'

I smelt gas. Something sickly sweet. Behind us, black smoke seeped under the door.

The old man looked up. 'If you want to know who you were in a past life, Esta, look at your actions now. If you want to know your future, look at your actions now. You are nothing more than your actions in this present moment.' He leaned forward and put both of his hands against my shoulders. 'Accept change, Esta. Embrace the sandstorm. Don't fear it.'

The door creaked.

'You wanted me to tell you who you were?' he said. 'I can only tell you who you are right now.' His hands lowered down my arms, and I felt him pass something into mine.

The whispering got louder. The smell of burning oil seeped up my nostrils, making me choke. I resisted the urge to cough.

'You are...'

I closed my eyes and prepared for the worst.

75

THE GIFT

ESTA BROWN.'

It took me a moment to respond. I thought maybe I'd mis-heard him. I opened my eyes. 'Say what?'

'That is all.'

'All of this to tell me my name?'

'That is all I know.'

'You said I was a Tulku. You said I wrote the story about the Jewel Island.'

Lama la shrugged.

'So what about Padmakara? Rudra? The monks I saw in my own memories. I was there, Lama la. I picked up the Orb... I mean the Vajra. I can see Rigpa Gompa, I can Carve, I can speak to you in a dream.'

'You are a Tulku Esta. You have returned. But to what end?'

'Cause and effect is complicated, right? That's what you were trying to show me. But now, somehow, you know I'm *not* Padmakara or Rudra? Who else could I be?'

'I only know who you are *not*. Not who you *are*. I would need to consult the *Annals* for clues. There must be something.'

I felt heat against my back now. Something was trying to get through the door behind me.

'How do you know who I'm not?'

'Rudra is trapped. He cannot be reborn. Padmakara... Padmakara... All I can say is that he cannot be reborn twice at the same time.'

At the same time? 'Simon,' I whispered. 'Simon is Padmakara.'

'I must consult the *Annals*. There will be something there... something I have missed.'

'Right. The Histories. I'll get them when I go back to Rigpa Gompa. Just tell me.'

'You'll never find them, Esta. They are beyond your reach.'

'OK. So *you* get them. How do I get you out of here?'

Lama la settled back on his mat. 'I am afraid that is something you cannot do either. The Eternal Knot binds my physical body and only Karma Chodron can untie it.'

The heat scratched painfully at the back of my neck as if a flame had been placed within a couple of inches of me. I refused to turn away from the old man, though. *The flame is in my mind.* 'I'll find a way.'

He nodded. 'I know you will. But hurry. We have an impatient visitor.'

The room started to fade. 'Whoa, whoa!' I shouted. 'Hold up! Can't I do something here? In the dreaming Bardo thingy?'

He shook his head. 'In the Bardo of Dreaming? No. Dreams are fleeting and insubstantial. Whatever you do must be in the physical realm.'

'Right. It's just that *this*...' I pointed at him and then at myself. 'Whatever dreaming thing we're doing right now, was kind of the beginning and end of my plan.'

'The fate of reality rests in your hands.'

'Yeah. About my hands—'

He looked past me to the door. Raised a finger to his lips. 'Someone's coming. Do you hear them?'

I could hear breathing.

I thought of Bernard watching over me. Just me and him in a padded cell.

I shuddered.

Smoke was coiling around my waist now. I could feel it like slimy fingers caressing me. I looked up at Lama la. He was being gobbled up by it.

'Wait, Lama la. I'm trapped here. What do I do?'

'Come back, Esta Brown. You must come back. Everything depends upon it!'

And then he was gone.

I opened my eyes. Breathing heavily.

Everything had gone white... again, which was better than oily black at least. I rolled on to my side.

Still white.

The light in the cell room was on. I craned my neck to see the door.

It was open.

A face appeared over me. A tangle of amber hair.

'Oh Jesus! Oh my God. It's her!'

'Lily?' I croaked, squinting up.

Was this another Valium hallucination?

She called out in a sort of whisper-shout. 'Graham? Graham! I found her. Oh my god.' She turned me over. 'Esta, get up, let's get this awful thing off you.' She helped me to my knees.

'Lil?' I croaked. 'What are you doing here?'

'I never believed they'd do this! It's barbaric! Turn around. Let me untie you.'

I did as I was told. 'Lil?' I whispered. 'Simon's trapped. We have to—'

'I know.'

'I have to go back.'

'Why do you think we're here?' she said as she worked on the straps at the small of my back. She paused. 'What have you got in there?'

'Got in where?'

'Your hands. Something in your hands. Graham? Come and help me with these.'

More steps coming into the cell.

'Blimey. This is a flipping dungeon!' Graham said.

'Help me untie her.'

Now Graham's fingers worked against the strapping around my arms. 'Unbelievable,' he said as he tugged. 'I thought these things were illegal.'

'Yeah,' Lily replied. 'We'll write a letter to Amnesty... but maybe not right now? Let's get her out before he wakes up.'

'Hi Graham,' I said with my new husky voice.

'Hi,' he replied, straining to unfasten me. 'This is a proper mess. You OK?'

'Could do with a drink.'

'Got one in the car.'

'Wait. Before who wakes up?' I asked. 'How did you get in here?'

Graham tugged hard at one of my hands. I felt pain in my shoulder. 'They've put something inside these sleeves.'

I felt my arms loosen. My hands freed. I tried to flex my fingers, but there was something in them. Graham unravelled the straps. I brought my arms to the front and stared dumbly at my hands... and more to the point... what I was holding in them.

I turned to face Graham and Lily. 'Hi,' I said, my hands raised in front of me.

Their mouths both opened in shock. 'How on earth?' Lily whispered after a second. '... did you get hold of those?'

76

Small Windows

THE ORB AND THE Bell gleamed in the harsh strip lighting.

'What can you see?' I asked, staring at them both.

'The bolt and the hinge,' Graham said. 'But why would Bernard tie you up with them? What kind of sick—?'

'He didn't,' I said, Lama la must have put them there when he held my arms in the Bardo of Dreaming.

'So how—?' Graham and Lily both stood there gawping at me.

'Look. I don't know. But of all the things that have happened recently, I'm going with it, OK?'

They still didn't move.

'Now. You *did* come to rescue me, right? Or are you just waiting for the tour?'

The corridor was as dark as I remembered from earlier. Graham and Lily headed to the stairs.

'Wait,' I hissed. Graham turned. I jabbed a thumb behind me. 'What about the others?'

'The others?'

'I heard voices before. There are others locked up.'

'I checked. Everywhere else is empty. You were the only one.'

'No...' I said, sliding the viewing plate on one of the doors to the side. It was gloomy in there. Empty. 'There were definitely others.'

Graham walked back to me. 'Esta. We checked. Maybe they let the others go. Anyway, we don't have time. Come on.'

'Wait. There's someone in this one.' I went over to a door just opposite mine.

'Ah,' Graham coughed. 'Yes. Him.'

'We can't leave them inside. Give me the key!'

'I didn't lock it—'

'What do you mean you didn't lock it?' I slid the plate across. There was a body slumped in the corner. I made to open the door. But Lily put her hand on mine. 'He's a disgusting slime bag,' she said. 'But I think we should let him wake up in his own time.'

I stopped. Looked back through the viewing plate. The body was a thin one. One arm was beneath its head, one outstretched away from its body; in its hand was a bunch of rainbow coloured keys.

'Lily, what did you do?'

Lily wiped her mouth with her sleeve and raised both her eyebrows at me. 'Whatever it takes, remember?'

'Oh god.' I remembered the way Bernard had looked at her as she walked out of the canteen yesterday. 'You didn't?'

'He had a thing for red-heads, apparently.'

Graham slid an arm between us. 'See the sacrifices we make for you?'

I gaped at them both. 'Lil?'

'What?'

'Tell me you didn't—'

'It's not as bad as you think.'

'If he'd have touched her,' Graham said. 'He wouldn't be lying there sleeping if you know what I mean. Now I don't know how long those pills will keep him quiet for, so can we please go?'

We reached the top of two flights of steps, and Lily closed the door behind us. 'You sure you're alright?' she whispered. I nodded, still imagining her seducing Bernard and thinking that, taking everything into consideration, I'd probably had the better day of the two of us.

'So what happened after we... you know, flipped over?' I asked as we tiptoed through yet another corridor. This place was as warren-like as Rigpa Gompa.

'We saw it, Est!' Lily replied.

I stopped in my tracks. 'Odiyana? You saw Odiyana?'

'Just for a second. But we saw it! You vanished when you fell! Honestly. One second you were falling. Next second there was a blue line or something coming out of the rusty bit of metal and then it went misty and then... nothing.'

Graham stopped too. He turned, frowning. 'Could we possibly save the chit chat for later?'

'You saw me vanish?' I asked in an excited whisper, ignoring Graham completely. They'd believed me all this time without any evidence... and now they had actually witnessed it themselves! 'What else? What else did you see?'

'Enough!' Graham hissed, glaring at us both. 'We saw enough! But later! I'd rather not have this conversation in the back of a police car.' He turned, then lifted himself on to and over the reception desk. Lily followed him.

'And... how... How did you know they locked me up down there?' I asked. There was a swing panel on the desk surface. I lifted it up and walked through.

'You won't believe it,' Lily said. 'Graham, show her!'

'Hold on,' Graham whispered. 'There's a broken window through here. This is where we came in.'

We entered the office beyond the reception. There was the little window I'd cut myself on this morning.

'I did that,' I said proudly.

Graham grinned at me. 'Thought so. You little vandal.'

They had boarded it up with nails since I'd smashed through it, but not very well. Graham must have pushed it in from the outside and now the board lay leaning against the wall. The window itself was fairly small. Not much bigger than the one Graham and I had squeezed through into Gatley House last spring.

Graham looked at me. 'What you waiting for? A leg up?'

I grinned and pushed myself up. The effect of the Valium had mostly worn off, but it was still a bit of a struggle to squeeze through. I stumbled clumsily as my feet hit the ground. There was a stifled giggle on the other side of the window and I was about to whisper something witty in my defence when a loud ringing alarm echoed and the intruder floodlights switched on, bleaching the gardens white.

Graham and Lily tumbled out of the window one after the other like they'd been squeezed from a tube. 'What's the plan?' I whispered when the three of us were under the cover of the line of trees.

Security was out in force, torchlight beams pinging like crazy around the grounds as they searched for us.

'The car,' Graham replied, heading towards the wall.

'What?' I said, running after him. 'That thing still works?'

'I fixed it!' He ducked under a low branch. 'Sort of.'

We raced between trees, ignoring the shouts from the building. Up and over the wall — my legs still wobbly from the meds, so Lily had to help me over and I almost folded into three when I landed on the pavement.

Graham shot off ahead towards the Ford Escort, which was parked about fifty yards down the road. He was in the driver's seat and had the lights on by the time Lily and I reached it.

Neither of us needed telling this time. We heaved at the rear of the car to get it moving. The exhaust coughed, the engine spluttered and finally turned over. We climbed inside, me in the front, Lily in the back and the car jerked away.

77

CONSTELLATIONS

A PLASTIC COLA BOTTLE slid off the dashboard into my lap. I looked down at it. Glanced at Graham. He looked at me as if I were mad, nodding furiously. I downed the entire thing. When I finished, I looked at the empty bottle and burped for about five seconds.

Graham shook his head as if I'd done something outrageous, ran his fingers through his sweaty hair and laughed out loud.

'What?'

His face reddened, and his laugh became a cough. The car swerved a bit.

'Eyes on the road, boy!' a gruff voice said from the back seat.

I swivelled round. 'Harry?'

Harry Sparks was sitting next to Lily. He looked old, haggard. A bubble of spittle hung off his lower lip. He still had those piercing eyes though, and he was staring lasers at me. 'After all this, I don't want to hit a tree before we get there.'

'You brought Harry?' I whispered.

Lily nodded. 'Dream team.'

I nodded. Why not? He could see Rigpa Gompa like me and when I got back, I'd need all the help I could get.

Graham checked his rearview mirror and switched on his headlamps. The road sprang into life in front of us.

'Tell me what happened,' I said. 'What did you see at Gatley House?'

'Show her the notebook,' Graham said. 'It's in the bag.'

Lily reached into Graham's bag. She pulled out a few sheets of paper and a notebook.

'It was just a split second,' Graham said. 'But I got the angle. We can work out the rest from there.'

Harry reached forwards and patted Graham's hand. 'Good boy. You have a quick mind... I wish you could have seen it.'

I stared at Graham, then back at Lily. 'Seen what? What did you do? What's in the book?'

Lily opened the notebook and showed me a page with a bunch of random dots jabbed into the paper with a pencil.

I shrugged. 'What is it? Writing? Code?'

Harry leaned forward and placed a finger on the page. 'No.' He tapped the image. 'Constellations.'

I looked at Lily for clarification.

Harry traced his finger as if he were joining up the dots with an imaginary pencil. 'Recognise that?'

'It looks like a dot-to-dot outline of a hat,' I said.

'It's Ursa Major.'

'It doesn't—'

'The Plough?' Lily said. 'Graham mapped the constellations in the sky.'

'So, you saw something?'

Lily grinned. 'Just for an instant. To be honest, I didn't see much.'

'She was a bit more focused on you falling to your death,' Graham said.

'While Graham...'

'No offense or anything, Est, but I was looking up.'

'Harry told him to,' Lily said.

'There's always a moment,' Harry said, from the shadow of the back seat.

No one spoke for a few seconds, Harry's words hanging in the air. Graham took the turning off Wilmslow Road, switched his headlights back off, and slowed down.

'It was nighttime, Est!' Lily said, clicking her fingers. 'Just like that. Day to night!'

'Lil,' Graham said, turning briefly round to look at her 'Let me tell the—'

'Sorry. You go on.'

'Well, I looked up, and it was night. For, I don't know, a second or two.'

'He was going to take a photo,' Lily interrupted again. 'But I reminded him of the rusty hinge. Photos don't work, do they?'

'Yeah, so, she made me bring the pencil.'

'And it was... Graham?' Lily asked, smiling proudly. 'What was it?'

'It was a brilliant idea. OK? A lot better than the Spam.'

'Or the fluffy cuffs?'

'The cuffs actually worked.'

'For like, two minutes...'

'Guys!' I said impatiently. It was a relief to hear them bantering, but for god's sake, would they get to the point!

Graham placed a calming hand on my arm and smiled at the road. 'What we're trying to tell you is, I made a map of the sky directly above Rigpa Gompa.'

'That's great,' I said, without much enthusiasm. 'But what about the valley of Odiyana? The mountains?'

'No!'

'So what's the point? Big deal. You saw some stars.'

'It means,' Harry said, leaning forward again and jabbing his finger at a small 'x' beneath the main constellation, 'that there is your ticket. The Pole Star. The north. With the date and the time, you should be able to figure out its location on a map.'

'We don't need a map,' I said, pointing at the road. 'We know exactly where it is!'

'No. It means... if we need to,' Lily whispered, looking over at Graham, 'if they destroy Gatley House, break the connection, then there might still be a way. Using this to help us and Harry's notes, we might be able to find the physical entrance to Rigpa Gompa.'

I looked at Harry. 'Is that right?'

'Maybe. But I'm not saying it'll be easy. I knew where it was once. It was my job to hide it, but I don't think even I would find it again.'

'So? What does it matter then? It could take months, years... we might never find it. But we know where it is *now*!'

'We know, we know. It's just a... a... failsafe, Est,' Graham said. 'Just in case the worst happens.'

I slumped back in my chair. I should have been pleased at this discovery, but for some reason, I was annoyed. I wanted Graham and Lily to see Rigpa Gompa, but the fact that it could just be found somewhere here on earth somehow cheapened it. You know, a tourist destination on a map for anyone to rock up at, buy the t-shirt, leave crisp packets and cans of coke.

'Lily?' Graham said. 'She needs to see Charlie's maps. We're almost there.'

'Charlie's maps?'

Lily reached inside Graham's bag again. 'You wanted to know how we found you in there? Here.' She took out a couple of folded sheets of paper. 'Take a look at these.'

78

Charlie's Maps

I UNFOLDED THE PAPER on my lap. Charlie had drawn more floor-plans.

In one, I recognised the entrance hall and the waiting room, with the canteen off to the right. Next to it on the same piece of paper was what I guessed must have been the plan for the lower floor: a single corridor with a row of square rooms on either side of it. A dark seated figure was in the third room on the left. Charlie had drawn tiny hair lines coming from it, like a child draws the rays around the circle of the sun. 'This is how you found me?'

'We didn't know you'd be tied up, though,' Graham said angrily. 'We should have locked him in, Lil. We should have tied the bastard up.'

'How did she know I was there?'

Lily shrugged.

'She sees,' Harry said. 'The girl sees.'

'Look at the other one,' Graham said, as he weaved the car along the twists and turns of Boundary Lane.

I placed the second map on top of the first. The design was similar, except in this one the ground floor had a large open room instead of the reception area. A single long corridor led into the rest of the building. 'This is Rigpa Gompa.'

There were steps at the end of the corridor.

'Turn it over,' Harry said.

Charlie had sketched a warren of corridors with square rooms on either side of each passageway. There were two figures in separate rooms. One of them was, like me, a roughly drawn figure surrounded by light rays, the other, down a corridor that branched off the main one, had a face. It was only an inch in diameter. But it was a face. I lowered my head to it.

Charlie had drawn her stepbrother's face, the straight hair, the high cheekbones. He looked sad. Worse than that, he looked *haunted*.

He looked like his best friend had abandoned him...

An acid burn in my stomach rose as I looked down at Simon's image.

I had run away. Let them take him. And when the voices in the Bardo asked me what I wanted, what had I said?

Home.

Why didn't I fight harder? Why didn't I stand with him?

Sharp pain stabbed against my chest. What had I done?

What sort of person does that to a friend?

The sort of person who murders his master... an unwelcome voice inside my head replied.

Tears threatened. The image of Simon's face became blurred. I was finding it hard to breathe.

I felt a pressure against my shoulder. I jumped, let go of the map.

Harry leaned over to me. He whispered in my ear. 'The past does not define your future, Esta. It is defined by what you do in the present moment.'

'Hold on!' Graham cried.

The car hit the curb, jolted hard and screeched to a sudden stop, sending my head crunching against the back of the seat.

'Jesus,' Lily whispered.

'Sorry,' Graham sighed, turning off the headlights. 'Only way I can get it to stop.'

'No,' she said.

'What?'

'That.' She was staring at something outside of the side window. 'How are we going to get through that?'

79

— . —

Two-way Radio

SECURITY AROUND GATLEY HOUSE had stepped up big time since yesterday.

The perimeter fence now extended way beyond the immediate grounds to include the whole of Fletcher's Field. It was all metal and topped with rolls of barbed wire.

Lily was right. There was no way through that.

Climbing it was out of the question. We could ram it with the car but even then, I doubted it would budge, and anyway, I got the impression we'd have a regiment of soldiers pointing guns at us if we tried.

'Well, that went up fast,' Lily muttered.

Graham softly head butted the steering wheel and groaned. 'I didn't even think!'

'You reckon there's another entrance?' I asked.

'What do you mean?'

'Other than the one down at Grover Close?' I pointed along the fence to some dazzling lights at the far western end.

Graham glanced up. 'If it *is* an entrance, it'll be manned by soldiers like the other one. I don't know, maybe I could get another rope. There might be a spot back along the road where they can't see us.'

I had a crazy thought. 'Graham, can you get us closer?'

He didn't seem to hear. He kept on mumbling a bunch of half-baked plans. '... through the trees. I bet they haven't completed the fencing that way. There might be...'

'Graham!' I said again. 'Get us closer to that entrance.'

'OK, OK. What've you got in mind?'

'Just drive, will you?'

He turned the wheel, put his foot down gently. We hobbled off the curb and crawled another few hundred feet towards the bright lights.

'It's a gate,' Graham whispered as we came to a stop. 'And there you go. Three soldiers and another bloody dog. No way through.'

I gazed at it. 'Not unless...'

'What are you thinking?'

I was thinking about the look of abandonment on the drawing of Simon's face. I was *also* thinking about my lesson with Karma Chodron in the Great Hall and my hot and cold attempts at Carving since.

You had to visualise everything perfectly for it to work. Every obstacle, every crack in the ground, every twist and turn... I remembered the door of Rigpa Gompa. *You hit something at the speed of light; you flatten your nose.* I thought of Mr Blakely again. *Cause and effect. Maybe what goes around does always come around.*

'Gray?' I said, slowly folding Charlie's map of Rigpa Gompa into my jeans pocket. 'You reckon you could make them open that gate?'

'What? I dunno. Maybe, but the guards—'

'Let me worry about the guards.'

'And the dog...'

'Yeah, and the dog. Just keep it open for a second.'

'What are you going to do, Est?' Lily asked.

I checked my pockets for the Orb and Bell, then pulled on the door handle. 'A little trick I learned. Gray, I need you to angle the car so the headlights are pointing into the field.'

'I could. But... why? We'll draw attention.'

'I need to see the way obviously, and anyway, they already probably heard us half a mile back.'

He gave me a sarcastic smile, but reversed the car. The back wheels mounted the nearside curb. I got out, and he flicked on his beams. Their light flooded Fletcher's Field for maybe five hundred feet. Beyond was a line of security lighting that was strung up against the inner fence. Somewhere along that fence would be the little yellow 'DANGER OF DEATH' sign marking the gap Graham had cut. I was rather hoping the car's headlights would have picked it out. Given me something to aim for.

Full of doubt, I ducked back inside the Escort. 'Harry? You want to do this?'

'On my own if I have to,' he said and struggled out the other side with Lily's help.

I leaned back against the car and stared at the ground, illuminated by the headlights. There wasn't much to see, just broken earth, a two-stripe path disappearing into the tall grass, maybe some bits of discarded rubble. I gulped. There was probably another five hundred feet of absolute blackness between the two sources of light. I tried to recollect from the other day. *Had there been a ditch? Equipment?* Anything could be lurking in that darkness.

Harry put his hand in mine. I gripped it. He gripped back.

Graham and Lily got out. 'You certain about... whatever this is?' Lily said.

'Honestly? I'm kind of learning that certainty isn't all it's cracked up to be. Just... open the gate. Wide enough for us to both go through. That means you and Graham clearing out of the way... and the soldiers and the dog.'

'What are you going to do?' Graham hissed.

'Trust me. I'll get us through. But... I need you right out of the way. Understand?'

He turned to Lily. 'You think this is a good idea?'

Lily smacked his shoulder. 'Have you not learnt anything over the last few weeks, Gray? Just do what the crazy girl says and apply your considerable brain to figuring out how we get that gate open.'

'Alright!' he said, shaking his head. 'I'm thinking, I'm thinking!'

'You sure about this?' Lily whispered to me.

I nodded back. 'It's the only way.'

'What will you do if you get inside?'

'I don't know. Get Simon. Free Lama la. Save the world?' *And Dad?* I thought.

Lily smiled. 'You'll come back, won't you?'

I nodded. But if I'm honest, I wasn't thinking that far ahead.

'Because, whatever happens.' She glanced up into the night sky. 'You know, we'll come for you.'

'I know.' I glanced up too. The stars were faint. I recalled my physics teachers' lesson about how their light could take millions of years to travel to us. How some of them, even though they shined down brightly on us now, might have actually burnt out long ago. *All a matter of perspective.*

'Take this.'

I looked down. Lily was pulling a black oblong box from her jacket pocket.

'What is it?'

'Two-way radio.' She placed it in my hand. 'Graham's got another one. It's got a range of two miles. You hold down the button to talk.'

I weighed it in my hand. If Harry and I managed to get to Odiyana, I didn't think a two mile range would be enough.

'Just in case...' Lily said. '...you need a getaway car.'

I grinned. Placed the radio in my own pocket. 'Thanks, Lily.'

'Got it,' Graham said suddenly. 'Let's go.'

80

THE OLYMPICS OF BLAGGING

HARRY AND I WALKED hand in hand behind Lily and Graham as they approached the gate. The gate was a double one which opened outwards on two hinges. A bit like the door into the main hall in Rigpa Gompa. It was wide enough for a bus. Width wouldn't be the issue, though. It didn't really matter how wide it was if it remained closed.

'Do you remember the way?' Harry whispered.

I nodded and gulped at the same time. 'Course I do. Back of my hand.'

Graham and Lily reached the spill of light surrounding the gate. The dog's ears pricked up. One soldier stepped forward.

'Wait,' I whispered, my mind making a thousand calculations. 'Let's just hang back here.'

If Graham failed, what could I do? I thought about Carving into the middle of the gate at whatever speed I was capable of. Would that break the lock? It'd almost definitely break a few bones. Harry would probably shatter into a hundred pieces on impact. I was sure that Simon's life and probably the very fabric of reality depended on us getting through that gate. Despite that, blasting through it didn't seem a brilliant move.

Graham and Lily *had* to get it open.

The two of them reached the soldier. Graham began to speak. The soldier—a good half foot shorter than Graham—just stared at him while he talked. Graham finished what he had to say and pointed to the gate.

I shook my head. Graham was what some of the kids at school used to call a 'blagger'. I remembered the story he told Bernard. He was trying his charms now, holding up his left hand and pointing to his bare ring finger.

I took a deep breath and refocused on the ground between us and the gate. *Focus, Est. Blagging is Graham's job. Your job is not to die by steaming into a closed gate at a million miles an hour.*

You ever seen high jumpers at the Olympics when they're mentally preparing to go higher than ever? Bouncing on their toes, blowing air out of their cheeks? That was me... except I was holding the cold hand of an OAP who—in this world at least—could barely hop over a matchbox.

There was about ten feet of road to the entrance; a small curb; a fairly substantial pothole I could easily trip over; a couple of old wooden posts where the cow-gate used to be; a dog turd to the right — most likely supplied by the army issue Alsatian. Definitely wanted to avoid that. The dog *and* the turd. If you can imagine the mess stepping in a dog turd at the speed of light might make... just think what stepping in a *dog* would do.

The soldier turned and walked over to his friend on the other side of the gate. Graham, just like me, bounced on his toes. *The Olympics of blagging.* He glanced back at us. His face was half in shadow...

... but I reckon he winked.

I focused back on the ground by the gate. If it opened, I'd have to time it just right. They wouldn't open them the whole way probably, so we'd have to be perfect. Right through the middle. Like a dart — straight in to the eye of the bull.

'You need to aim a little to the left,' Harry whispered.

'What?'

'You ever Carved with another person in tow?'

'No.'

'You have to account for my weight, or we'll curve to the right. You ready?'

'How do you know—' I stopped mid-sentence. The gate was opening. I don't know what he'd said, but Graham had got the gate open. 'Harry?'

'Yes.'

'Just tell me when.'

I took a deep breath. Closed my eyes. Visualised the route to the gate. Adjusted a couple of feet to account for Harry.

Waited.

The base of the gate scraped gravel as it slowly opened.

Not too soon, Est. Not too soon.

I heard Graham theatrically shout: 'Aha! There you go!'

Took a deep breath. Placed my palms together. 'There is no—'

'Stop,' Harry hissed. 'Wait.'

I tried to keep the route clear in my mind. It was already beginning to fade.

A split second later, Harry whispered, 'Now.'

I said the words...

... and we Carved through space and time.

In my mind's eye, I watched as the darkness blurred together with the electric glow of the security light. I caught a glimpse of Graham and Lily leaping aside; the Alsatian yanking on its lead, jaws open in mid-bark.

A sharp pain sliced through my right arm. There was the dull sound of snapping wood.

The vision became a billion spots of white noise.

I opened my eyes and breathed.

There was a light ahead of us and darkness all around. Harry was with me, breathing hard and bent over, leaning on his cane.

I looked back. The gate was satisfyingly distant.

'We made it!' I whispered. I spun towards Gatley House and smiled. There was the silhouette of a Hawthorne tree. 'We bloody made it!'

'Your arm OK?'

I checked my left arm. The sleeve of my shirt was ripped. There was a gash. But I didn't feel the pain *because I could flipping well fly! And,* I thought proudly, *every time I look at that scar, it's proof!*

'Mr Sparks?' I said when I'd stepped off my cloud. 'Can you walk?'

'You shouldn't be able to do that, you know,' Harry said as we made our way to the DEATH sign.

'Karma Chodron can do it.'

'In Odiyana. Siddhis don't work here so well, though.'

'Well clearly they *do*, because...' I threw a thumb back at the gate we'd just sailed through.

He stopped. 'I've only known one other person capable of moving that fast in the human realm.'

I took his arm. There was torchlight waving at the gateway now. I reckon I'd snapped some the gate off with me as we Carved through and they were wondering what in hell had done it.

'Well,' I said. 'Now you know two.'

81

—.—

Keys to the Front Door

THE GAP IN THE fence was still there.

Harry and I slipped through and into the bushes beyond.

The place had changed since we'd last been here. The trees and sleeping-beauty hedgerow were all gone now. The house, thankfully, was still intact, but everything around it had been cleared away and it stood out like a boil, or some sort of cancerous tumour.

I looked left. Some trees at the southern side of the lawn still made the thinnest of barriers between us and all the activity on Grover Close. The Weeping Willow remained too. Harry seemed particularly happy to see that.

I knew why. I bet the army wasn't in the business of carefully removing memorial stones.

'How are you feeling, Mr Sparks?'

'I get stronger the closer we come. My eyesight is no better, though. Can you see the way?'

My heart sank. The fencing around the house was gone, the shopping trolley was gone. They were hardly going to let a rope stay in place, were they?

'It's not there,' I whispered.

'What isn't there?'

'The rope.'

'What do we need the rope for?'

'There's no other way up to the roof.'

'Why would we need to get in through the roof?' he said, pointing a finger down at my feet.

I looked down. A mist was rising. Above it... both my pockets were glowing.

'I believe,' Harry said, tapping his cane against my hip, 'you already have the keys to the front door, my dear.'

PART SIX

The Advancing Shadows

82

The Shadows Advance

I REMOVED THE BELL and the Orb from my pockets and watched as electricity played along their surfaces.

A freezing breeze snaked through me, bringing with it the smell of wood smoke and something else, something vinegary. I barely noticed the mist expand around us, although it must have done because when I took my eyes off the objects, there were pale shadows on the ground.

It was early morning, and I was standing in disturbed snow outside the courtyard walls of Rigpa Gompa. Same place where I'd seen the army of Black Sadhus a thousand years ago. Thick mist surrounded the Gompa; its windows mere ghostly squares, with only the snow-covered roof floating above. Here and there, pillars of smoke curled upwards towards the peak of the mountain.

Other than that, it was quiet.

Still.

I took out Lily's radio. Pressed the orange 'call' button. White noise. Of course. We were on our own.

I frowned, glanced to my right. Harry was nowhere to be seen. I cursed. Had I flipped alone?

I checked the ground for prints. There were plenty. Some of them pretty huge. I thought of the Rakshasa and looked up again quickly, scanning the grounds. No sign of any creature... just yet. I didn't want to be out here any longer than I had to be though.

I hurried to the courtyard entrance.

Stopped.

Out of a confusion of marks in the snow, a set of regular human prints led off towards the track that went down into the valley; just ahead of them, a single hole in the snow. *Harry's cane.*

I took another glance back at the Gompa. The mist was thinning now. The place looked peaceful, asleep. *Stable* even. Had we already passed through the Bardo? God, I hoped so. I had decided I didn't like Bardos.

I checked my top pocket for Charlie's map, then followed Harry's tracks to the edge of the plateau.

I found him at the top of the steep path. He was leaning on his cane, looking at the valley stretching out below us. My attention was drawn to the mountain path as it wound down from light into shade.

I pictured the procession of monks hauling up Rudra's carriage: that golden curtain, the ruby ring. *Had that been me behind the curtain?*

Despite Lama la's reassurances, I still had a sneaking suspicion that he hadn't told me everything he knew. Or that maybe there was simply stuff he just didn't know.

Why had I been drawn to Rudra's carriage?

Rabjam had said Rudra was trapped in some kind of hell, so if I wasn't Rudra, why had Trisna—the goddess of desire no less—brought me straight to him?

'Are you ready to fight?' Harry said, interrupting my thoughts.

I looked at him guiltily. His cane was raised. He gripped it with white knuckles. For a second, I thought he was going to smash it over my head and send me down the mountainside. Instead, he held it out, pointing down into the valley.

I peered along its shaft. 'What am I looking for?'

The sun had cleared the mountains, but the valley bottom was still in shadow.

'You see them?'

'See who?'

'The shadows.'

I looked again. The valley bottom seemed to ripple.

'They're advancing.'

Dark clouds flowed along the valley, like some horrible muddy river bubbling upstream towards us.

Harry lifted his cane up, angling it up towards the eastern mountains. Oily clouds seeped over them, spilling down the valley walls to join the rising tide below.

'We have about twenty minutes before we're buried shoulder deep in Mamo. Can you Carve back to the Gompa?'

I tore my gaze from the darkness swelling up beneath us. 'I can take us to the wall. We'll have to open the door in it though.'

I held out my arm for him to take hold of. He looked down at it, winked, and placed his own hands together. 'Don't worry,' he said. 'I'll get the door.' He murmured something and, to my astonishment, disappeared in a puff of snow.

83

THE SIDE DOOR

I CARVED AFTER HIM, stopping with my nose an inch from the wall just right of the door.

'Close... but no cigar,' Harry said, wrenching the door open. 'Don't worry. You'll get better with practice.' He walked through. 'And if you're going to survive the next few hours, you're going to get plenty of that.'

Full of surprises, that one.

He was already hammering at the main door to the Gompa by the time I'd Carved to the steps leading up to it.

'No answer,' he growled. 'Cowards.' He kicked the base of the door and yelled at it as if the mere force of his voice would open it.

I looked back across the courtyard. Any minute, black shadows would appear over the top of the wall. If we were stuck out here when they did, I doubted it mattered how fast we could Carve, we'd be wiped out in seconds.

Harry looked up at the walls of the Gompa, shielding his eyes against the sun. 'We could climb...'

'Or,' I said, 'we go in the side entrance?'

'Side entrance?'

I frowned. 'This was your place, right? Come on.' I took him round the corner to the door Lama la had once brought Simon and me out of.

Harry scratched his head. 'I don't remember...'

'It's some sort of basement thing in your old house, I think. Little window?'

I pushed at it; the door didn't open, but it did budge.

'The utility room?' Harry sounded a bit disappointed.

'That's what it was?'

His eyes lost their fierce blue, and he seemed to gaze dreamily at it. 'It's where Carol hung the laundry.'

I shoulder barged it, but bounced off. Tried again. This time there was a faint splintering noise, but otherwise I just succeeded in dislodging Lily's radio from my pocket. It landed in the snow.

I booted the door. 'Mr Sparks. A little help?'

No response.

'Mr Sparks?'

He'd turned round to stare at the courtyard. 'Trees,' he said. 'In the summer, she'd string a line between them. I always told her she was silly, hanging clothes on this side of the house. Barely got any sun.'

I stared down at the radio lying in the snow. If only Lily and Graham were here now. They'd have a plan. I thought of the cans of Spam, the fluffy handcuffs, the spider-man crawl up the wall. Even a rubbish plan would have been an improvement on this.

I glanced at the top of the border wall again. No tendrils of black seeping over yet, but... 'Harry. The door?' I slammed a foot against it again, Bruce Lee style. More creaks, but no joy.

'She said she liked the view... But there was no view. Just a hedge...'

God, was he flipping back into Gatley House? I nudged him.

He looked at me with a smile. 'There you are,' he whispered, and raised a hand to my face.

I took a surprised step back and slapped him on the cheek. I'm not proud of hitting an elderly man. I can't say I planned it, my old little violent streak, I guess. 'Oy!' I shouted and pointed at the wall. 'Mamos! Remember!'

The slap kick-started him. If he *had* been flipping back into Gatley, he was well and truly back with me now. He looked at me, then the door. Put his hands together, closed his eyes, muttered something under his breath and became a blur...

Crack! The door split in two. Harry reappeared, kneeling over the splintered remains.

I nodded appreciatively, *why didn't I think of doing that?*

'You go,' he growled, rubbing his shoulder. 'Free Lama la. I'll hold off whatever tries to come through here.'

I stepped over the door and headed for the stairs that led up into the gompa. Halfway up, I turned. Harry wasn't bothering to fix the door. He stood in the opening, stick in both hands.

Outside, the brightness of the morning had already faded as if a cloud had passed over the sun. Flakes of snow drifted down at Harry's feet. He looked up at me, his eyes burning madly again. 'What are you waiting for? Run, goddamnit.'

84

THE BLACK CLOUD

I SHUT THE DOOR at the top of the stairs and took off along the corridor, stopping at the flight of steps going up to Lama la's study. A strip of light filtered through the curtain over the entrance to Padmakara's shrine opposite. I stood there for a few long seconds, eyes flitting up and down the dark corridor. No noise from either direction.

I chewed my lip, then slid the curtain aside.

The room was cold. A single butter lamp sputtered away at the far end, making dancing shadows against the bare walls and lighting up the immense face of Padmakara. He glared down at me, the massive Orb in his right hand flickering gold.

He looked nothing like the meek-looking monk I'd seen in my memory. Maybe he'd bulked out in middle age? A thought sent a shiver up my spine: *If anything, he looks more like Rudra.*

I'd wanted to know who I'd been in a past life, but Lama la's little lesson about the complexity of history made me ask another question, and this time it was a question for the statue.

Who are you?

The statue didn't respond. 'Nobody knows anything, do they?' I whispered to it.

I peered over the shrine and down through the gap in the floor to the base of the statue and the Great Hall. When I'd left, there had been hundreds of lamps lighting up the place, now just a few spots of light remained. The sand mandala was scuffed and smudged beyond recognition, and from this angle at least there was no sign of the Dharmapalas. I ducked back and brought the map to the candle.

The ground floor with the Great Hall was obvious enough. But what about the other floor? In the car, I'd assumed it had been a plan of the floor I was on now, a part I'd maybe not visited before, but now I was up here, the rooms that Charlie had drawn didn't match up at all. According to the map, I should have been right at the spot where Lama la was being held and there should have been more rooms lining the corridor. But there had only been one set of stairs leading...

Cellars!

Rigpa Gompa had cellars! Of course it did! That would explain why Karma Chodron had seemingly disappeared when she took Lama la away.

I pictured the journey to the end of the corridor. I'd never be able to Carve down the spiral staircase; way too complicated for me to visualise accurately. I'd have to stop at the bottom anyway, because I'd never seen a set of stairs heading beneath ground. But... I looked back down at the map. Where else could it be?

There was a whistling sound from below. I leaned back over the shrine. A breeze blew out the remaining candles, plunging the hall into darkness, and from out of the black cave-like room, a single high-pitched note rang out. That was followed by the ringing of a bell and the steady thump of a drum.

The Dharmapalas *were* down there and they were summoning the protectors!

Over the noise of their music, the sudden machine-gun-fire of hailstones beat against the walls of the Gompa. Then the unmistakable moaning of the Mamo and the teeth grinding *scrraaape* of what could only be a Rakshasa.

The black cloud had finally arrived. Rigpa Gompa was under attack again.

85

Trap Door

I RAN TO THE doorway, lifted the curtain, closed my eyes, visualised the route and said the words. The rising screams and the sound of the hail slowed to a dull roar, like the sound of the sea in a shell; the dark walls of the corridor warped around me.

I skidded to a stop on the second step down the staircase, and the world became sharp and hard again. A high-pitched wailing spiralled up the stairwell.

I stared down into black. Took three or four quick breaths. Pulled the Orb and Bell from my pockets. They still glowed, just enough to light up a fragile sphere around me.

I headed down.

The furious drumming and chanting from the Great Hall was loud at the bottom of the stairs. The shadows were as thick as Marmite though, and the Orb and Bell barely gave a foot of vision. I placed them on a step and took out the map again. There had to be a way down in to the basement. Charlie's plan showed the corridor I was in now—I squinted down at the drawing—*Was there a mark right at the end there?* Had Charlie drawn a mark by the stairwell? A secret door?

I picked up the Orb and brought it to the wall, tracing its vague glow up and down, side to side. No sign of a door.

A single long high note from the horn blasted down the corridor, making the hairs on my arm rise. *That'll be Sera,* I thought.

The horn suddenly stopped; the drumming and chanting all stopped as well. Raised voices, the whine of tables being pushed against the floor. Shouting.

I swore. Returned to searching the wall. There *had* to be a way down.

A scream.

I looked back into the darkness. A human scream came from the Great Hall. *Sera.*

A crash. Splintering wood. A sudden stream of stinking, hot air filled the corridor. *The demons have broken through their defences.*

Pitch black shadows formed into shapes around me. Tiny specks of scarlet twisted and swirled like the spitting embers of a fire; chattering voices echoed from wall to wall; the stench of rotting flesh burned the inside of my nostrils.

I backed up against the wall, one arm reaching behind me for the bell I'd left on the stairs. The darkness pressed in, shrinking the tiny circle of light from the Orb even more. The foul-smelling breeze grew into a stronger wind that tugged at Charlie's map. The walls whispered: *Depresta, Depresta, Detesta...*

The swirling embers seemed to blink at me.

A sudden gust ripped the map from my fingers, whipping it away.

Footsteps.

Something crashed into my thigh, bounced off, and thudded to the ground with a squeal.

'Tubten?'

The young monk was picking himself up off the floor. I held out my free hand to help him up.

'Tub!' came a shout. 'Don't let her touch you!'

I looked up.

A figure stood at the edge of the light, spear pointed at me. 'Tubten,' it said. 'Get up and get over here.'

I raised the Orb a little higher to illuminate my face. 'Karma Chodron, it's me.'

The nun pushed Tubten behind her. 'Get out of the way.'

There were more footsteps. Rabjam and Sera.

'Esta?' Rabjam whispered.

'Rab, is everyone OK?'

'What are you doing here?' Karma Chodron hissed.

'Where's Simon?'

Karma Chodron's silhouette raised its spear a little higher. 'He told us how you let Trisna inside...'

'What does that matter now? We have to free Simon and Lama la.'

'You did this!' Karma Chodron said. 'Rigpa Gompa stood safe for a thousand years before you came.'

'I didn't mean to... It's not like I just gave—'

Scrraape.

I stopped. Turned toward the Great Hall.

'Raksha,' Sera whispered. 'A Rakshasa inside Rigpa Gompa.'

Karma Chodron whirled round to face the noise. Before she did, her eyes flicked down to something at my feet. It was only the briefest of glances. It would have been easy to miss, but...

I followed her eyes. Lowered the Orb. Its glow reflected off a ring of metal.

The handle of a trapdoor.

There was a sound like fingernails on chalkboard from down the corridor. The others shifted their stance to face whatever was coming.

I took the chance. Dropped to a crouch and heaved at the ring.

The trapdoor flipped open.

Stone steps led down into darkness.

I grabbed the Bell and dived through; the door slamming shut above me.

I slid a dead bolt across—hardly any match for Sera if she decided to double in size, but it might give me a few seconds—then turned and made my way down into the dungeons of Rigpa Gompa.

86

—·—

The Dungeons of Rigpa Gompa

AT THE BOTTOM OF the stairs was a dimly lit passageway. Heavy wooden doors lined on either side ten feet apart.

Lama la and Simon had to be behind two of those doors.

Charlie had drawn Lama la in a room about halfway down the main corridor. Simon's room had been at the end of a series of twists and turns.

The sound of splintering wood from above. The trapdoor still held, but probably not for long.

The lamps in the dungeons were brass goblets, each filled with oil and a single wick. Twenty feet away, two of these lamps stood on either side of what I guessed was Lama la's cell door. I closed my eyes and Carved the distance.

The door was solid. I tugged at a metal hoop. It didn't even budge in my hands. I banged on the door, shouting: 'Lama la!'

No answer.

'Even if you opened it.'

I jumped.

Karma Chodron was standing right behind me. 'You wouldn't be able to free him.'

She was about six feet away; her spear pointed at me. Behind her, Rabjam and Tubten were hurrying down, tendrils of black smoke curling down the steps after them.

'We have to get it open!' I said, still tugging on the hoop.

Karma Chodron jabbed the spear at me. 'Move away!'

'Bloody hell Karma Chodron. You really think *I'm* the problem here?' I pointed up at the ceiling.

'You let her in! You gave away the Kila!'

I released the hoop. 'Yeah? Well, I seem to remember you weren't much help at the time!'

'It wasn't me who handed over our only weapon.'

'I had to wake you up. Remember that?'

The tip of her spear wobbled. 'I was concentrating on the ceremony!'

'What are you doing?' Rabjam called.

He and Tubten had made it to the bottom of the stairs now. Ankle deep in smoke.

Karma Chodron glanced over her shoulder. Strengthened her grip on the spear. 'I've got this Rab. Go back upstairs and help Sera!'

'KC?'

'Rab. Damn it. Go back!'

'Listen to yourself,' I said. 'You want to lock us all up? Who next? Rabjam? Tubten?'

'KC,' Rabjam said carefully. 'What if she's right about Lama la? Maybe we should—'

'And what if she's wrong?' Karma Chodron snapped.

'At least let me get Simon!'

'You don't know what you're doing. Free him, and you could be making this a thousand times worse.'

There was another long, drawn out *scrraaape* from above.

Tubten whimpered. 'Exactly how is this going to get worse, KC?'

'Who are you, Esta Brown? Why are you here?'

'I don't know,' I said. 'But I know that we're all on the same side. We all want to stop this...' I glanced up at the ceiling again. '...this chaos.'

Her eye twitched. Her knuckles flexed against the shaft of her spear. 'If you were the tulku of Padmakara, you'd fight with us.'

I spread my arms wide. 'Fight? What with?'

'The Vajra and Bell.'

'That's Simon, remember? Not me.' I held up the objects. They glowed. But really faintly. 'I can't get anything out of them!' I looked back at Lama la's door. 'Rab, is Simon's door the same as this one?'

Rabjam. 'I don't know. Most of them just have deadbolts on the outside. Why? Esta?'

I placed my hands together, bowed my head and closed my eyes... Karma Chodron might hold the key to Lama la's door, but not Simon's.

87

— . —

Carve Race

THERE WAS A CLATTER of wood on stone just as I began to Carve. Karma Chodron must have realised what I was doing and dropped her spear so she could do the same.

The walls of the dungeon rose and bent as I cut through the damp air. In my mind's eye, the corridor ended at a sort of T-junction. I slowed... a bit too late, grazing the wall. I opened my eyes, catching a glimpse of the next row of doors. This corridor was about forty feet.

There was a flash of blue as Karma Chodron rushed past me. Surely heading for Simon. I just had to follow.

I Carved after her, her blue robes rippling as she surged away.

Twenty feet to a left turn. This time I didn't stop at all. I tilted my body, kicked at the wall, and spun off it. The smudge of blue that was Karma Chodron was already at the next corner. I saw the briefest flash and was there in a millisecond; I turned...

... and went flying head-over-heels.

In the slow motion blur, I could see Karma Chodron backed up against the wall, the foot I'd tripped over still raised in the air. I had time to tuck the Orb and Bell into my body and curl up into a foetal position.

I opened my eyes.

The passageway snapped into vivid solidity again just before I collided with the stone floor, grazing pretty much every bit of exposed skin.

I raised my head just in time to see Karma Chodron push away from the wall and become a blue stripe down the passageway towards me. Before I could react, a bare foot struck my stomach, making me curl up even more.

I heard a bolt slide. The creak of a heavy door.

Karma Chodron grabbed my hair, forcing me up, and dragged me across the floor. 'I don't know who you are. But I can't take the risk.'

'Karma...' I grunted. 'I can help.'

'Enough of your lies!'

There was a shout from behind one of the doors. Simon must have heard us.

I didn't have the energy to fight Karma Chodron. She was much too strong for me. So, instead, I dropped the Bell on her bare foot. It had the desired effect. She briefly loosened her grip enough for me to get my palms back together.

The passageway ended in a blank wall a hundred feet down. Nice and straight. Easy to visualise.

I closed my eyes and Carved free of Karma Chodron.

But Carve where?

I swiftly searched through the slowly fading mental image of the passageway.

Bingo.

There was a door about thirty feet away with butter lamps on either side of it. That had to be him. I headed towards it.

There was a frazzle of energy at my back as Karma Chodron split the air behind me. I wouldn't have time to stop and work the lock... so I took a leaf out of Harry's book, nudged to the right to make an angle, turned sharply as I reached the door and kicked out at the wall.

At the very last instant, I turned my shoulder and braced for impact.

88

STAY PUT AND DON'T GET KILLED

THE DOOR SPLIT. I opened my eyes. The world snapped into focus and everything sped up. Momentum slammed me in to a straw mattress that lay against the far wall.

'Esta?'

I stood up. The room spun. Ringing in my ears. A couple of Simons gawked at me from the smashed door. Something warm trickled down the back of my neck and my arm hung down at my side like some sort of stage prop.

'Esta?' Simon asked, his voice all echoey. 'What the hell are you doing?'

I thought about that for a second while I swayed on my feet. *What* was *I doing?*

I thought about throwing up. Thought about falling down. I reckoned serious pain was probably on its way, but for the moment, I was just numb.

I cocked my head at Simon. *So what happens now?*

When I was about seven, I came back from school in a right state.

I'd fallen off a swing. Properly scraped my knee. It hadn't hurt. I was just shocked and embarrassed and by the time I'd run home I was so exhausted I could barely see. I had no key, so I curled up on the step to wait for Mum or Dad to come home.

It was Mum who peeled me off the front step where I'd fallen asleep. When I woke up, I was in the kitchen and she was dabbing my knee with a cloth. A trail of blood droplets ran from the front door up to my knee.

Now it stung like hell. 'How come I didn't feel it?' I asked her through clenched teeth. 'How come I ran all the way home and never felt it?'

'Magic juice,' she told me. 'Your body pumps you full of it in an emergency. Makes you invincible for just long enough to do what you have to do.'

'But it hurts now.'

'Of course it does. You did what you had to do. You got home. That was your superpower today, Est. But even superheroes have to pay the price, eventually.'

So, I stayed on my feet while the room tried to tip me over, while Simon gawped, while Karma Chodron bristled in the doorway. There would be a price to pay. But I promised to pay it a little later.

'What are you doing?' Simon repeated.

'Coming to save you?'

Sccraaape.

Simon exchanged a look with Karma Chodron. A flash of fear crossed her face. She said something to him I couldn't hear, then stepped back into the passageway.

She bowed, put her hands together, but before she could Carve away, a tidal wave of smoke took her.

Voices echoed out in the corridor. Mocking laughter, poisonous words.

Simon screamed out and tried to follow her. I had to drag him back into the room with my one good arm. 'Wait, you idiot!'

Simon shrugged me off him. Prepared to launch himself out of the door again. But something made him pause this time.

The shadows outside were gaining shape. Twisting into unpleasant forms, filling the corridor with hundreds of those maddening, blinking eyes.

He turned to face me, face white as a sheet. 'We have to help.'

I nodded. 'I know. Hold this.' I handed him the Orb. 'Now. Help me with this arm. I bust it.'

'What are you doing?'

'Just help me lift it up, will you?'

I chomped down on my lip to stop a scream as Simon lifted my broken left arm up to meet my right.

I joined my palms together. 'I need to get something. In the meantime, stay put and don't get killed.'

89

It Has to be Simon

I CARVED BACK UP the long corridor. This time through a cloud of vile-smelling smoke.

I opened my eyes when I reached the corner where Karma Chodron had grabbed me. The smoke was only knee deep here, no more than a black stream. Gleaming beneath its surface, just where I dropped it, was the Bell.

If we were going to escape from this, I had to get it to Simon.

I bent to pick it up.

'Tubten! Stay behind me!'

Sera. Somewhere to my right. I grabbed the Bell. If Sera and Tubten were coming, maybe Rabjam was here too. If I could find them, bring them together with Simon and the Orb and the Bell, then we had a fighting chance against the Mamo.

Scrraaape.

I froze. Glimpsed the yellow of Sera's robes through a dirty mist. Tubten cowering behind them. Beside her, a flash of white as Harry swiped at something with his glowing cane. His hair fanning out around his head.

A clawed arm swooped out of the darkness.

He parried it. Staggered backwards.

I quickly checked behind me. A river of smoke filled the passageway back to Simon.

A terrible roar. Tubten screamed.

Something clattered at my feet.

Harry's broken cane skidded to a halt against my shin. I stared at it for five long seconds.

It no longer glowed.

I looked up. Sera, Tubten and Rabjam were backing away from a Rakshasa. The creature was too big for the space, but somehow it had squeezed itself in. Its two arms tore at the ground, dragging the rest of its body forwards, the walls and ceiling disintegrating around it.

I had to do something, or it would bring the whole Gompa down on top of us.

I rang the Bell.

Its sound was pathetic in the darkness, about as effective as a bicycle horn on a jumbo jet.

It had never worked for me. I looked down at my useless arm.

I was no good to anyone here.

It has to be Simon.

I swore, glanced back at the retreating Dharmapalas, then turned and headed into the cloud of Mamo.

90

BEEN THERE, SEEN THAT

THE SMOKE THICKENED AROUND me into soft, greasy flesh. Half-formed Mamos emerged out of it: long limbs stretching out, taking shape and solidity. Their eyes bulging, their teeth chattering, their red tongues quivering.

I could sense their greed, could smell their disease, and I knew what they craved. *Fear. Pain. Misery.*

Their sickness oozed out, infecting everything around them. They tried to cling to me with their oily fingers. Hissing, cracking voices singing and whispering:

'*Detesta Brown. She invited us in.*
She wears the crown. It's made of tin.'

I pushed forward, feeling the weight of the Mamo as they became more solid, more real. Their sharp fingernails catching my shirt, slithering through my hair.

'*Depresta Brown. This is the end.*
She murdered her father. She killed her friends.'

It was like wading through estuary mud, dragging me down, dragging me in.

I swiped at leering faces that bent and twisted in the smoke.

'*Bound by hatred and bound by bone.*
Esta Brown is all alone.'

The fingers became hard, the bodies of the Mamo jagged and bony, nearly fully formed now.

I glimpsed something between their writhing limbs. Simon, his face golden in the glow of the Vajra. He was battling his own tide of smoke, lashing out at it with the Orb.

'Don't breathe!' he shouted. 'Esta! Don't breathe it in!'

I held my breath. Dragged myself through the sea of arms and legs. I had to get through. Had to get through.

But my eyes were becoming dim, and my lungs were burning up.

Sccrraappe.

The black shape of another Rakshasa. At the end of the passageway. Bony limbs illuminated every time Simon swung the Orb towards it. A dash of colour in its skull cup. A strip of bright blue cloth.

'*I'm so scared, Daddy!*' the Mamo whined around me.

Another wave of smoke broke and crashed against the walls and it was like I was drowning in a grey sea.

'*No, Daddy!*' the Mamo wailed. '*I'm too scared.*'

I stopped struggling. Someone solid stood in my way. An ugly figure, its face sneering at me hungrily, its features folding in on themselves, contorting first into my dad and then, like it had changed its mind, into something, leaner, sharper, more weasel-like... I squinted at it. It took a moment to realise what was forming before my eyes, what nightmare shape the Mamo had decided to become.

Bernard?

I straightened my back, ignoring the clawing fingers trying to pull me down. 'Really?' I said incredulously. 'Bernard? The orderly?' I reached down for my useless left arm.

'*Feel the fear,*' the Bernard lookalike mocked, bringing his odious face up to mine; hot, sticky breath streaming through its yellowing teeth.

I shook my head at it and whispered through gritted teeth. 'Did you...' I lifted my left arm, pain shooting down my body. '... miss a meeting?'

The Mamo cocked its head.

I locked my hands together and visualised the corridor ahead.

Bernard sneered and opened his mouth: 'Depresta Br—'

He didn't get to finish.

I Carved right through him. He came apart as if he were sodden paper, dissolving back into the sludgy smoke from where he had oozed.

'Been there,' I gasped, opening my eyes. 'Seen that.' Then collapsed to my knees.

I'd only Carved five feet. Enough to obliterate the Bernard Mamo, but not to escape the rest of them.

Their grip thickened around my ankles.

'Esta!'

I looked up. Ahead of me, Simon was desperately trying to fight off his own tangle of demons.

'Simon!' I croaked with the very last wisp of breath I had. I flung the Bell as hard as I could towards him.

I opened my mouth and breathed in the acrid air.

There was a dull thud as the Bell hit the hard stone floor. I tried to look, but the smoke bit at my eyes. There was a rattle, perhaps the sound of the Bell bouncing a couple of times, maybe skidding against a wall.

The poison snaked inside of me. My ears filled with a hundred whispers about death and hate and fear and disgust. I squeezed my eyes shut, punched the ground like a three-year-old.

'Pick it up!' I sobbed. 'Simon, pick it up!'

91

Rakshasa Are Not Just For Christmas

TING.

Quietly, like a cowbell way down in the valley.

Ting, ting.

Gaining rhythm.

Ting, ting, ting.

Louder. A crackle of static electricity.

And words. Chanting in a low melody.

The pressure of limbs against my body melted away.

I opened an eye. The passageway was clear. Swimming-pool-blue light washed the stone walls and floor.

Seated right in the middle of it was Simon, Orb in one hand, Bell in the other.

I grinned… and coughed out a lungful of hot, stinking air. My eyes streamed. I spat the polluted air onto the floor and sucked in fresh oxygen. Retching and gasping until the poison was all out.

When I'd finished, I rolled on to my back, chest heaving. Lay there for a minute, letting my muscles relax and staring up at the ceiling, enjoying the silence.

I frowned. *Silence?*

The ringing and the chanting had stopped. But in their place was some sort of rumbling that made the stone beneath me shiver.

Where was Simon's smiling, triumphant face looming over me?

Sccrraappe.

The sound grated on my bones and froze the breath in my lungs. I turned on to my right side and stared down the passageway

Sccrraappe.

The smoke and the Mamo were gone. But the dark form of the Rakshasa was still there. And, for some reason, Simon was walking right towards it. He'd left the Orb and Bell on the ground behind him.

The stones vibrated.

I pushed myself up and limped down the corridor after Simon.

'Simon!' I called.

He stopped about fifteen feet from the Rakshasa. Stood there staring at it. It didn't seem to notice he was there.

What are you doing?

I reached the Orb and Bell, picked them up. The Bell made a dull clunking noise. The thing was dented and the sound it made might as well have come from an old door bolt.

'Simon!' I hissed.

He didn't respond. Just stood still, watching the Rakshasa as it made odd, darting movements at the end of the passage.

I swore, then hobbled over. 'We have to go,' I whispered when I reached him. 'Lama la will know what to do.'

Simon shook his head. Pointed at the beast.

And now I could see.

Karma Chodron was still alive. Her robes were missing a strip and were stained in blood. She was pinned against the wall, trapped between the two great arms of the beast.

The Rakshasa roared. Lunged.

There was a flash of blue and Karma Chodron appeared just inches away from its closing fangs.

The thing shook its head, turned and prepared to lunge again. Karma Chodron bowed and disappeared. The beast refocused and went for her again.

A deadly game of cat and mouse.

Each time the thing lunged, Karma Chodron Carved away from it like a matador side-stepping a raging bull. But she could only Carve a few feet before hitting flesh. Obviously the Rakshasa was built of firmer stuff than a Mamo. No sooner had she disappeared than she appeared again and the Rakshasa adjusted itself for a clear shot at her.

'She's not going to last for long,' Simon said.

I tried to hand him the Orb and Bell. 'Can't you try at least?'

He took the Bell off me, without taking his eyes off Karma Chodron. 'It doesn't work on that thing. We have to distract it. Give her a chance.'

'What?' I looked around for something we could use as a weapon. I thought of Harry's cane back down the passage. If I could bring my arm up, I could be there and back—

'Hey!' Simon shouted, clanking the Bell at the monster.

Karma Chodron looked up at the sound, but the Rakshasa ignored him and lunged again. She managed to Carve, but this time she wasn't fast enough. The Rakshasa lifted its head. Blood dripped from one of its fangs.

'No!' Simon jerked forward.

I grabbed at him, pulling him back. 'What are you doing?'

He whirled round, his face ablaze. 'She's got the key to the eternal knot. Lama la's the only one who can stop this now.' He struggled out of my grip. 'And she's the only one who can free him!'

'Wait for the others!' I pleaded. 'Sera's coming.'

'No time.'

'This is suicide.'

He looked at me. Eyes wide with fear.

'Simon...'

He gave me a weak smile. 'Thanks for coming back.' He turned to face the Rakshasa. 'But you should probably go now.'

I wanted to pull him back with me. There had to be another way, but I was too weak. Simon took a couple of steps, looked down at the Bell in his hand. Considered it.

For a moment, I thought he was going to play the Bell again. I even held out the Orb for him to take off me. Instead, he lifted it and hurled it at the monster's head.

I watched as the glowing metal sailed away in the dim light.

It struck the Rakshasa's jaw. It flinched and turned its coal red eyes towards us.

Simon screamed and waved his arms over his head in a mad danced.

Rage rippled across the beast's face. It turned, and one arm snapped out towards Simon, cutting off his voice in an instant. Claws wrapped around him and flung him against the wall.

'Simon!' I shouted, my throat hoarse. I tried to pull my arm up again so I could Carve to him.

But pain ran through me like a sword and I fell to my knees.

The Rakshasa shifted around to smother Simon with its massive arm. It raised its head, opened its jaws, and made an ear-splitting screeching sound.

Simon held up a puny arm to protect himself.

Then the head of the Rakshasa dropped to feast.

92

Beautiful Esta

THERE WAS A NOISE like a thousand fog horns all blaring at once.

Then a blinding flash.

Like someone setting off a camera flash bulb right in front of your eye, so that, for a moment, it's like the light has entered your brain... filled it up, pushing out any thought or memory.

Then it faded away, leaving a hundred dazzling mini rainbows in its place.

A gentle whisper caressed my ears:

Beautiful Esta...

Nope, I thought. *Not listening.*

Can you see?

I closed my eyes. I didn't want to see anything. But a green valley emerged far below. A mountain rose before me, a path cut into its sheer slope.

What do you desire, Esta Brown?

A line of monks climbing the impossible path.

I can show you...

We were back. Back in time to the caravan marching up the mountain; back to the owner of a hand with the ring on its finger.

Trisna had always known what I had really wanted. She'd tapped into the deepest part of my mind.

What do you yearn for?

All this time, I thought I'd been searching for Dad... But there had been something even more deeply ingrained into my mind, something carved in, deep as the words on Dad's memorial stone.

I hadn't been searching for him.

The hand: its golden ring, the rest of the body hidden behind the curtain.

The thing I had been yearning for was...

...a return.

Trisna's voice.

It was you who gave me the Kila. You who opened the realms.

'Who am I?' I whispered.

There was an avalanche of giggling. Then: *You are what you desire, Esta Brown.*

See...

And now, replacing the valley, was an image of Rudra as he stooped over the corpse of his master.

I floated over him as he approached the shrine, his eyes red with tears. Watched as he reached out, his face darkening, plucking an object from the table, squeezing his fist around it.

The Orb.

Rudra had taken the Orb from the shrine. He had lifted it, just as I had lifted the exact same object that night in Gatley House.

'He's in hell,' I whispered. 'He can't come back.'

Yesss, whispered a chorus of voices.

The image died, replaced with a white Orb rippling against a black background.

What do you desire, Esta Brown?

I tried to blink away the image. But as it faded into black, I could hear the voices whispering:

Ruuddraaa...

93

THIS ISN'T OVER

THE SOUND OF FOOTSTEPS woke me. The ground was reassuringly hard. Definitely not floating anywhere.

I sniffed. The air was clean. As clean as a dungeon can be, anyway. I turned my head to the left.

The Rakshasa had disappeared. In its place: two spots of glowing light on the floor and a dark Simon-shaped shadow lying unmoving against the wall.

'Simon?' I whispered.

The shadow groaned.

I shifted my gaze right. Two figures were coming towards me out of the darkness: one, wide and heavy looking, the other tall and thin. Each carried something. The tall one held something large and dark and obviously heavy in one hand, the other cradled a body in its arms.

'Simon?' I croaked, trying to push myself up. Failing.

'Shh,' the tall figure said as it reached me. It placed the heavy object down with a clunk of metal on stone. 'Drink this. You'll feel better.'

A little dry laugh escaped my lips. *A kettle,* I thought dimly. *Rabjam dragged a kettle down into the dungeons? Course he did.*

Rabjam poured tea and placed the cup to my lips. It smelled of chicken soup. I sipped. Warmth trickled down my throat. My left arm tingled with feeling. *Man, this stuff is good.*

'Simon?' I asked after I'd downed half the cup.

Rabjam nodded and refilled my cup. 'I'm going to him now. Sera? Make sure she drinks it all.' He dragged his kettle away.

I don't know if it was the effect of the tea, or if my eyes were just getting used to the dark but I could make out colours in the gloom now: the yellow of Sera's robes and the red of Tubten's in her arms.

'Is he OK?'

She lowered him down next to me so his head rested against the wall, too. 'Sleeping.'

I wiped a streak of dirt from his cheeks. They were wet. I glanced back at where Rabjam was serving Simon his tea. They were talking. Good sign.

I looked up at Sera. 'What happened?'

'Lama la happened,' she said. 'Karma Chodron freed him.'

I gave a satisfied sigh. 'So what was the noise? The light?'

'He must have blown the conch. Raksha trembled at the sound. Then...' She made a swatting gesture.

I closed my eyes for a second and smiled. Tubten stirred against me. The weight of his head dropped to my shoulder. 'And you?' I asked. 'How are you, Sera?'

'I've faced Raksha before,' she said. 'My bones are strong. I don't break so easy.'

I suddenly remembered the way Harry's broken cane had landed by my feet. *Oh no.* 'Mr Sparks? What happened to the old man?'

Sera paused before answering. 'Angry.'

I looked up, surprised. 'Angry?'

She nodded.

'As in, *alive* and angry?'

She pointed a thumb over her shoulder. 'Broke fighting stick. Trying to fix.'

'Thank God. Where is he?'

Before Sera could respond, there was a rush of air, a flash of blue and Karma Chodron —ragged, bloody and out of breath—appeared.

She looked me up and down. 'Can you move your arm?'

I nodded. The tea was doing its job. I had feeling back in it. I flexed my fingers.

'Good. We have to go to the Great Hall. Can you remember the way?'

'I think—'

'I'll bring the others. You take Tubten.'

'Give us a sec. I'm just finishing my tea here.'

Karma Chodron glared down at me. 'If you let him come to any harm, I'll do to you what Lama la did to the Raksha.'

I looked over to where Simon was slowly getting up.

'Can't I see with Simon first?'

'No!' she shouted. 'Don't you understand?' She put her palms together. 'This isn't over!'

Then she held Sera's hand, and they both disappeared in a rush of blue and yellow.

94

REUNION

I DIDN'T CARVE THE whole way back to the Great Hall. For one thing, I couldn't visualise all the twists and turns of the dungeons and for another, I'd still not figured out how to climb stairs during a Carve either. They were tricky to navigate in normal time, let alone at the speed of light.

Karma Chodron sped past me a couple more times, once to carry Simon, then again for Rabjam.

I, on the other hand, took a couple of wrong turns and gave myself a few more bruises, each time managing to shield the still sleeping Tubten from major damage.

By the time I finally found the Hall, Tubten was blinking awake, and the others were already assembled in a horseshoe shape around Lama la's throne. Around them, filling most of the hall, was a wall of pearl-coloured light.

'Esta!'

Simon limped over to me, his clothes muddy, his face grimy, his crystal blue eyes shining in the lamplight. For a moment I thought he was going to hug me, but he stopped awkwardly a couple of feet away as if there were some sort of invisible shield between us.

He wiped his brow. 'Erm,' he stuttered. 'We...' he rolled onto the balls of his feet and sort of bounced there as if waiting for something.

I looked down. Tubten was staring up at me from my arms. 'Hello lady,' he said. His face cracking into an enormous, snotty grin.

I laughed and dropped him to his feet. He scurried off, and I was suddenly smothered in Simon's arms. His face buried against my neck, breathing heavily. 'You came back,' he breathed. 'You came back for me.'

I smiled and wrapped my arms around him. 'You crazy bugger,' I whispered.

He pulled away and looked at me with glistening eyes. 'How did you know?'

'Know that you're a crazy bugger?'

'Know that I'm safe. That I'm not Rudra.'

I felt a frost touch my cheeks. Shrugged. 'I just did.'

His smile returned, and he hugged me again. Kind of squeezed the air out of me, actually.

'When you've finished?' came a dry, impatient voice. Karma Chodron was glowering at us. 'Get over here.'

95

THE CAUSE OF CHAOS

THE SEVEN OF US—ME, Simon, Harry and the four Dharmapalas—stood in silence, feet on the mess of coloured sand left over from the broken mandala.

Lama la was seated on his throne, purple robes around him like a tent, his lined face poking out, all grim and stony, misty light pouring from an Orb and Bell he held. 'Well?' he said after a while. 'What are you just standing around for? Get to work.'

The effect of his words was immediate. Sera immediately dropped to her cushion and picked up one of the long horns. Rabjam sat down beside her and began leafing through his prayers. Two more Tubtens appeared and picked up a hand drum each.

Karma Chodron didn't move, though. She stayed put, staring glumly at her feet.

'We have all been deceived,' Lama la said, as if reading her thoughts. 'Karma Chodron. We have all made mistakes.'

'But... I locked you up.'

Sera blew into the horn. A long, loud, tuneless blast.

Lama la waited for it to subside. 'Your intention was to protect. So was mine.'

She bowed her head even lower, not taking her eyes off him.

Lama la nodded back. 'Time is against us, now though and of course...' he glanced at me. 'The Kila is gone.'

Subtle. Thanks.

Rabjam looked up from his seat: 'We still have the symbols. Tubten could repair the mandala?'

Lama la sighed. 'Ah. Yes, the ceremony. Of course.'

When it was clear he wasn't going to add to that, Rabjam elbowed Tubten and pointed down at the scattered sand on the floor. 'Make another one, Tub.'

The boy put down his hand drums, closed his eyes, and suddenly three of his brothers flickered into life. Each one seemed to know their job, because, while the original Tubten picked up his drums again, the others set to work.

The rest of us moved out of their way as one Tubten swept up the sand around our feet; another collected up the tools they'd used to sift the coloured sand before; and another one started re-drawing the outline of the wheel of life.

Lama la watched everything from his throne. 'Everything is changing,' he murmured. 'And yet nothing has changed.'

'What's that supposed to mean?' Simon whispered.

There was a loud click. Harry Sparks had tapped the remains of his cane against one of the tables. 'It was you, wasn't it?'

Karma Chodron lifted her gaze from the floor to Harry.

Harry was staring directly at Lama la. 'It was you who opened the Bardo of Becoming.'

Karma Chodron scowled at him. 'You don't know what you're talking about!'

Harry walked forwards, ignoring her. 'You got the Dharmapalas to remove the symbols from each realm, didn't you?'

Karma Chodron's frown deepened. 'So we could end the chaos!'

Harry shook his head. 'Removing them *caused* the chaos.' He paused. 'Isn't that right, old friend?'

Lama la tipped his head a little. Could have been a 'yes', or he could have been merely cricking his neck.

Karma Chodron switched her gaze to Lama la. 'That isn't true.' But she said it like a question.

Finally, Lama la spoke: 'The White Sadhus would have stolen them, anyway.' He looked at Karma Chodron, then at Rabjam. 'You know. You saw them.'

'White Sadhus?' Simon asked.

'The White Sadhus,' Harry explained, 'are a sect of disciples who remain loyal to Rudra.'

An icy shiver ran down my spine at the sound of that name again. 'Why would they still be following Rudra?' I whispered back. 'He's... you know. In some forever hell thing.' I looked around me for confirmation. Rabjam nodded. I looked at Lama la. His eye twitched.

'So what do they want with the symbols?' Simon asked.

'From what I know, the symbols were the keys to each realm.' Harry said. 'While they were in place, the Wheel of Samsara turned as it always has. The law of cause and effect intact.' He raised his cane, pointing at Lama la. 'Removing them broke the chain. An old master like you would know that.'

'I had no other choice. The temples in each realm were weak. No match for an army of White Sadhu. Rabjam, you saw them?'

Rabjam bowed. 'Everywhere we went, master. White Sadhus were either there already, or followed us.'

'Then you know why we had to gather the symbols here. It is the only safe place for them.'

'But why? Why now? Why do they want the symbols?' Tubten asked.

There was silence while Lama la appeared to contemplate this; just the crackling sound of the protection circle, Sera's gentle chanting, and the tapping of a hand drum. I glanced at Simon, catching his eye. He looked quickly away.

It was Harry who broke the silence this time. 'Chaos.'

Everyone now turned to him.

'If the link between cause and effect is distorted. Consequences are unhinged from their causes.'

Lama la's gaze dropped to his lap.

'Mr Sparks?' Simon asked. 'What are you saying?'

'He's saying,' Rabjam answered, 'that while we remain in the Bardo of Becoming, the link between cause and effect is broken...'

'I know that's bad, but...?'

'But... it means, until we leave the Bardo, there's nothing to stop Rudra from escaping hell.'

96

The Whispered Lineage

THE GREAT HALL WAS hot, the air musty with incense and candle smoke. No one moved. Each of us quietly getting our heads around what Rabjam had just said.

Simon took a step towards Lama la. 'I want to get this clear, because I'm confused. A group called...' he looked behind him at Harry.

'The White Sadhu,' Harry supplied.

Simon looked back towards Lama la. 'Right. The White Sadhu are trying to free this... murderer, Rudra from hell by breaking the law of cause and effect?'

Lama la tilted his head to one side.

'And so you could stop them, you got me and the Dharmapalas to remove these symbols from their temples... which was the exact same thing they were trying to do in the first place.'

Lama la nodded.

'Isn't that kind of...?' He left it at that. But we all knew what he wanted to say. What the hell was the old man up to?

'Why?' Karma Chodron whispered.

Lama la finally spoke: 'It is not so simple, Karma Chodron. There are wheels turning within wheels and—'

'Don't!' she screamed suddenly. The sound of her rage filled the Hall. 'Don't try and blind us with words! You made us open the Bardo so that Rudra could be released from hell?'

Lama la shuffled on his seat, reached for his tea. Sipped. 'Karma Chodron, the histories do not tell the full story of the battles between Rudra and Padmakara. Rudra should have died centuries ago. But Padmakara—'

'*Should* have died?' Karma Chodron asked. 'You mean he's still alive?'

Lama la looked up at the ceiling and whispered quietly to it. 'There are always consequences... no matter how long... no one cannot escape their sins.' Then he lowered his gaze back to Karma Chodron. Her expression was dark and full of thunder. 'Rudra has gradually become more powerful in his prison. The defences around him have weakened as the old certainties have crumbled.'

'Prison,' Karma Chodron snarled. 'Padmakara only put Rudra in prison?'

'I can't excuse what he did. I can only find a way to make it better.'

'What are you hiding?'

He nodded, wiped his nose with the sleeve of his robes. 'I know, I know. But it is difficult to speak of truths that have lain silent for so long.'

'Talk anyway.'

'Every Abbot makes a vow of secrecy.' He blinked a few times and then carried on. 'But you are right. Now is the time to speak.'

'Old friend?' Harry said. 'Tell us what you know.'

Lama la cleared his throat. 'Karma Chodron is right. Rudra lives.'

There was an intake of breath from beside me.

'Not only does he live, but he has found a means to influence the world. He cannot act himself yet, but... as you have seen... he is gathering an army. The White Sadhus. And unless we do something—it is inevitable—they will find a way to release their master.'

'So, you helped them!' Karma Chodron said coldly. 'That's why you wouldn't let us conduct the ceremony. Give Rudra more time to escape?'

'Karma Chodron,' I snapped. 'Shut up, will you?'

She whirled round to face me. 'You don't understand what he's done! What he's *trying* to do!'

I didn't back down. 'Haven't you learned anything? Let him speak.'

'He lied!'

'Maybe there's stuff *you* don't understand!'

Karma Chodron rolled her eyes.

'He just saved us all, didn't he!' Simon added. 'Completely wiped out a couple of Raksha... Rakshash... whatever those things were!'

'And *he...*' I said, nodding at Simon. '... another guy you locked up by the way—was prepared to sacrifice himself for you just now. So, why don't you get off your high horse and shut your mouth?'

Karma Chodron froze, her mouth half open as if to spit something angry back at me. Instead, she closed it. Swallowed. And to my surprise and relief, bowed her head slightly to me and turned to face Lama la. 'I'll listen.'

'So, back up. Rudra was defeated?' Simon asked. 'But he didn't die. He was put in... in prison?'

Lama la nodded. 'Eventually. At first, Rudra defeated Padmakara. Killed him in the first war. But thirty years later, Padmakara returned.'

'Reborn?' Simon asked. 'A Tulku.'

Lama la nodded. 'Padmakara's first Tulku continued the battle. He was defeated a second time, but the second Tulku finally subdued his old brother.'

'How do you know this?' Harry asked. 'I've read the *Annals*. They say Rudra was subdued and defeated. There's no mention of prison.'

Lama la closed his eyes. His head dipped. 'Ah. The *Annals*. Stories written by the victors.'

'They're lies?' Karma Chodron said.

'No. More like a skilful version of the truth. Passing down that which will benefit those in the future.'

'Lies then,' she muttered.

'How do you know this?' Harry asked.

Lama la tapped his forehead. 'Other truths are passed down orally, from master to disciple, in an unbroken line. It is called: The Whispered Lineage. Every abbot of each temple of the six realms holds this transmission.'

'So, what happened? Are you saying Padmakara didn't defeat Rudra after all?'

'No. But in victory, Padmakara showed pity on his brother.'

'Pity?'

Lama la looked up. His eyes were open and sad. 'Perhaps it wasn't pity. At the last, when he was finally defeated, Rudra begged his brother to spare him death. He knew what sort of rebirth would be in store for him after his horrific crimes. Avichi Hell.'

'Avichi Hell,' Tubten repeated with a shudder, as if he was recalling visiting the place.

'Instead of killing him and allowing cause and effect to ripen, Padmakara locked his brother away in the depths of Mount Meru itself. An ironic and cruel punishment. Bring me some more tea, Rabjam.'

Rabjam refilled his cup. Lama la blew on the surface, knocked the lot back in one gulp and held out his cup for more. 'Rudra always wanted to be lord of the Gods, so now he was imprisoned in the very realm he had hoped to command. A prison in which he would live for eternity to reflect on his deeds, a prison in which, even if he wanted to, he could never die to serve the correct punishment his own actions had in store for him.

'The Whispered Lineage tells us that one day Padmakara will return and, in a show of great compassion, will wield the Vajra, the Bell and the Kila to vanquish his brother and allow him to extinguish his past deeds in the proper way.' Lama la sighed.

'Lama la,' I asked. 'Why did you open the Bardo of Becoming?'

'And why won't you let us end it!' Karma Chodron added.

'Because, if we are to defeat Rudra, we must first embrace chaos for a brief time. It is the only way.'

'You want to free him from his prison?'

'Just like the White Sadhu want!' Tubten said.

Lama la raised a finger. 'True. But. When he is released, he will be old. Hundreds of years old. And physically weak. The White Sadhu plan to release him during the Bardo of Becoming, then allow him to die and take a new rebirth, whilst the chains of cause and effect are weak. They will allow him to regain his strength, avoid Avichi Hell altogether.'

Karma Chodron kicked one of the prayer tables.

'We, on the other hand,' Lama la continued. 'Will free him from his bondage. But the moment he is liberated, we will conduct the ceremony, reinstate the law of cause and effect and....' he paused. 'Then I will do what I should have done right at the beginning.'

'What's that?' Simon asked.

'I'll kill him.'

97

The Tulku of Padmakara

THERE WAS A GRATING *Scrraape* outside as if to draw a scratchy line under Lama la's words.

But even the sound of a circling Rakshasa somewhere outside the walls of the Gompa hardly registered with me right then.

'You,' I whispered. 'You're the Tulku of Padmakara?'

Lama la tried to take another sip of tea, but his cup was empty. Rabjam didn't budge though, so he carried on, dry-mouthed. 'Padmakara was a great master, but he...'

'You let Rudra live?' Karma Chodron said, staring up at him, wide-eyed.

'He confused kindness and compassion. In this life—Karma Chodron, I have taught you—that compassion is difficult. It is hard, and it sometimes means doing things you would rather not. His sin was not stupidity or recklessness. His sin was innocence. All those lives ago, He was not tough like you are. He was naïve.'

'You!' Karma Chodron shouted, turned violently away from him. There were tears in her eyes. 'It was you!' Everyone else was silent. Stunned.

'It's true. I am him. But... I am not the same man who showed mercy to Rudra. There have been many lives in between, and in this life, I can fix the mistakes of my former self,' Lama la said finally. 'And, with your help, that is what I intend to do.'

Karma Chodron glared at her feet for a moment. 'How long have you known?' she asked.

'I have always known.'

'And yet.' She raised her head. 'You have never acted before.' Then, without waiting for a response, she strode away. Down the central aisle of the Great Hall, towards the edge of the protection circle. I watched her until she stopped in front of the door, now just a puny square in the middle of a wall of shimmering silver. Shadows slid and shifted on the other side of it as if behind a sheet of water. Sounds like the sifting of sands blown by a scorching desert wind, bringing to my mind the realm of Hungry Ghosts again and that emaciated looking dog in my dreams.

Lama la is Padmakara? Rudra still lives?

The walls shivered and creaked as something pushed against them from the outside. The world was cracking apart out there. Chaos, uncertainty. Reality bending into crazy shapes. *And Lama la is Padmakara? And he let Rudra live?*

'We cannot sustain the protection circle forever,' Lama la said after a while. 'I know the circumstances are difficult, but if we are to defeat Rudra, we must act now. While we still can.'

98

---·---

NOT WITHOUT HOPE

'WE ARE NOT WITHOUT hope,' Lama la said. 'We have all eight keys and we have the original Vajra and Bell.'

Simon winced. Held up the battered thing. 'The Bell's a little bruised actually,'

'Rabjam?' Lama la said, pointing at the Bell. 'Can you fix that?'

'I can try.' Rabjam held his hand out for it. 'May I?'

Simon handed it over with no hesitation.

'There are many obstacles,' Lama la said. 'But there is one goal. We must retrieve the Kila. Without that we are defenceless.'

'What about them?' Tubten asked, pointing at us. 'We don't know who they are. What if they're bad?'

'How can we be bad?' Simon protested. 'Rudra is in prison. So we can't be him, can we?'

There was a rush of air. Karma Chodron appeared again, spear in hand. 'Tub's right,' she said. 'We don't know who they are.'

'We have no time to debate something we cannot know. Esta and Simon must help you get the Kila back,' Lama la said.

'She was the one who handed it over!' Karma Chodron said, pointing at me.

'Oh, give it a rest!' I snapped back.

Karma Chodron ignored me and approached the throne. 'Master, let the four Dharmapalas fight Trisna. You trusted us to enter the realms. You can trust us with this.'

'Trisna is out there in the human realm. A realm Esta, Simon and Harry understand.'

'But each of us were born there!'

'It has been longer than you think, and England is not Tibet.'

She pointed her spear at Harry. 'What about him? He could guide us. Esta and Simon could stay here. Safe until we return.'

'No,' Harry said. 'Outside of Odiyana, I'm an old man. I'd be no good to you.'

'But we don't know who they are! Who they might become!'

'Karma Chodron. You can't defeat Trisna without siddhis,' Lama la said. 'She will destroy you all with a flick of her hand.'

Karma Chodron looked stunned. 'What do you mean?'

'Beyond the courtyard walls,' Lama la said. 'You will become woven into the human realm. You will obey normal, human physical laws.'

'No brothers?' Tubten said.

Lama la shook his head. 'In the beginning, none of you will be able to express your siddhis.'

Karma Chodron's shoulders dropped. 'So,' she said. Quiet now. 'How are we supposed to get the Kila from a goddess if we have no powers?'

'You can't. Not without Esta.'

All eyes on me.

'Because for some reason,' Lama la said. 'She can Carve in the human realm as well as Odiyana. Without her, there is no hope.'

99

Two Books

KARMA CHODRON GLARED AT me, then back at the abbot. 'So. What do we do?'

'All of you must leave the Gompa.'

'Who will maintain the protection circle?' Karma Chodron asked.

'I am the abbot of this temple. I will stay behind.'

'I will stay with you,' Rabjam said.

Lama la folded his arms. 'I will stay. Alone. You must enter the Human Realm. Find Trisna. Take the Kila and return it.'

There was a *whumping* sound outside. Candles guttered in a sudden current of air. Everyone stared at the wall.

'Wings,' Tubten whispered.

'That is a Garuda taking flight,' Lama la said. 'You must leave as soon as you can before things become even more unpredictable.'

'You're sending us out there?' asked Tubten, with a quivering voice.

'Tubten, Rigpa Gompa is not safe anymore. There will be more sustained attacks and I can't protect you all.' He cast his gaze around our little semi-circle. 'You must enter the Bardo. You must do it now. Mara is at his most powerful where there is uncertainty, so you don't want to be there for long. Harry? You know where to take them?'

Harry nodded once. 'The Waymarker.'

'Does it still stand?'

Harry nodded. 'Last time I looked.'

'Good. That will give you temporary protection. Seek shelter there first. But White Sadhu will know our location now. You will need to stay quiet until you locate the Kila. They mustn't know who you are. You must try to blend in.'

'Wait,' I said. 'We can't just walk into the Bardo. I've been there. It's impossible. Nothing makes sense. Nothing stays the same for longer than a few moments.'

'That is why you must listen to my guidance as you go. Rabjam?' he flicked a finger towards the wall behind the shrine. 'The hidden library.'

Rabjam got up and Lama la whispered instructions to him. Rabjam nodded, then slid behind the shrine and opened a door in the back wall to a room behind.

'The Bardo Thodol,' Lama la explained, while we waited for Rabjam, 'When I read from it, the words will guide you through the confusion of the Bardo.'

Rabjam returned with two books.

Lama la opened the top one: a silver-bound book. 'When I recite, listen to my words, focus, do not let the voices of the demons distract you.' He looked at me. 'Ignore Mara's visions. The Bardo is Mara's home. He wants to confuse and corrupt.' He held up the book. 'Listen only to these words.' He placed a forefinger on the first page, licked his lips, then glanced up at us. 'Now!' he said, pointing at the door. 'Don't come back without the Kila.'

No one moved.

'There is no time for farewell. Every moment the Bardo remains open is an opportunity for Rudra to escape. Find Trisna. Find the Kila. Come back to me.'

Finally, Rabjam bowed low. Then, the others did the same. Tubten sniffed and rubbed his red cheeks.

'Uncertainty is out there,' Lama la said. 'Do not fear merely what you do not know. You have faced danger before, Tubten and you have friends who will protect you.'

'I want to stay,' he whispered.

'They need you, Tubten. To protect them.'

'What can I do? I'm only a boy. And I don't have my brothers.'

'Times are strange, Tubten Yeshe.' He looked up at the other Dharmapalas. 'Understand this. The Kila has the power to bend reality itself. While Trisna has it, it will give her enormous power. But there is a chance for you to even things up a little. The Kila is like a magnet. The closer you get to it, the more powerful it's distorting influence. If you are near enough, it may loosen the bonds of cause and effect enough to allow your siddhis to return. So, you see. There is hope. Now...' He made a shooing motion with his hands. 'The window to leave diminishes.'

The Dharmapalas bowed and backed away. Harry went. Simon did too. I took a last look around me and started after them.

'Not you.'

I turned round.

Lama la was staring at me. He held the second book Rabjam had brought. 'Take this.'

I took it off him. Heavy, wrapped in dark blue cloth. 'What is it?'

'You wanted to know who you are?'

'I thought you said it was pointless to speculate?'

'I also said that there may be clues.' he patted the book. 'in here.'

'The Blue Annals?'

'These are the Histories. They may explain who you and Simon once were. Knowledge is power. We need all the help we can get. Take it.'

I partly unravelled it. Stacks of thin pages full of spidery writing. 'Not sure if I'll understand them this time.'

'Your father could.'

'My Dad's gone.'

He touched my hand. 'If there are answers. They will be in here. If you want to know who you are, you must unlock them. Who knows, knowing may change everything.'

I looked back at the others. They'd reached the door. Karma Chodron was watching us. 'What about right now? How can I be certain one of us isn't... working for the other side?'

Lama la waggled his head. 'The only certainty is change and change is woven into the fabric of the universe.'

'What's going to happen?'

'The gods will win. The devils will lose.'

'Great. Thanks. Any other words of wisdom?'

He closed his eyes. 'Just... be yourself, Esta. That's all you can do.'

Then he lowered his gaze to the silver book and was silent.

After a minute, I bowed my head to him, turned and headed for the pale light of the protection circle and whatever lay beyond it.

100

— . —

TAKING OUT THE ARROW

MIST HUNG IN LAYERS around my ankles; the floor crunched under foot. Lama la's whispered chanting followed me through the mist. His voice never raised, his words staying with me as I caught up with the others.

'Oh noble one, the time has now come...'

The floor became soft and malleable closer to the door I got. At the farthest reaches of the protection circle, the two worlds of Rigpa Gompa and Gatley House had fused together in a blurry mishmash of shapes and colours. I walked in a daze, looking down at the book in my hands. *I know who you are...*

I wasn't Rudra. I wasn't Padmakara. But I saw them in my memories. I chose the Orb. I had siddhis that no one else had. *Who am I?*

Voices seeped through my thoughts: *that you yearn for... a return...*

I stumbled on. What if the voices were my own? What if the mind of some stranger was stirring deep within me somehow? A black shoot pushing through the soil of my own memories. *Listen to Lama la!* I told myself. *Don't get led astray.*

And just like that, the whispering stopped. Replaced by the Abbot's sing-song voice.

'... face to face before the Clear Light...' he sang.

I picked my way through the ever-shifting space; tripping over obstacles that both were and then suddenly weren't there.

Eventually I reached the main doors—a big oak thing in Rigpa Gompa and a boarded up front door in Gatley—half listening to Lama la's song and half listening for noises from outside: a low, guttural growl. It could have been a demon, or the engine of a machine. Impossible to know which for sure. Maybe both at the same time?

Listen to the song.

'...spotless intellect is like a transparent vacuum without circumference or centre.'

Tubten reached out and held my hand. The warmth and solidity of it was reassuring. 'Lama la wants us to go out into that?' he whimpered. 'We'll be ripped to pieces.'

'Quiet!' Karma Chodron whispered, placing her hand on the door as if checking its heart beat.

'Listen to the words, Tub,' Rabjam said. 'Can you hear the words?'

'... all things are like the void and cloudless sky...'

Tubten nodded.

I nudged Karma Chodron to one side. She stared fiercely at Simon, then at me. 'You know my loyalty is to Rigpa Gompa, not you two?'

I grabbed the iron ring handle. 'Fair enough.'

'If either of you betray Rigpa Gompa, you betray me.'

'Yeah. Well, it's easy to make threats when you can travel at the speed of light, Karma Chodron.' I flashed her a smile. 'But remember, you're going to lose all of that as soon as we leave this place.'

Karma Chodron flinched as if I'd pinched her. I shivered at my own words. If there really *was* some evil mind growing inside me, then I would need someone to stop me. If I couldn't do it myself... *If not Karma Chodron,* I thought, *then who?*

'Wait. Lady?' Tubten tugged at my shirt. 'Lady?'

I looked down at him. 'What is it, Tub?'

'What's in the book?'

I looked at Simon. 'Maybe a clue.'

'Who you are? Do you know? You and him,' he said, pointing at Simon and me. 'Are you on our side or his?'

I shrugged. 'At the moment? I don't know.' I turned to Simon. 'What about you? Do you know?'

He held out the Orb for me. 'I know this is yours.'

I let him place it in my hand: the object that tied me to Rudra. The object I had chosen right at the beginning of all of this.

Except, I thought, *it wasn't the beginning. The beginning was a thousand years ago when Rudra killed his master.* I looked down at the young monk. What had Lama la told us? *Embrace the uncertainty.* I smiled. 'Tub?' I handed Simon the Orb back. 'You know what the first thing you do is when you're shot with an arrow?'

He shook his head.

Simon frowned at the Orb. Then, I think he understood. He smiled and took it. Then handed me the Bell. Because... what did it matter? Nothing was decided.

Not yet.

I winked at Tubten, pulled at the handle. 'Let's get that bloody arrow out, shall we?'

The door creaked open.

Suddenly, Lama la's voice became even clearer than before: '*At this moment, know yourself. Abide in that state.*

One more glance at Simon.

'*I too, at this time, set you face to face.*'

Then we stepped out...

... into the Bardo of Becoming.

KEY TERMS

WHILST THIS IS A work of pure fiction, the world of Esta Brown and co. is heavily influenced by Eastern mythology. Particularly Tibetan.

This is by no means an educational guide on matters of Tibetan Buddhism, and I play pretty fast and loose with the culture in order for it to fit my story.

Anyway, because many of my readers have wanted to know more about some of the Buddhist ideas and concepts I have used, I include this appendix to satisfy that itch!

contact@rnjackson.com

Alaya consciousness – 'Storehouse consciousness' where the karmic seeds from one's previous actions are stored.

Ashura – The Titans or Jealous Gods.

Blue Annals – Written in 1476 by Go Lotsawa Zhonnu-pel. The histories of Buddhism in Tibet.

Dharmapala – A protector of the Buddhist religion. They are typically wrathful deities, depicted with terrifying iconography in the Mahayana and tantric traditions of Buddhism. The wrathfulness is intended to depict their willingness to defend and guard Buddhist followers from dangers and enemies.

Eight auspicious symbols – a sacred set of eight auspicious signs or symbols representing the qualities of enlightenment.

Eternal knot – A symbol of the ultimate unity of everything. The intertwining of wisdom and compassion.

Garuda – A legendary bird or bird-like creature in Hindu, Buddhist and Jain faith.

Hidden Valley/Pure Land – The idea that there are certain 'pure lands' concealed in the world, ready to open when the time is right.

Kila – a three-sided peg, stake, knife, or nail-like ritual implement. Its blade can be used for the destruction of demonic powers.

Mamo – Female spirits that represent the natural forces that respond to the human misuse of the environment by creating obstacles and disease.

Mara – The principle of chaos and confusion. Mara is the demon who tried to distract the Buddha from achieving enlightenment.

Meditation – The practice of focusing the mind.

Odiyana – The name of Padmakara's *Pure Land*.

Orb – This is a made-up word that Esta uses to refer to a *Vajra* (see below)

Padmakara – An 8th Century master who brought Buddhism to Tibet. Sometimes known as the second Buddha / Padmasambhava / Guru Rinpoche.

Rakshasa – Blood thirsty demon. Hindu origin.

Rinpoche – (pronounced *Rimposhay*) An honorific title for a spiritual master.

Rigpa Gompa – The main temple that protects the valley of Odiyana. 'Rigpa' refers to the true nature of mind and 'Gompa' is the word for 'temple'.

Rudra – The name of a being that became disturbed by arrogance and pride to become a powerful demi-god.

Samsara – A universe which is divided into the *Six Realms*.

Sand Mandalas – Ritual images made of coloured sand that represent the spiritual universe.

Six Realms – The six lands of *Samsara*: Gods, *Ashura*, Humans, Animals, Hungry Ghosts and Hell.

Siddhis – Magical powers that are the product of certain forms of meditation.

Trisna – The goddess of desire. Or 'Thirst'.

Vajra and **Bell** – Ritual objects that represent compassion and wisdom.

About R.N. Jackson

Amongst other things, R.N Jackson has been: shot at in Kashmir by separatists; saved from kidnap in France with the use of a Brazilian hunting knife gifted by a bare-knuckle fighter for the Mafia; leader of expeditions to Northern India, Nepal, Thailand and Japan; a student of some of the greatest living masters of Tibetan Buddhism.

His day job involves managing the Religion and Philosophy department at one of the UK's leading independent schools.

He has a beautiful wife and three talented children.

Get in touch... Get free stuff and find out more about him and his books!
Point your camera at the QR code to find out more!

www.rnjackson.com
Facebook: www.facebook.com/rnjacksonauthor

LEAVE A REVIEW

Thanks for reading EBBoB. I hope you enjoyed it.
Your support makes it possible for this independent author to continue creating.
If you liked what you read, please leave an honest review wherever you bought this book.
Your feedback is invaluable.
Thankyou
If you want to get in touch with me, I read all emails and respond personally.
You can reach me at: contact@rnjackson.com

Also By R.N. Jackson

Legends of the East Series:

The Eyes of Mara: Prequel novella

The Search for Jewel Island: Book 1

Esta Brown in the Bardo of Becoming: Book 2

Other Titles.

Meditations on: Madness: A collection of Flash Fiction

Mr Pig and Mr Rat Discuss This and That: Beautifully illustrated humorous Buddhist poetry.

Free Stuff

Read the essential prequel to The Legends of the East series.

A search for truth. A house with a gruesome past. A disturbing secret that could tear the world apart.

Excerpt

The Eyes of Mara Chapter 1

"THEY CALL IT THE murder house," Simon Taylor said, settling himself on the wall edge, his feet dangling halfway down to the thorns below. "We should go in before dad pulls it down."

Charlie Bullock heaved herself up, peered down into the painful-looking thicket five feet below and wondered what she was doing scrambling up walls at the age of eighteen. This particular wall, of all places, with her annoying step-brother of all people.

She perched herself next to him, "It's just a rundown old building like all the others."

"This one's different," he said. "This one's got history."

"Every house's got a history, idiot."

Simon grinned at her. A big, wide, stupid grin. "Not like this one, Sis." He left that phrase hanging in the still, early summer evening air. They both peered through the tangle of branches towards Gatley House. A three story detached mansion, ivy running wild up the crumbling brickwork, surrounded by trees, hedgerows. A jungle of a lawn to its front that might have once been hosted garden parties.

"Dad told me all about it," Simon said. "It was owned by this old guy and his wife. They lived here since the 1950s. He went crazy, talking about other people living with him."

"You believe anything. Dad just spreads these rumours so kids like you don't go exploring where they're not wanted."

"He went crazy," Simon continued, ignoring her. "Dad says he killed his wife. And couldn't live with the guilt. Then..." He paused and licked his lips. "Took out the floor in one of the rooms upstairs."

Charlie shook her head. "So?" Charlie asked. Trying to sound like she was bored. Trying to sound like vertigo wasn't actually making her dizzy and nauseous. She gripped the wall more tightly.

"He put a hook in the ceiling. Tied a rope to it. And... you know..." He wrapped a pretend rope around his neck, tugged it and made a croaking sound.

Charlie rolled her eyes, but despite herself, she found her gaze drawn to one of the first-floor windows. Simon was enjoying this. He'd enjoy it even more if she freaked out now.

"Who does that?" she said. "Think about it. You want to kill yourself, why go to the trouble of taking out a floor? Just stand on a chair and kick off it."

She didn't have time for this. Her art exam was in a week, and she still hadn't finished her portfolio. She glanced behind her and began planning how she could slide her leg back over the wall.

Visiting Gatley House had been Simon's idea. He'd said it would be the 'perfect thing' to draw for her final assessed piece: *"The heart of the thing"*

Mrs Hartley had told the class that they had to make sketches of objects that were imperfect in some way. She'd shown them things like old logs, chipped cups, rusty cutlery.

Things with character, Mrs Hartley had said.

So far, Charlie had only managed to sketch a bunch of rotten fruit. Apples mainly. They weren't even rotten, just had a few bites taken out of them.

She wasn't exactly big on imperfections. Whether it was the clothes she wore, the hairstyle, or the company she kept. Hence why she intended to leave Simon to his ghost stories and get home to get ready for the Pub tonight. You didn't look like Charlie Bullock without it taking at least a couple of hours in front of the mirror.

She took perfection seriously.

"Dad said he left one beam running across the room so he could walk on it. He put the rope over his neck..."

"Simon! Enough, okay?"

"Apparently something to jump off."

"You're a sick little boy," she sighed, but a shiver ran down her spine as she imagined the old guy, mad with grief, rattling about in that dusty old mansion. Driven to jumping off into a floorless room with a rope around his...

"It's just a ghost story," she said. "And Mrs Hartley wants Still Life of imperfect things, anyway."

"What's Still Life?"

"Things in a bowl. I don't think this..." She swept a hand out towards the old building. 'is what she had in mind exactly."

"I bet there's loads of stuff in there you could draw. And dad said there's definitely a room without a floor."

"I wouldn't go in there if you paid me."

"Only cos you're scared," Simon said.

Charlie inspected her little brother. Fourteen years old, and right in the middle of early brat-hood. Or, she thought about her step Dad—head as round and bald as a bowling ball, gorilla arms bursting out of his work shirt—maybe this was the best it got. Maybe Simon would *devolve,* like his dad had.

"No," she said, lowering herself off the wall, finding an edge of stone for her heel. "I don't want to go inside, because it would ruin my clothes." She jumped to the pavement. Simon followed her, smarmy grin still smeared across his face. A grin that, in Charlie's experience, nothing would peel off.

Even with the matching blonde hair, Charlie consoled herself with the thought that no one would ever mistake them for actual brother and sisters. Her mum had had her before moving in with Simon's dad and they'd played at happy families for fourteen years. But surely... no one would pair them up as related by blood. He was like a different *species.*

She should just draw a picture of her family. That should fit Mrs Hartley's 'Imperfection' brief.

She waited for a couple of cars to swish past, then crossed over the road. Simon at her heels like a dog.

They reached the junction of Oak Road. Just a five-minute walk to the five-bedroom monstrosity her step dad had built for them before her mum finally filed for the divorce.

It was an all-square shaped thing, with white plastering, Greek columns and even a couple of stone lions guarding the gate. Couldn't have been more different from Gatley House.

She glanced back. The tiled roof of the old building peered through the branches of the trees on the other side of the wall.

She wasn't going to admit it to Simon, but Charlie knew a bit about Gatley House and the truth was, she *was* scared of it. Always had been.

She'd walked past it for most of her eighteen years on her way into Gatley town, or to school, and she vaguely remembered when someone had owned it. Ten or more years ago.

She remembered the stories people used to tell about the couple who lived there. Some retired military couple from India.

One day when there'd been an ambulance. You could see the blue flashing lights sparking through the trees from her Primary School. There had been a hundred different stories about what had happened the next day in the playground. Even though all the adults and the newspapers had said: "heart attack".

But there had been *police-tape*. Even eight-year-olds know you don't have police tape for a heart attack.

Every day Charlie walked past over the years, she could see it slowly sinking into the ground through neglect. A crumbling fossil, a dark relic.

And on winter days, when all the leaves were gone from the trees, if you stared at it from the right angle, its dusty windows would stare back at you.

Point your phone camera at the QR code to read the essential prequel for the Legends of the East series. FREE.

Printed in Great Britain
by Amazon